To PATRICIA;
BEST Wishes
DAN

THE

CANDLE

ROOM

IMAGINE Colourd
PRESS

DANIEL K. GENTILE

COPYRIGHT

ImagineCloud Press
P.O. Box 1955
Wrightwood, California 92397

ISBN-13 978-0692608807

ACKNOWLEDGMENTS

In loving memory of Marsha C. Rajacich,
a true thinker.

A special thank you to Steven J. Pope for his invaluable
guidance during my early years as a lawyer and his
steadfast commitment to honesty and integrity. And,
of course, a very special thank you to Whitney for her
tireless editing and insight, without which the
completion of this book would not have been possible.

ONE

AN obvious target for the pint-sized hoodlums, Oliver Randall Pearce sought isolation during morning recess, hoping to protect himself from the fifth grade thugs. They'd eventually find him, tease him for being a fat, freckled, red-head and, as usual, he'd do nothing to resist their assault. His indifference offended them and often provoked further hostilities in the form of a shove to the ground or kick to his rear-end. The teachers and proctors turned a blind eye and his mom and dad couldn't care less, instructing him to lose weight and act like a man and not a sissy if he wanted to prevent it. Over time, he learned to deal with humiliation by not dealing with it. If he ignored the idiots long enough they'd move on to some other fat kid.

Ollie's parents provided the bare minimum in terms of guidance, and less than that in terms of love. They preferred–actually insisted–that he and his younger brother, Andrew, keep out of their way and, when at all possible, out of their sight. Discipline was usually exacted by belittling Ollie, and they disciplined him often. Andrew was too young to feel the pain of criticism. He was punished the old-fashioned physical way, which Ollie would have opted for himself if he had a choice.

Ollie's lips formed into an odd permanent smirk, the result of a nerve disorder which he had since birth. On occasion it was confused for a smile, clearly a contradiction to his troubled young life. If he had it his way, he'd never smile. His smirk not only pissed off the bullies at school, but on one occasion Ollie's inebriated father felt compelled to demand that Ollie wipe off the shit-eatin' grin. When Ollie didn't–because he couldn't– Dad belted him. Mom looked on, said nothing.

As he reached teenager status, Ollie's scarlet face and heap of unkempt fire-red hair managed to fade to a less dramatic burnt orange. This small favor, however, was offset by his bulkiness, which took a decided turn for the worse. Thick and dumpy, he struggled for air as routine movements challenged his ballooning body.

But unlike others his age, he didn't dwell over his physique, attributing his failings to the cards dealt to him by whomever or whatever in the universe happened to be in charge of dealing the cards. He accepted himself for what he was and never struggled internally over who he should be.

Predictably, he shunned social rules and did little to adapt to the trends others followed. His existence played out in the seclusion of his bedroom. Friends, family and even the opposite sex, were irrelevant distractions and were not part of his general plan. A bucket of Neapolitan was far more appealing than human companionship.

When he was fifteen, his mother's health deteriorated due to the effects of liver disease and she died unexpectedly in her sleep. Her death was difficult for Ollie, but not in the love-loss kind of way. He never experienced the typical mother-son relationship. He existed, and that's about it as far as she was concerned. Occasionally, her maternal instincts stepped in and she defended Ollie against some of the abuse by his father, but this was unusual, and it only seemed to occur when her friends were around.

The Pearce family had very little structure, but what it did have, she provided, albeit reluctantly. She managed to keep the home somewhat clean, and she always had plenty of cheap fast food for the kids. Her passing meant that Ollie and Andrew would have to fend for themselves, as their father was a detached drunk, consumed with his own interests, and unwilling to be tethered to the responsibility of taking care of his boys.

After her death, Ollie encased himself deeper into his shell. He rarely acknowledged his father's presence and spoke little to Andrew. Their small house, located in a secluded area west of Columbia, South Carolina, was now filthy–as was he–and the living conditions would have been considered unbearable for most people. Not Ollie. He never complained about a thing. His father was kind enough to throw a few bags of junk food on the table and keep the utilities on. Ollie walked to school, walked home, and went to his room to play video games. Nothing else was necessary.

After finishing high school, misfortune struck again when Ollie's father was killed in a freak accident caused by a malfunctioning heater which exploded in the barn. The barn was engulfed in flames, and his father and their horse, Bonnie, had no hope of escaping before the rescue crews arrived. Luckily, Ollie and Andrew were asleep in their small house in front of the barn and were uninjured.

Ollie was distraught by the tragedy, but only because he would lose the few remaining parental tokens which his father provided. He would no longer be given the necessities and was now expected to find employment, contribute to the society which he felt abused him, and associate with people who would never mean a thing to him. This was not Ollie, and he had to get as far away from that life as he could.

Shortly after his father's death, he split, leaving Andrew behind for social services to deal with. He'd never return, and made no contact with anyone from his past, including Andrew.

The change of scenery was positive for Ollie. Over the next thirteen years, he managed to become a self-made millionaire by trading stocks, options and futures out of his small, rented adobe three thousand miles away in Burbank, just north of Los Angeles. Still a loner, he conserved energies most would expend developing relationships, and utilized them instead to master the stock market. The Internet, and a few streaks of luck, allowed him to prosper without a care in the world of what anyone thought of him.

Sadly, the fruits of his accomplishments did nothing to enhance Ollie's personal life. Generating a profit by trading stocks was no different than advancing to the next level in a video game. He played with vigor, but when the game was over, he'd turn it off and go to sleep, only to resume playing the next day. The cycle was endless and to him, there was no other viable alternative. He was numb and having all the money in the world wouldn't change that. His winnings piled up without any plan or desire to enjoy his success.

On October 14, 2010, tragedy struck one last time, when Ollie was found bludgeoned to death in his home. His neighbor called the authorities when the odor became unbearable.

Two responding officers entered through the unlocked front door after efforts to communicate with Ollie were unsuccessful. It was immediately apparent there had been a violent attack. Dried blood was splattered throughout the living room and kitchen. His body was discovered on the kitchen floor at 2:12 p.m. A homicide team was dispatched with the medical examiner not far behind.

The scene was horrific. A metallic smell permeated the air and the thick, putrid stench from the decaying body hovered like a morning fog. Ollie's head was pummeled with a blunt object. His hands, bound tightly with plastic ties, prevented him from fending off his attacker who viciously amputated his feet above the ankles, discarding them into the kitchen sink. His giant carcass, punctured with multiple stab wounds, lay motionless, drained of its blood.

Barely discernable was Ollie's once plump reddened face, now distorted and blackened by the ravages of after-death, but still managing an eerie smile. He wasn't simply the victim of a senseless murder; he suffered torture beyond comprehension.

The lead detective, Jarred Cranston, an eighteen-year veteran with the LAPD, concluded that there was no forced entry or obvious struggle, despite the condition of the body, as the limited furnishings in the home were in order and defensive wounds on the victim were not visible. Robbery didn't appear to be the motive, given that a small stash of cash, a watch, and a coin collection of unknown value were found in open view on his bedroom dresser. The victim was partially clothed, lying face down on the kitchen floor. He had ligature marks around his neck. A dark flannel scarf, tightly wrapped between his upper and lower jaw, kept him quiet during the ordeal. No fingerprints were recovered, but investigators found several shoe impressions–which didn't surprise them due to the amount of blood distributed throughout the scene. The victim appeared to have been murdered approximately eight to ten days before the discovery of his body.

Few personal items were the home and other than the basic information provided by his landlord, the LAPD knew little about Ollie or the extent of his wealth.

Interviews with neighbors revealed nothing remarkable. He had never spoken to them, and after ten years of living in the same neighborhood, they didn't even know his name. He was rarely seen leaving, except to retrieve his mail. He kept to himself, had no visitors, other than occasional delivery services, and he had no vehicle.

According to the landlord, Ollie paid his rent on time, and never complained, other than when he had an ant infestation a few years back. His rental application reflected that he was self-employed as an investor and he had no credit history.   No emergency contact information was provided, and the space on the application for the nearest relative was left blank.

The landlord quickly let the investigators know he expected to be paid every dime which he incurred cleaning up the bloody mess. He insisted that if he couldn't rent out the home due to the butchering of his former tenant, he'd sue the hell out of the LAPD for not protecting his property, the lack of protection to Ollie being of no moment to him.

A computer found at the scene was taken to the lab for testing and data extraction.

As far as weapons, a butcher knife smeared with dried blood appeared to have been the instrument of choice for removing Ollie's feet. The knife was part of a set maintained in a wooden block located between the rear burners on the stove. No other obvious weapons were found.

Over the course of the next few weeks, the LAPD reached out to the public for help and requested that any information related to the crime be reported to an anonymous tip line. Although dozens of tips poured in, most of them were useless and lacked credibility. The detectives followed up on a few promising leads, but in the end, they were stumped.

TWO

THE Los Angeles firm of Fleming, Fleming & White, was a bad apple in the legal profession. Its founding partners measured success by how competently they could convince their clients to part company with their wallets—not by productivity, analytical skills or prowess in the courtroom, and definitely not by doing what was in the best interest of the client.

An associate lawyer spending fifty hours preparing and filing a motion in the L.A. County Superior Court, would earn the firm upwards of fifteen thousand dollars—a partner, at least twenty-five for the identical motion. Add another hundred to two hundred buckaroos per hour for clerical staff and the billings multiplied. Whether the filing had any likelihood of success, or whether it even had any material impact upon the ultimate outcome of the case, had zero relevance. It was all about the fees baby, the fees.

Fleming, Fleming & White, required all associates to bill a client for reviewing a file even before they had the file. The clock began to run while the associate waited patiently for Assistant Number One to organize and index the file so the attorney could understand it. Assistant Number One billed her hourly fee while she in turn waited for Assistant Number Two to take her sweet time figuring out how to operate the firm's state-of-the-art, thousand-function digital color copier/ scanner/ printer/ stapler/ hole-puncher/CD player and fax machine so she could copy documents to give to Assistant Number One to organize and index to give to the associate attorney.

The firm recognized the profitability of reinventing the wheel in all legal matters and did so with the patience of a saint. Redundancy was critical. Allowing a member of the firm to handle a project in solitude, thus obviating duplicative billing by Assistant Number One and Two, and oftentimes Three, Four and Five, was taboo. Associates conferring with partners regarding a client's matter, partners conferring with partners, assistants conferring with paralegals, etc., were multi-billable events encouraged by the firm, even if said conferences occurred under the watchful eye of the local bartender. Dreaming about a case justified time-and-a-half billing; a nightmare deserved triple time.

FF&W was an insurance defense firm and their insurance company clients paid what was billed and rarely asked questions. When they did inquire, they were assured that all billings were necessary and in furtherance of protecting the client's and their insured's interest.

Zachary E. Morgan, Esquire, the firm's newest associate, was hired fresh out of law school. He was immediately indoctrinated into the FF&W protocol, but after a few short weeks on the job, he learned to despise everything that had to do with the firm. His view of the legal profession differed drastically from that of the more seasoned associates. They ignored ethical considerations in favor of generous salary increases and prestige. FF&W offered both, but under the circumstances, Zach wanted neither.

He developed a fascination for the study of law after one of his friends was killed and his brother-in-law paralyzed several years before during a robbery. The charges against the perpetrators were dismissed based upon a constitutional technicality. Zach was outraged by the legal system and thought, perhaps naively, that he could make a difference if he became part of it.

He was 25, and worked as a data processor when he started law school. His wife, Sasha, was a second grade teacher and they were parents to a young daughter, Amanda. They earned enough to afford the monthly payments arranged by Jefferson School of Law, a small night-school located in West Los Angeles. Students at the school were typically family types with existing careers, hoping to climb the economic ladder. Obtaining a legal education on a part-time basis at Jefferson was a long shot, but to Zach, doable.

In the four years that followed, his family endured one sacrifice after another. Personal time together was a luxury. Sasha undertook the lion's share of raising Amanda. Zach, the absentee dad, avoided total alienation by providing occasional emotional necessities– too exhausted to offer more. Surprisingly, their marriage remained intact, even strengthened by the challenge.

Zach was obsessed with his studies and graduated with honors, earning his Juris Doctor along with twenty-six others in his class. Passing the bar exam several months later was anticlimactic. He finally accomplished his dream of becoming a member of the California State Bar.

Insurance defense firms offer new associates immeasurable experience handling civil litigation matters. Preparing and scrutinizing discovery documents, drafting motions, evaluating claims and researching legal issues are integral to gaining basic knowledge into the world of lawyering. Law school teaches how to analyze facts and apply them to the law—not how to practice law. This can only be learned in the heat of battle.

Zach understood that, as a new lawyer, he wouldn't see the light of day in a courtroom or even speak to a client for several years. However, he was fired-up and ready to barricade himself in a skyscraper office somewhere, anywhere, tending to Lady Justice.

The 35-member firm of Fleming, Fleming & White, was not the first firm Zach interviewed with after passing the bar exam, but it was the last. Most of the other firms frowned upon his education from the small, unknown school and preferred to hire the Stanford, Pepperdine, USC, or UCLA grads. But J. Robert Wharton, managing partner at FF&W, took a liking to Zach's work ethic and hired him on the spot. Completing law school while supporting a family impressed him. Zach had exactly the type of qualities FF&W wanted. With a little grooming, Zach would do just fine in the litigation department.

He was expected to bill sixty hours per week, at a starting rate of two-fifty per hour. This equated to fifteen thousand in fees to the firm every week. His monthly salary was less than half of one-week's billables, but far more than he earned as a data processor.

Sasha and Amanda became the first casualties of Zach's new profession. To reach his quota, he worked fourteen, fifteen and sometimes eighteen hours per day, ignoring all that mattered, including his family. Welcome to the practice of law.

His supervising attorney was K. Sanford Filbert, a short, stocky man, mid-forties, with thin, greying hair, greased to a comb-over which failed miserably to conceal his baldness. Thick, prickly, black wires grew out of his ears and meandered down toward his lobes, obviously never having been trimmed. He wore the same suit, or something very similar, every day: tan, tweed jacket, heavily worn at the elbows and fraying on the sleeves, a white shirt, paisley green tie, blue oversized slacks and casual dark shoes with thick rubber soles. He'd been with the firm for over ten years as a paper pusher and motion writer and was elevated to supervisor three years ago.

Filbert was definitely not an expert in any specialized field and had never even appeared in a courtroom, but he had marching orders from the FF&W brass and he followed those orders to a T. His job was to mentor the less experienced associates regarding the preparation of pleadings, discovery and motions. He paid particular attention to teaching them how to bill for every minute of their time, and then some. The associates aptly nicknamed him "Ticktock."

It was no secret that Filbert's primary function was to supervise the churning of fees. All associates received his words of wisdom at one time or another: "If a plaintiff is owed money for an injury, he'll eventually get it, but there ain't no way in hell he'll get a penny until we get our money first, and if we do our job right, we'll get more than he does."

FF&W rewarded Filbert with handsome annual bonuses based upon the billings of the associates he trained. His job was secure and he did it well.

Filbert threw Zach into the fray immediately after

he was hired. His first assignment was to prepare discovery which addressed the allegations made by a plaintiff who sued FF&W's client, Formost Trucking Company, Inc., for wrongful death after the plaintiff's mother was hit head-on by one of Formost's trucks. The eyewitness accounts, police reports and the sworn statement of the driver of the truck, confirmed, without dispute, that the driver had fallen asleep and crossed the median, colliding with the victim's vehicle, killing her instantly.

Although Formost was FF&W's client of record, its real (and paying) client was Insurico, one of several transportation industry insurance carriers. FF&W realized that Insurico had a contractual duty to protect Formost, regardless of its undisputed liability for the accident, and it would make Insurico pay for such protection by employing all legal machinations available.

Zach did what Ticktock instructed him to do. He spent dozens of hours combing through the police reports, medical histories of the truck driver and the victim, witness statements and background checks, public records, credit histories, property ownership reports and every other document given to him by

Filbert. He crafted hundreds of interrogatories and document requests, witness summaries and issued numerous deposition subpoenas seeking the testimony of the plaintiff, other members of her family, witnesses and potential witnesses. His tedious work, which he completed to perfection, would have no impact upon any material issue involved in the case since the firm's client was clearly liable. However, FF&W was paid for every minute of it.

Three weeks after Zach was hired, Filbert reported him to the senior partners after it was discovered that he failed to bill for all of the time he spent preparing a routine motion. Zach defended his actions by reminding Filbert that he recently prepared identical motions filed by the firm on behalf of three other clients and almost had the motion memorized. Therefore, it only took him two hours to prepare the last one—not ten hours as with the first one.

"Too bad," Filbert said sternly, his chubby face turning beet red almost to the point of igniting, "we bill for everything around here. One client should not receive the benefit of work which we did for another client. If it took you ten hours to prepare the document the first time, you bill at least ten hours the first time, the next time and the time after that even if it's the same goddamn motion, and even if you can recite it verbatim without notes while taking a shit. You'll cost the firm big dollars doing it your way, and we can't have that, and we won't have that, so get used to the program and don't ask questions." Filbert spoke loudly and quickly and his rant sounded scripted, no doubt having been used many times before. Zach was intimidated as he listened to the lecture and had no response other than to inform Ticktock that he'd be more careful in the future.

Near the end of his first month at FF&W, Zach was disillusioned by his short career, unable to sleep as his mind raced to find legitimacy. He understood the game and how it was played. Very little, other than unnecessary billing of the insurance companies for legal terrorism against legitimate plaintiffs, was accomplished in the world of insurance defense at FF&W.

So when Zachary E. Morgan, Esquire, decided to spend his seven-minute lunch hour meeting with J. Robert Wharton, it was not to let him know how much he appreciated the opportunity to be a part of the magnificent firm of respected FF&W lawyers, or how honored he was to have his name on the firm's marquee and letterhead. Instead, it was to politely advise Mr. J. Robert Wharton to go fuck himself and his crooked firm.

THREE

AS expected, Sasha became unglued. She threatened physical violence and made it abundantly clear to Zach that he'd better march down to the offices of FF&W and graciously apologize to Mr. Wharton, kissing his hairy bare ass if necessary. She demanded he undo the damage he caused and get his job back or he'd be involved in his first divorce case.

Still in shock himself over what he had done, Zach couldn't blame her, but he couldn't comply with her demands. He'd spend one of many nights on the couch.

Sasha was strong, compassionate, and insisted upon order and routine and was never one to conceal her opinions. She was groomed and manicured to near perfection. By no means vain, just disciplined, self-confident, and in tune with her mind and body. She enjoyed the kind of inner-peace most people struggle their entire lives to find.

When Zach was introduced to her by her brother, Dillon, he was stunned by Sasha's natural beauty, accented by her huge, captivating brown eyes, long slender legs and olive skin. It was a brief introduction, but long enough for their pupils to momentarily track each other's, a sign of mutual interest. Why or how Dillon kept her a secret for nearly two years since they became friends, was a mystery Zach would get to the bottom of later. He was smitten.

Soon thereafter, they met at a party, each with a group of their own friends. This time, the collision of their eyes prompted warm, playful smiles and one-on-one conversation. The lively party slowly faded into a silent movie which they watched in the company of each other–Sasha and Zach, Zach and Sasha. Nothing else mattered that night.

They hit it off immediately, much to the chagrin of Dillon. His sister began to occupy more and more of his best friend's time. Within a year, the two were inseparable and moved into a small apartment in Culver City. After a month of living together, they tied the knot on a whim while on a short vacation in Vegas. The next year, Amanda was born and their family was complete.

Nowhere was the grass greener in Sasha's mind.

But Zach's antics at FF&W jeopardized Sasha's orderly process of protecting her family and she didn't like it one bit. The life she and Zach envisioned while their family endured considerable sacrifices to put him through law school was at great risk. In keeping with her nature, she would not sit idly by as he did his best to screw things up.

The next morning, Zach and Sasha aired it out. Zach had time to think and Sasha had time to cool. They met in the kitchen before Amanda woke up for school.

"I'm sorry Sasha, but it's a fee mill. We perform needless legal services at substantial expense to the clients who are kept in the dark over whether the so-called services are productive or useful. It's highway robbery..."

Sasha interrupted, "Listen dumbass, if you haven't noticed, the clients who you feel so sorry for happen to be insurance companies, most of which are crooked themselves. If they didn't want to pay the fees, believe me they wouldn't pay them. Maybe a thief taking from a thief is the nature of the beast in the legal world... the screwing you get for the screwing you gave. Or... maybe paying outrageous legal expenses is just their way of easing the guilt they feel after treating their own customers like shit. I'm not a lawyer but if you can't handle making money off of others, you picked the wrong profession. Why you didn't figure this out four years ago when you had the brilliant idea of becoming a lawyer is beyond me." Sasha was steaming. The night alone in her bed did nothing to quell her anger.

"Sasha," he said softly, "this may sound naïve and cliché, but I got into this business to try to help people, rich people, poor people, small businesses, big businesses, anyone who needs help. Being productive and making a difference, even only a little difference, is what I had in mind. FF&W is in the business to help themselves, not others, and I don't want any part of it. I'm sorry… honestly I am, but I just can't function in that environment…"

Sasha interrupted again, "Cut the save-the-world crap, Captain Justice. Don't you think you could have… one, discussed it with me first… and two… given it just a little more time and thought before you decided to humiliate yourself, and quite likely destroy any semblance of a reputation which you had… don't you? A month? You threw it all away after only a month on the job?

What the hell was going through that scrambled mind of yours, Zach?"

He knew she was right but conjured up a rebuttal. "Okay, but it's not the end of the world. I can start my own little firm. We have enough in savings for me to set up shop... hang out my own shingle. There are cheap answering and secretarial services that lawyers use and, with current technology, legal resources are inexpensive. I'd be calling my own shots, taking cases I want to take and not engaging in oppressive legal warfare every day of my life."

Sasha, again at the ready, jumped in, "Hello Mister Lawyerman, you have no clients, and in fact you've never even spoken to a client in your short legal career. You have zero reputation, and you haven't even stepped foot in a courtroom and wouldn't know the difference between a sledge hammer and a gavel."

"Furthermore, given your escapades at Fleming, you're probably blackballed by the legal profession. Under these very real circumstances, how the hell do you think you can swing that new brilliant idea of yours, Coun... sell... or?"

She continued matter-of-factly, "Perhaps you

haven't been paying attention around here, but we have a growing daughter, bills, rent, and things that require that we—not just me—but we earn a livelihood. Opening your own practice is absolutely, positively, and in no uncertain terms, out of the question. You, sir, need to get off your ass and find another job, possibly with a firm far, far away from the one you pissed off. Maybe the further away you are from Fleming, the less likely you'll be the subject of ridicule by your colleagues."

Any argument Zach had, he'd lose. He conceded. "Fine, I'll do it your way if that's what you want," Zach shouted, patronizing her, but not ready to give up his crusade. He'd spend the night on the couch again.

Sleep didn't always come easy, particularly after the robbery which killed his friend Abe and paralyzed Sasha's brother, Dillon. He relived those events over and over and time didn't seem to heal the pain. The tragedy five years ago, and the ensuing botched criminal prosecution, is what got him interested in the law in the first place. But at this very moment, he was no longer convinced that the legal profession was where he belonged.

FOUR

NEVER one to say no to a cold beer, Dillon Shepard accepted the invite and joined his buddies at Karl's Brewery, an authentic German pub tucked away on Grand Avenue in L.A. The July Southern California heat and the mere fact that it was Friday meant he'd be inebriated within an hour.

Zach and Abe were already seated at a small table in the corner of the noisy bar, when Dillon arrived. The tall pitcher of Hefeweizen, and the full frosty mug waiting for him, caused his mouth to water as he approached the table. He greeted his companions with a fist pump as he grabbed a slice of orange and squeezed its juice into the mug. After chugging the cold beer effortlessly, he licked the foam from his lips, said nothing, and then poured himself another, guzzling half. He was now ready to socialize.

Dillon was in law school but worked as a

paralegal with Litzer/Brown, a small boutique law firm downtown. The firm was highly respected for its prowess in wrongful-death cases. Its deceased founders, Jack Litzer and Steven Brown, won numerous record-setting verdicts in both state and federal courts. Their success perpetuated a solid reputation with the defense bar. Once a new case was filed by Litzer/Brown, serious settlement negotiations with the opposition began, oftentimes resulting in a substantial payout within a few weeks or months. The longer the defense took to settle, the more zeros the settlement check had to have. Dillon was assured employment as an associate with the firm, and a substantial salary, once he finished law school.

Friday was dress-down day at the firm. The partners and their staff called it quits by three in the afternoon. Dillon didn't complete his work until five, after which he met up with Zach and Abe.

When they graduated from college together a few years earlier, the three of them made a pact to hang out, sans their wives and/or girlfriends, at least once a month. Sasha was Dillon's younger sister and she and Zach were recently married. Despite the change in their familial relationship, Dillon and Zach still considered each other best friends rather than relatives. They and Abe enjoyed their little reunions which they spent arguing about politics, sports and just about any other controversy at-issue on that particular day.

The patrons at Karl's Brewery were generally professionals involved in the financial, real estate and legal business. They'd meet there for a beer or two after work. The atmosphere was always pleasant and typically festive.

Karl Gruben, the owner of the bar, had only one incident of violence in seventeen years when Sal Rasmussen, a drunken pharmaceutical sales rep, decided he no longer liked to be in the presence of lawyers, particularly the one that ate him alive on the witness stand earlier that day.

He sued his company for wrongful termination after he was fired for dipping into the company's anti-anxiety medication for personal use. Under cross-examination, the company's lawyer took a total of sixteen minutes to get Sal to admit that he not only used the drugs himself, but that he had a list of clients he sold the drugs to on the side. Sal was so humiliated by the rapid dismantling of what he felt was his multimillion dollar slam-dunk case that he abruptly left the witness stand in the middle of testimony, gave the finger to the jury, the judge and the attorneys, including his own, and stormed out of the courtroom. Sal's destination was the first bar he could find and that bar happened to be Karl's.

Unfortunately, Karl's was also the bar of choice for the post-trial celebration of Sal's former employer and its successful legal team. When the lawyers congregated at a table in the corner of the busy pub, they didn't notice Sal sitting with his back to them at the end of the bar, with three shots of tequila ready to inhale. After three quick snaps of his head, Sal consumed what he needed to take off the edge. He then casually looked around the bar and was stunned when he saw the smiling bastards that just ruined his life. With no other weapon in sight, Sal grabbed an empty pony-keg from behind the bar and hurled it at the attorneys. He missed, but the team of four lawyers rushed to Sal, surrounded him, and beat him senseless.

Karl was sued by Sal for failing to maintain a safe environment for his customers. Sal lost again. But Karl promised the next time something like that happened, he'd fire his Smith & Wesson in the air to nip it in the bud like they did in the saloon days.

Since that incident, six years earlier, the pub had no major disruptions. However, Karl's luck would soon change.

At approximately 11:45 p.m., Dillon, Zach and Abe had enough to drink, and their little party was winding down when two armed men, wearing masks depicting Richard Nixon and Bill Clinton, entered the pub and violently demanded that the patrons put their hands up and keep quiet. The thugs went to each table and gathered the terrified customers' valuables, throwing them into a backpack. They made it perfectly clear that if anyone flinched, he or she would die. Karl wasn't on duty that night, but his Smith & Wesson was.

After collecting the spoils from approximately half of the customers, one of the men grabbed the Smith & Wesson, which was plainly visible behind the counter, and began firing randomly as he and his accomplice hurried out of the pub. In the end, the barrage of bullets managed to kill three men and injure one. Abe was one of the men killed. Dillon's life was spared, but he was shot twice in the back. Zach miraculously managed to avoid the gunfire by diving into a nearby booth as the shots were fired.   The scene was a bloodbath.

News of the shooting consumed local and national airways during the next few days.   The perpetrators became known as the Grand Avenue Killers and the LAPD was on a manhunt.

Dillon was in a coma for two weeks before regaining consciousness, but he was temporarily unable to speak.   He watched as the staff worked on him.   Like a cadaver, he never flinched when poked with needles and catheters and never moaned as the dead skin from his gunshot wounds was peeled, cut and sutured.   The perfect patient.

But his eyes were wide open, alert, almost quivering, expressing his utter desperation as he lay there helpless and in fear.   No medical testing could reveal that Dillon was silently screaming from the top of his lungs. Not from pain, but from the claustrophobic panic and terror one would feel if buried to his neck in sand... unable to escape, cries for help unable to be heard.   Why didn't he perish like Abe–instantly–before the thought of dying could enter his mind?

A battery of tests and evaluations lead his medical team to conclude that Dillon suffered a complete C-1/C-

2 cervical vertebra injury. He'd be permanently paralyzed from the neck down.

Sasha and her family were inconsolable. They were very close and the tragedy was beyond the realm of comprehension. Zach did his best to help his new extended family cope, but he was overcome by survivor's guilt, worsening as the events continued to replay in his mind. He agonized over what he could have done to protect his friends, but had no answer. The shooting occurred rapidly and his flight to safety, and the instinct for self-preservation, was triggered involuntarily. He had no time to look out for the welfare of Dillon or Abe.

The partners at Litzer/Brown offered a modest reward for any information which would result in apprehending and convicting the perpetrators. They also assured Dillon's family that his desk would always be there for him should he decide to return to the firm regardless of any disability he may have.

Seven months after the robbery, the Grand Avenue Killers were captured when a tip came in by a friend of the suspects who decided that the $20,000 Litzer/Brown reward was worth more than friendship. According to the tipster, the two men were believed to have the masks, the murder weapon, and some of the stolen jewelry hidden in their apartment in East Los Angeles.

The LAPD ran a search of the suspects and determined that one of them was on parole after an assault-and-battery conviction. They immediately dispatched several units to the apartment to conduct a parole search, at which time they discovered the incriminating evidence under a sofa. The suspects, two Caucasian brothers in their early thirties, were apprehended without incident and charged with several counts of first degree murder, attempted murder and robbery.

Zach and Sasha's family were ecstatic over the news of the arrests and during the months to come, they monitored the prosecution and attended many of the pre-trial hearings. They were sickened by the sight of the killers in the courtroom and the smug, evil looks on their faces. The brothers expressed no remorse, and in fact seemed to relish the fact that the family members of their victims were themselves victimized by their acts of violence.

Nearly a year to the day after the robbery, the

court considered a motion to suppress evidence filed by the brothers. Accompanying the motion was also a request that the court dismiss all charges.

The evidence sought to be suppressed was the physical evidence obtained after the LAPD entered the apartment upon receipt of the tip. The defense argued that the brother who was on parole was actually discharged from parole several months prior to the search of his apartment, but that the LAPD failed to update its records to confirm the discharge.

As a condition to parole, all convicted offenders must consent to being searched at any time without a warrant. However, since the suspect was not in fact on parole, a warrant was required prior to the search of the apartment. As there was no warrant, the defense argued, all of the evidence obtained at the apartment had to be excluded, and since there was no other evidence linking the brothers to the crimes, all charges had to be dismissed.

After considering the prosecution's opposing argument, which essentially minimized the technical parole search violation and emphasized the callousness of the crimes and the need to keep the brothers off of the street, the judge stunned the courtroom by granting the motion and dismissing all charges. The judge openly acknowledged he was not happy making the decision, but that he was forced to do so in deference to the constitutional rights of the defendants, which rights were violated when their apartment was searched without a warrant.

Zach, Sasha and her parents were blindsided and, to say the least, outraged that the killers would be walking out of the courtroom as free men. In their minds, the failure to procure a warrant–a simple technicality–could not possibly have such catastrophic consequences. No answers were offered to the family by the prosecution team who hurried out of the courtroom after the ruling. Sasha and her family would spend the second worst day of their lives in anguish.

Over the months that followed, Zach found himself immersed in the law and its idiosyncrasies, hoping to find some rationalization for the injustice which occurred. He could not, but his interest in the legal system was forever piqued. He wanted to become a lawyer.

FIVE

RANDY Blake attended Jefferson with Zach, completing his final year as Zach finished his second. Unlike Zach, Randy, fifteen years his senior, already had a prosperous career in the banking industry. Law school to him was a hobby, borne solely out of curiosity.

While attending Jefferson, Zach and Randy shared observations in the school's tiny library about their law professors, novel legal issues, and whom, amongst their fellow students, had no chance of passing the bar. They became good friends. Randy had a wealth of advice for Zach ranging from family life to the principles of mergers and acquisitions.

Out of the blue, Randy called and suggested a get-together to chat about all things legal. As Zach was still very much unemployed since the events at FF&W ten days prior, he took the laboring oar to drive the twenty-five miles to a Starbuck's near Randy's bank.

The two quickly became reacquainted, having lost touch after Randy completed law school. Randy was quite a bit heavier than Zach remembered, and Zach appeared thinner than Randy remembered. Randy attributed his weight gain to the good life, which he admitted included a daily supply of Venti Caramel Frappuccinos with whole milk and several dollops of whipped cream. Zach's weight loss, on the other hand, was his body's reaction to the diminished appetite one experiences after nearly destroying a marriage and a career in one fell swoop.

The two caught up on family, business and gossiping about the success or failings of their former classmates. Zach then laid out the entire FF&W debacle, start to finish.

"You're kidding me," Randy said with a snort-like laugh. "You told him to go fuck himself–were you out of your freakin' mind? Brand spanking new associates do not do that and expect to have a prosperous legal career. I may not be as brilliant as you when it comes to the law, Zach, but business is business, and pissing off the big guns will get you nowhere. You take what's out there as a young lawyer. Do your work, don't ask questions, don't complain, get your paycheck, and go the hell home." Randy snickered throughout his lecture.

"Besides, most insurance companies reap what they sow. Why the hell would you be sticking up for them? They're number two on the list of the most hated professions, lawyers being number one. As far as I'm concerned, you should steal from them all day long if you can get away with it."

"So, what's in store for you now? Has Sasha kicked your ass out of the house after that impulsive blunder? If not, she should have."

"Not sure," Zach quietly answered as though just scolded by his father. "I pondered the idea of starting my own practice, but just the mention of it drew hellfire from my lovely wife. She insists that I get experience with a big firm. In fact, she thinks I'm interviewing as we speak. Perhaps I'll see what I can find with a PI firm. At least I'll get a sense of accomplishment when an injured client receives a settlement. I don't know… I'd like to dance to my own music."

"Well champ, you better lower your expectations and take Sasha's sage advice. Get a job and learn from mentors before you venture out on your own. If you do it any other way, it'll be suicide. Just a word from the wise."

Randy slurped the thick remains of his Frappuccino and glanced at his watch. "Damn, I'm late–sorry to cut this off Zach, but somebody's gotta earn a livin' around here. Hey, if ya ever want a teller job, let me know, now that your legal career's been flushed down a shit-hole." Randy belted an animated laugh as he stood up. Zach couldn't help but to smile, welcoming the comic relief. "Take care of yourself my friend and give Sasha my best. We'll have to do this again, so keep in touch."

Zach watched as Randy darted across the street to Commercial First Bank, envious of his friend's contentment and stability.

The 10 freeway is a nightmare to be avoided, but Zach didn't mind killing time in traffic. It was better that he endure the gridlock in his 12-year-old Corolla than to come home early to face Sasha without having found employment.

As he sat motionless behind an El Camino, bouncing about as its driver showed off its custom hydraulics, Randy called.

"Hey Zach, I was thinking about your situation after I got back to my office. I might possibly have a line on your first and only client. I received a call yesterday from a young man… I believe his name is Andrew. He indicated he was from Texas and that he had a large sum of money to deposit into my bank. Hang on… let me look at my notes here. Yes, Andrew Pearce. He said he was expecting to inherit a substantial amount of money and he wanted to place it with Commercial First. When I quizzed him about where this money was coming from, he said that the public administrator, whoever the hell that is, informed him he was the sole heir of the estate of his brother, who was apparently murdered several months ago. Poor guy."

"I gave him my condolences and inquired as to when he expected to receive the money and how much. He wasn't sure, but said there are things still needed by the public administrator to complete the process. I told him I couldn't help him until he had the money in hand, but that I would be delighted to place it in our bank once he got things worked out."

"Anyway, he asked if I could give him the name of an honest local lawyer to help him through the legal mumbo jumbo. I told him there's no such thing as an honest lawyer, but I'd check around and call him back."

"So," Randy paused, "Ya interested?"

Zach listened intently, but was distracted by the booming sound from the El Camino after the driver rolled down the windows and cranked up the volume.

"Am I interested? Are you kidding me? Let me understand this… you just chewed my ass out and told me to continue with my job search… now you want me to start accepting clients?" Zach spoke loudly with a finger in his left ear and his left elbow controlling the steering wheel while he held his phone in his right hand. His car easily kept pace with the parking lot traffic. The El Camino rumbled with vibrating bass, perfectly choreographed and in sync with its now dancing hydraulics. Zach wished his Corolla was equipped with heat-seeking missile capabilities to permanently stop the racket.

Randy responded, "Yeah, yeah, I know, but guys like you never listen to good advice. They do things the hard way and usually get burned. I'm trying to help you, if you want the help."

"I appreciate the consideration, Randy, but

seriously, how much legal work could a sole heir possibly need when dealing with an inheritance, even if the dead guy was murdered? It's not like there'll be family infighting, illegitimate children making claims, or a scorned lover feeling left out. I'll make a couple hundred dollars in fees, tops... not even enough to pay for the new tires I need on this piece of shit I'm driving.

"Don't know, Counselor, but if you wanna be in business for yourself, you have to start somewhere—give the man a call before he finds a real lawyer. I'll also talk to the higher-ups here at the bank and try to get approval to send ya some small collection matters. Don't worry, I'll forget to mention to them your brief and prosperous career at FF&W."

"Alright, alright, Randy, why not? Shoot me an email with the Texan's info and I'll get the scoop from him. As to any collection cases, that would be fantastic. If this pans out, I'll owe you big time. Thanks for looking out for me."

Traffic eased and Zach was finally able to pass the El Camino. The driver looked over as he gripped his cookie-sized steering wheel, grinning at Zach while bobbing his head to the thumps of the music. Zach smiled back at the happy man, feeling bad for the thought of firing a missile at him.

He exited the freeway near a strip-mall-style office campus, situated in a commercial district in Culver City, a few miles away from his home. He passed it every day on his way to L.A. ... a perfect place for an office. Sasha would never agree, but he thought he'd check it out anyway, especially after his discussion with Randy.

From all appearances, the main office building located in the Culver City Professional Centre was quite a bit older than other structures in the area. Of the thirty or so suites, several were vacant and available, ranging in size from six hundred to three thousand square feet.

The on-site manager was willing to show the available units, but noticeably frowned at Zach's unannounced visit which, according to the large, florescent "BY APPOINTMENT ONLY" sign hanging crooked on her office window, was expressly prohibited.

Her hair, starched to hardened plastic, was pulled back tight enough to force her eyebrows to relocate close to her hairline. Bright red lipstick sloppily covered her thin, nearly non-existent lips.

She unlocked the doors to a few of the units and

allowed Zach access, but didn't accompany him during his inspection, as one would expect from a property manager working hard to market available space. Her crossed arms, lack of interest in conversation, and her please-hurry-up-and-get-the-hell-out-of-here attitude told Zach she was still irritated by his impromptu visit.

The seven hundred square-foot suite, too small for Zach, adjoined a three thousand foot space which was perfect, but well above his anticipated budget. He had no desk or office equipment and surely didn't need anything more than two hundred feet but he settled on the twelve hundred foot unit, at a price of two bucks per foot, not including common-area expenses.

A little paint, some used furniture, a few books to make it look lawyer-office like and he'd be ready for the grand opening of the Law Office of Zachary E. Morgan.

"I'll put the lease together and email it to you. You'll need to complete and return a tenant application, along with a check for the first month's rent, and the security deposit in an amount equal to the first month's rent. This totals forty-eight hundred." The manager glared at Zach as if the two-bit lawyer couldn't add it up himself. She then handed him an application which reeked of cigarette smoke. The lingering vapors, coupled with the yellowing white paint in her office and her smoker's breath, was a dead giveaway that compliance with the no-smoking-inside-office-buildings law effective in the state of California, was not being followed in the Culver City Professional Centre.

"If your credit checks out and you're approved, you can take possession as soon as you're ready." She handed Zach a business card which identified her as Miss Pharout, which she pronounced, "far out."

"One other thing, you should be aware that we have a strict policy of receiving rent on time. This means receiving it, not mailing it. It must be in our office by the first day of the month, not the second or third... the first. Time is of the essence. If you're not making enough money from your business to pay rent, you'd better get it from Mom or Dad or another source 'cause we'll throw you out of here in a heartbeat. We've had lots of wannabees who think they can start a business with a nice suit, a computer, a few phones, and a copy machine, but they quickly fall flat on their faces and can't pay the rent. We nip failure in the bud and have zero tolerance for the inability to pay."

After she finished her monotone disquisition without taking a single breath, she looked Zach dead in the eyes and concluded, "Do you still want the place–yes or no?"

Her deep, whisky drinkin', smoking-like-there's-no-tomorrow voice was intended to be intimidating and it was. Zach clenched his jaw but managed to maintain control, as returning the inhospitality in kind would prove pointless. He politely smiled. "Thank you, I'll get you what you need as soon as my application is approved," as though being approved was a foregone conclusion: fired after a month on the job, no income, little savings–which will decline even more after paying the rent and security deposit–one possible client generating, at best, enough fees to pay the janitor to wash the windows, and a wife on the verge of filing for divorce, who will quite likely hire a hit man to toss him off the Santa Monica pier when she finds out what he's up to.

He pondered whether he needed a shrink to help him out of his funk rather than his own practice. He'd think long and hard before inking his name on Miss Far Out's lease.

SIX

"GOOD afternoon, Andrew, this is Zach Morgan, attorney at law. Randy Blake at Commercial First Bank gave me your name. I understand you're in need of legal assistance in connection with an estate matter."

Andrew took a moment to absorb the unexpected call, then responded, "Oh, yes, yes, I did ask Mr. Blake for help. I didn't hear back from him so I was actually in the process of tryin' to find someone on my own. Thank you for gettin' back to me."

"No problem at all. I hope I can help you," Zach said with enthusiasm.

"Yeah, me too. Here's my situation. I live in Austin, Texas, and I'm the beneficiary of my brother, Ollie's, estate. He was murdered in L.A. recently and it appears I may be the only heir to a large amount of money. I haven't seen him in over a decade so this all came as a shock to me. Someone from the county found me here in Texas and voilà."

Voilà'?... Zach thought, a rather odd term to use while discussing the murder of a brother.

"I see. Well, I'm so sorry about your brother. I know this must be a difficult time for you so let me see what I can do. First of all, are you aware of any problem which requires the services of a lawyer?"

"No, not that I'm aware of anyway. I just want to make sure all things are buttoned up properly and that after I receive the money I invest it for my future. I'm only 23 and I have no idea what to do with this kind of money. I'm also a babe in the woods when it comes to legal mumbo jumbo."

"How much are we talking about?" Zach inquired.

"Well, the public administrator's office wouldn't give me an exact number, but after beating around the bush with a clerk this morning, I shit my pants when she hinted that it exceeds four million dollars."

Stunned by the amount, Zach hoped it wasn't a cruel joke concocted by Randy. He paused, gaining composure. If it was a joke, he'd play along. If not, he needed to sound like a real lawyer to his first potential client.

"Wow, quite a large sum of money. I can see why you'd want an attorney to help you. Why don't you do this, send me what you've received from the administrator and I'll look into it for you? My hourly rate is two hundred dollars and you'll need to sign a retainer agreement. As far as investing the funds, Randy and I can help once you actually receive the money, assuming of course you're entitled to the inheritance."

"To start, I'll need two thousand dollars. This should get us through the preliminaries so we can see where you stand."

"That's a big problem, Mr. Morgan. I have no money... none. I'm living in a sleeping bag in a campground run by a charity. I use a pay-as-you-go cell phone, which may be out of minutes before we even finish this call. The campground has a general delivery mailing address, so you can send the retainer agreement here. But I have no money to send you."

Fantastic, my only client has no money. Randy, you ass, Zach mumbled to himself.

"Well, what do you propose as far as payment,

Andrew? Since you're dealing with the county, the process could drag out, and the expense may be significant. Further, if others decide to come out of the woodwork to claim a piece of the pie, there might be litigation. In such case, you'd be looking at tens of thousands of dollars, and quite possibly much, much more."

Andrew jabbed, "What happened to the two thousand dollar quote? And, I thought you lawyers didn't get paid until you win the case?"

"Not this type of case. You're referring to personal injury cases which are handled on a contingency or percentage basis and this is no personal injury case."

"It is to me, Mr. Morgan, since I'll be devastated personally if I don't get this money. Four million dollars, are you kidding me? Take it away and I might just do a swan dive from this pine tree standing next to me."

Andrew continued, "How 'bout you bend the rules a bit and agree to fifteen percent of the take, due and payable only when I receive the four mill? This way, you'll do a better job helping me knowing you're gettin' some of the prize."

Zach rapidly calculated his fee, nearly causing

smoke to blow from his ears. Fifteen percent; six hundred thousand dollars; six hundred K; six hundred big ones; Randy… I love, love, love you, Zach thought, trying to contain himself.

"Alright, Andrew, I'll do you a favor under these unfortunate circumstances and give you a break from my normal practice. But this is no slam-dunk. You yourself said you were told you may—underline—may, be the only heir. As I said, if there are others, this could get ugly and if it gets ugly, I reserve the right to increase my percentage. Send me the documents and I'll get the retainer agreement to you. No money up front." Zach would have to figure out what a retainer agreement looks like.

"Oh, one more thing, Mr. Morgan, I don't have anything pertaining to my brother, or anyone else in my family for that matter. My parents died when I was young and I bounced from foster home to foster home and haven't seen Ollie since he left South Carolina a long time ago. I don't really have anyone to talk to about this but you."

"No problem," Zach said, feeling sorry for his client, "I'll also send you a disposable cell phone with prepaid minutes to allow us to keep in touch. It's gratis, so don't use it for anything other than speaking to me or someone from my office." Zach didn't disclose that the only "someone" from his office, or more accurately his non-office, was him.

His excitement was tempered, disclaimed by the thought of Sasha. She wouldn't allow him to act like a fool at the expense of his family and she'd have his hide. Despite this, he was consumed with the thrill of defiance, a foe from his teenage years. Sheer impulse put his unauthorized plan into action in a matter of only a few hours. He watched what he was doing but felt—and some part of him hoped—he wasn't actually doing it. Surely, he thought, his misdeeds would be justified after Sasha learned he would soon become chief general counsel for a very wealthy young client. Surely, she'd understand.

SEVEN

THE sales pitch to Sasha would take place over a steak dinner washed down with at least one bottle of the finest cabernet, which, given his current financial condition, happened to be Two Buck Chuck.

He fired up the BBQ, uncorked the bottle, splashed the wine into a beer mug and waited for his beautiful wife to come home to discuss his rise in the ranks of the legal profession.   As usual, Amanda barricaded herself in her room, blasting unintelligible hip-hop from her stereo.   Zach, usually irritated by the noise, found himself tapping to the beat, grinning ear to ear and happy just like the man in the El Camino.

Sasha walked in, surprised to see him home, having ordered him to pound the doors of potential employers day and night until he became a loyal and obedient member of a new law firm.   It was only four o'clock and he most certainly could have been more productive. She was not pleased that he was sipping wine and wearing his filthy BBQ smock imprinted with the faded words, "CHEF DAD," the "CH" nearly invisible.

"It's early, you'd better have good news and that good news better be in the form of a large employer and large salary," Sasha barked, discarding normal pleasantries.

"Well, no on the employer front, but I am glad you asked, baby cakes. Good news is the order of the day. In fact, I have excellent news. We're going to be rich, rich, rich." The wine had already kicked in. "Go give your daughter a big hug and kiss and get yourself into something more comfortable, then I'll tell you how your wonderful, brilliant husband changed the course of our future."

"Oh pu... leeze, you're drunk, Mister, and that description of yourself is not generally accepted." She tossed her purse on the couch and went to her daughter's room, greeting her with a warm hug while multitasking as she picked up a dirty glass and turned down the volume on the sound machine she wished she never gave her for Christmas.

After changing to sweats, she reappeared in the

kitchen, was handed a full glass of wine by the still smiling Zach and took a seat across from him at the small, laminated dining table. The now overcooked steak remained on the grill drying out to leather.

"Let's hear it," she ordered.

Zach described the meeting with Randy, which he insisted was in fact a job interview, not an unproductive, fun get-together with an old friend which would have gotten him into trouble.

He went on to explain, with some exaggeration, the discussion with Andrew about the horrible tragedy involving his brother and how desperately Andrew needed his legal expertise. He concluded by detailing the hefty fee he would earn for his services.

"Not bad for my first client, eh? I'll receive a copy of the file within a few days and a signed retainer agreement. I'll then start working with the public administrator to sort it all out. Once it's done, we'll be in hoooog heaven. My first client will put us in the black for years and years and years... new house, new car and plenty of moolah in the bankaroo."

Zach, showing the consequences of his over-consumption of wine, was uncharacteristically pompous.

Sasha listened quietly as he slurred through the remaining events of the day, declining to utter a single word until she could take no more.

"Time out." She jumped in. "So let me understand this." Zach didn't like the tone in her voice and knew he was headed for another tongue-lashing. He was not the life of their little celebration party as he had hoped. His excitement instantly evaporated.

"You have no idea when–or even if–this supposed fee will be paid, but you do know that not a single penny will be paid up front; you're draining our small life savings and leasing an office based upon this speculative fee; you're terminating all efforts to find other employment based upon this speculative fee; and the client whom you've unilaterally decided to hang our financial future on is a twenty-three-year-old, penniless, homeless man living in the woods over fifteen-hundred miles away who, for all you know, may be feeding you a crock of scheisse while injecting chemicals into his arm… does that about cover it, Mister EF DAD, 'cause I wanna make sure I got it all?"

Zach, surprised by the pinpoint accuracy of her summary, became defensive and paused while he carefully crafted what would be a lame response. "Sasha, c'mon I need to start somewhere for cryin' out loud. I think this guy's for real. Lots of lawyers have successful toaster practices and I don't know why you think I'm less capable than they are."

"What the hell is a toaster practice? You're drunk."

"They take whatever pops up." Zach smiled and Sasha couldn't resist a grin and hesitated before responding.

"It's not that I don't believe you're capable, Zach," Sasha said, now less agitated, "It's just that we have a family and commitments and you have no experience. I'm afraid of what it will do to us. I'm not doubting that you can be successful, I'm just completely in the dark—as are you—as to what is required to thrive in the legal business. I may be wrong, but you can't just pass the bar one day, tell a senior partner at a prestigious law firm to go screw himself a month later, and expect me to have confidence that you possess the knowledge or experience to start your own law practice."

"Believe me, I respect you, and I'm aware that you would do anything for us. I just think you need some

OJT under your belt before you think about doing this."

Zach responded, "Well, Randy guaranteed he'd send some collection cases from his bank." Slight misrepresentation, as Randy guaranteed no such thing. "That'll bring in some cash too."

After a long pause, Zach looked at Sasha, her eyes fixated on her glass of wine, contemplating. "Please, hon, let me give it a try, I promise I won't let you down."

Sasha looked up, frustrated. "Ugh, to put this behind us once and for all because I'm convinced you'll never shut up unless I do, I'll make you a deal which is not subject to negotiation. I'll give you six months, and not a day longer, to show me you can make enough money to at least pay the bills for your little adventure. Our savings will only pay two to three months' rent and maybe some of your incidental expenses. Therefore, you better start bringing in money now if you expect to stay afloat beyond a few months. If you can make it work in six months, I'll get off your ass for a little while. If you can't, you're done and you'll hit the interview circuit... capiche?"

Her sudden compromise triggered goose bumps. Ecstatic, he grabbed her shoulders and looked her in the eyes, her face blurry from the effects of the booze. "Sasha, I love you more than words can express, and you are right about one thing—I'll do anything and everything I can to provide for you and Amanda. This means so much to me and you won't regret it. If it doesn't come together in six months, I'll abandon my silly plan, I promise."

"Well, this is against my better judgment, Zach, but I really do hope it works out for you, and us." Although she said nothing of the sort, she was actually excited for her drunk husband.

* * * * *

"Oh for Pete's sake, you have a fifty-two-percent vacancy rate in this center, you've approved my credit, I'm holding a check for forty-eight hundred dollars and I'm ready to sign the lease. I just need the term to be six months, not one year. I'll even agree to extend for a year after the six months is up, but I can't do a one-year lease, not yet anyway."

Miss Far Out shot back, "Well, sir, we only do one-year leases here. We're not flexible on this issue, regardless of our vacancy rate. If, after one year, the rent is paid on time, we'll let you extend for another year. But we don't do six-month leases. Therefore, if you want a six-month lease, go somewhere else."

Zach pleaded, "I guarantee all rent will be paid in a timely manner during the six-month period." Zach lied. "So what's the big deal? Six months' rent is better than no rent, which is exactly what you'll receive if I go somewhere else, right?"

"No. I'm busy and you're wasting my time. Sign, or don't sign, the rules are the rules." Miss Far Out stared at Zach as she waited for an answer. Her arms were tightly crossed and her upper body drooped back as though she was about to levitate. Zach considered thumping her on her tight, shiny little head, poking her eyes like Moe did to Curly, and bolting out the door.

He signed the lease, handed it to the bitch from hell along with his check, and prayed to the lord almighty that he'd get the money from Andrew or other clients in less than six months to avoid the wrath of Sasha.

It took him a few days to paint and decorate the office and to acquire used furnishings and equipment, including a telephone system. He hoped to graduate to an automated answering service sometime down the road, but for now, he'd be his own secretary. He placed ads in the local newspapers and on Internet sites offering legal services in all areas of practice.

On February 1, 2011, the Law Office of Zachary E. Morgan opened for business.

EIGHT

AMONG other functions, the Los Angeles County Public Administrator handles the estates of those who die in the county without wills or known heirs. Upon death, the PA's office will appoint a deputy administrator to investigate the decedent's affairs in an effort to ascertain next of kin and potential heirs. The administrator will also do what is necessary to marshal and protect assets until heirs can be located and a probate concluded.

The investigation into the estate of Oliver Pearce was assigned to Shelly Presley, a 22-year veteran of the PA's office. Over the years, she developed a compassion for the families of those who died in her jurisdiction. Many of the next-of-kin were distant relatives with little or no recollection of the decedent. In a few cases, the heirs purposely lost contact with the decedent and couldn't care less about his or her lonely death. Not surprisingly, their lackadaisical feelings toward the dearly departed quickly turned to feigned grief, sorrow and mourning once it was disclosed that something of value may be passed down to them.

Presley didn't have much to work with, other than the computer found at Ollie's home. Techs at the crime lab conducted an exhaustive analysis of the computer which contained hundreds of downloaded investment reports, as well as thousands of colorful charts, countless articles written by Wall Street talking heads, and a vast arsenal of other materials one would expect to find in the possession of a successful individual investor.

Books such as *How to Buy Short in a Bullish Market*, *How to Create and Keep Wealth Through Online Trading*, and *A Foolproof Guide to Timing the Market*, were loaded onto Ollie's hard drive.

He held seven accounts with three different online brokerage firms. Four of the accounts were used to deposit his profits; the other three were investment accounts. The funds in the latter accounts were used for trading in the electronic market.

A review of his transaction history reflected that

Ollie was a serious day trader. He flipped securities shortly after he purchased them, sometimes within a few minutes, rather than holding them long term and allowing an orderly appreciation in value, as recommended by conventional wisdom. A good day trader anticipated and profited from quick market fluctuations. Even a small percentage gain in price could mean a substantial profit.

Ollie also participated in short selling securities. He'd sell shares he didn't own yet. If the share price fell below what the buyer paid him, he would buy shares from someone else at the lower price and cover the prior sale by giving those shares to the original buyer. In other words, he pre-sold the shares for more than what he ultimately paid for them, thus generating a profit.

This repetitive trading on a daily basis rewarded Ollie with massive accumulated wealth. He wisely learned to hedge his investments to prevent them from quickly evaporating when market conditions unexpectedly went in the wrong direction.

The records revealed that Ollie began his career as an investor with approximately one hundred twelve thousand dollars, the source of which was not known. According to Presley, his liquid assets at the time he was murdered approached $4,300,000, equating to a return on his investments of over thirty-eight hundred percent in a little over ten years. Stunning.

As for other assets, Ollie had little. Most of his furnishings were either old and dilapidated or destroyed by the blood splatter. He had $425 in cash at his home, a few DVDs and electronics, including a television, computer and two video game systems, having a combined best-guess value of $1,500.

The coin collection found by the police consisted of twelve Susan B. Anthony dollars, worth about twelve dollars.

His computer also stored other personal, but seemingly unimportant files, such as a few old photographs of Ollie and his family. Another file, entitled, "Misc.," held hundreds of scanned invoices and receipts for utilities, groceries, computer supplies and other purchases over the course of thirteen years. Each invoice was categorized and the details incorporated into a lengthy spreadsheet.

It was clear Ollie was a data packrat, consumed with what he earned and what he spent. Presley found this odd, given that his life appeared to be as exciting as a stop sign and there was no need for him to worry about depleting his massive cash reserve.

One notable item found in a file, identified only by the letters, "CSC," turned out to be the key to locating Andrew and discovering more information about Ollie. The file contained a scanned newspaper article published in the Columbia, South Carolina, *Tribune* on December 16, 1997.

The article detailed the horrible accidental explosion and fire which killed Mr. Pearce, leaving behind his two sons, Oliver Randall Pearce and Andrew Sean Pearce.

The younger Andrew was placed in child protective services, having no other family members to care for him, except Ollie. According to the article, Ollie refused to be a parent to his younger brother and moved out of state.

Although sympathetic to the tragedy, the author wasted no time pointing out their father's long arrest record, which included assault, spousal abuse, car theft, and the distribution of illegal and prescription drugs to minors.

A reader's comment under the article offered the

following condolences: *"Good riddance. The drug dealin' scumbag should have been roasted earlier. He was a cancer to our schools and our community."*

Other files stored on the computer were evaluated by the LAPD, but disregarded as having no known material impact on the murder investigation.

The task of locating Andrew turned out to be more routine than Presley thought it would be. The Department of Social Services in Columbia, provided the names of the foster parents who cared for Andrew over the years since the fire.

The most recent family, Stanley and Rebecca Johnson, took him in for several months about five years ago. He left town after he reached eighteen.

Andrew sporadically contacted the Johnsons, but only when convenient to him. He'd call... broke, and they'd send him small amounts of money from their social security stipend. Finding employment to earn his own money was difficult for Andrew, particularly since he didn't spend a single day seeking employment.

According to the Johnsons, Andrew moved around quite a bit, but settled down as an unpaid camp counselor in Austin, Texas. They gave Presley the telephone number and the mailing address for the campground and offered to help her any other way they could.   Presley decided against disclosing the fact that little Andrew was going to be a very rich man.

NINE

RAY Mason had consumed far too much malt liquor when the two police officers approached him as he slept off his hangover in an alley.

He was known amongst the homeless as Scooter, a nickname given to him based upon his mode of transportation–a customized, two-wheeled, foot-powered scooter capable of carrying his worldly possessions in several attached old milk crates.

Scooter was, perhaps by necessity, a punk. Tattooed from head to toe, his long straggly brown hair partially concealed his bushy, out-of-control handlebar moustache.

Seventeen years ago, he was forced onto the streets when his family was evicted from their apartment in downtown L.A. Scooter was only a teenager and learned to survive the hard way. Drugs and alcohol infiltrated his young life and petty crimes were committed to support his addictions. He had no one to turn to and crack and booze provided the perfect escape, which he initially found exciting. But he quickly learned that he couldn't escape the escape. He had no way out. There would never be a way out.

He was now thirty-four, but could pass for fifty or older. The hot California sun, coupled with his lifestyle, took its toll in a major way.

Scooter earned his living by panhandling on random corners or freeway off-ramps, holding one of three hand-written signs. He wanted repeat customers and believed a variety of messages would keep them interested. This was his protected trade secret which he alone developed, and he made it clear that if he caught any of his competitors doing the same thing, all hell would break loose.

His selection of signage depended upon the day of the week. The Monday and Wednesday sign, made of crumpled brown cardboard, contained the words, "*Proude Vitnam vet in nead of a meal, Plese Help!!!*" The Stars and Stripes was crudely drawn over its torn bottom edge. Despite his business acumen, Scooter neglected to consider that even if he were fifty, as he appeared to be, he would have been too young for service in Vietnam.

For Tuesdays and Fridays, he would solicit customers by displaying his fancy white cardboard sign, which read: *"outa gas….. my famlie is Strandid anithing will Help!!!"* More false advertising, as he had no car and no family.

His patrons were greeted the remainder of the week with a large red-and-white poster board he would spin to get their attention. He stole this idea from a furniture-store guy he saw doing a spinning routine while dancing. Scooter wanted to look just like him but he couldn't spin every day, given that it would tire him out, and he was never able to duplicate the talent of his idol. He usually spun the sign too fast and without coordination, such that it could only be read by customers waiting at long intersections. It had the words: *"I will due anithing U wunt me 2 due for a warme meal, and I meen anything???"* Under the words was a smiley face.

On the spinning-sign days, he received requests from smart-ass customers to do jumping jacks, sit-ups, underarm farts, impersonations and animal sounds. He had to sing opera and Christmas carols and even do the robot. One client paid him five bucks to light his moustache on fire. Scooter complied and wound up in the emergency room with first degree burns after it spread to his hair.

When he began his panhandling career, he'd approach each driver and flat out beg for money. This practice quickly ended when a pissed-off customer driving a new BMW kindly told him, "I got some money for you, you piece of shit... let me get it." The generous customer then reached under his seat for his .45, aimed it at poor Scooter and fired over his head, blowing out his eardrums. As he hauled ass, Scooter read his customer's lips, "Now get the fuck away from my car, you worm." Needless to say, he learned to keep his distance and only approach customers when authorized.

Although his customers came first and service was always with a toothless smile, Scooter hated the rude and obnoxious people, every stinking one of them.

Fortunately, living on the streets didn't require much money. Restaurant and grocery store dumpsters supplied Scooter with a smorgasbord of free, rotten food, still edible, and oftentimes quite tasty. Cash was needed only for his cold brew, and his thriving panhandling business provided enough cash to cop a buzz on a daily basis.

As he lay drunk in the alley, the two officers gently kicked him to see if he was dead. Scooter groaned and slurred, "Wut da fuck," which told them he was not. Too bad, they thought.

"Get your ass up and put your hands behind your back," one of the deputies commanded.

"What the hell'd I do?" He complained, yelling a few expletives as he struggled to get to his feet.

"Loitering, drunk-in-public, to name a few." They proceeded to handcuff him and muscle him into the squad car. The scooter mobile and all of his personal and business belongings stayed behind to be picked through and taken by other transients.

During processing at the county jail, Deputy Cramer, the jail supervisor, observed what appeared to be dried blood covering Scooter's jacket and pants. To the layman, the blood could pass for the kind of stains one accumulates while living on the streets for over a decade. But to the trained deputy, the stains gave him reason to inquire. He handed Scooter jail garb to change into in exchange for his clothes.

"Mr. Mason, could you please tell me why you

have blood all over your clothes? ... and don't lie my friend."

Scooter, less inebriated than when arrested, was still hostile. He shouted, "I ain't your friend, asshole, and I don't speak to pigs, ever. You want to talk to me, you get me a lawyer."

"Oh I see, so you're gonna lawyer-up, eh? It's your right, but it won't make things any easier for you, you slimeball. We'll take this up later." Deputy Cramer yanked Scooter's handcuffs and pulled him toward the holding tank, tossing him into the cell.

Undaunted, Scooter yelled, "You can lock me up all you want pig, but it ain't gonna change the fact that that son-of-a-bitch deserved what he got and I'd do it again. I'll let you have it too if you come back here and fuck wit' me you jackass."

Deputy Cramer absorbed the comments made by his prisoner, then packaged the bloody clothing in an evidence bag and delivered the bag to Detective Susan Rogers, who happened to be the first detective he ran into at the station.

"Not sure what, if anything, we have here, Detective. I think you may want to check it out. We picked up this drunk over on South Victory Boulevard wearing these clothes, which appear to be stained with blood. Don't know if it's animal blood or human blood, but to me it looks like blood, and lots of it."

"Yep, sure does," Detective Rogers said, examining the items. "Who is this guy?"

"His name is Ray Mason, lives on the street. No priors, but we haven't completely checked him out yet. We thought he was just another drunk littering the city. The arresting officers failed to take note of the blood. Anyway, Mason volunteered to me that the victim deserved it and he'd do it again. Not sure what he was talking about. He zipped his lips pretty quick and asked for a lawyer."

"Hmm... let me do some checking," the detective replied as she continued to examine the clothing. "Find out where he was picked up and get back to me. I'll go out and take a look around."

TEN

COMFORTABLY situated in his new office, Zach wasn't quite sure how he was supposed to practice law without being fed a daily supply of billable files by Ticktock. No clients waited for him in the lobby and his calendar was clear. Until now, the excitement of hanging his own shingle consumed him and the reality of running a practice for a profit, or just to break even, was a worry for another day.

Not wanting to be bothered with the minutia of business matters, Zach did the one thing any young lawyer would do under the same circumstances: lock the office door, dim the lights, put his feet up on his used desk, sway back in his used executive chair, close his eyes, smile proudly and drift off to sleep.

His heart palpitated when the phone rattled like an old fire alarm. The ringer option on the used phone system was never adjusted to a modern professional tone and the volume shrieked at maximum level.

He abruptly came out of his temporary coma and grabbed the phone. While tilting up from the horizontal position in his chair with his legs still extended, he lost his balance, causing him, his coffee, the one sentence retainer agreement he prepared for Andrew, and the telephone to come crashing to the ground. His chair rolled to the other side of the office as he was dumped out of it.

In the chaos, Zach stumbled to articulate the appropriate office greeting. "Shit. Hello... I mean Law Office of Zachary Morgan, sorry about that, may I help you?"

"Wow, are you okay? I'm not sure what that was all about but it didn't sound fun. Yes, good morning, this is Shelly Presley with the Los Angeles County Public Administrator's Office, is Zachary Morgan available?"

"Yes, this is he. Your ears must be ringing, as I was just about to give you a call when one of my staff spilled hot coffee, causing a bit of a ruckus." Zach learned at FF&W that simple white lies are perfectly acceptable in the legal profession. If necessary, major fabrications are also appropriate as long as they're made verbally.   If it's not in writing, it didn't happen.

"Thank you for calling.   I assume you'd like to discuss the Andrew Pearce matter?" Zach stuttered–heat overcoming his face as he realized he was finally providing legal representation on behalf of his first client.

Holding the handset to the phone with the cord stretched like a tightrope while kneeling on the floor in his dark office, coffee burning him where coffee shouldn't be, and speaking to the woman who would be instrumental in cutting him a very large check if he didn't manage to screw things up, was not a promising grand opening for his new office.

"Yes I would," Presley responded.   "As you know, we have an interesting case here.   Your client appears to be the sole heir and in line to receive several million dollars from the estate of his brother, Oliver Pearce, or Ollie, as I understand he was known as. According to Andrew, he and his brother hadn't spoken in years and he wasn't even aware of the death.   County records from South Carolina and elsewhere suggest there are no other family members, except a distant cousin of Ollie's father."

"Obviously, what makes this case unusual, other

than the murder itself, is the nature of the murder…
rather macabre."

"Yeah, I agree. Definitely not your garden-variety probate matter," Zach said, adding his two cents. "I read a few of the press releases, but if you have any additional information as to what happened, perhaps you can share it if you don't mind?"

"Oh certainly."

Presley then described Ollie's peculiar and reclusive lifestyle, and provided a brief overview of the crime and the way Ollie was tortured.

"There are other details I'm not privy to, but you're welcome to speak to Detective Cranston with the LAPD who's handling the investigation. I'm not sure what, if any, additional information he'd be willing to disclose to you."

"Thank you, but I don't think I'll need to involve myself too much in the gruesome part of this case. If I need further specifics, I'll give him a call."

"Now, getting to the logistics of the estate, what do you need from us? Whatever it is, I can assure you we'll do what we can to provide it to your office, ASAP." Zach was beginning to get into the rhythm of zealously representing his client.

"I appreciate that. I'll put together an information packet and a claim form for you to review. A petition to administer the estate was filed shortly after death. Once we receive the information from your client, and other documents we're waiting for, we'll act expeditiously to close it out with the probate court and distribute the proceeds. To the extent there are any creditors, they'll have the statutory period to present their claims to the court. I doubt we'll have any claims though. Ollie was meticulous about paying his bills and didn't appear to owe anything to anyone."

Presley continued, "Counsel has been appointed to take over from our office and you'll deal with him going forward. Given the manner of death and the large amount of money, this case will be monitored closer than others. Standard procedure. Overall, I anticipate a routine process which should conclude within the next few months, assuming no complications."

Zach was mindful of the six-month deadline imposed by Sasha, but declined to ask Presley whether the "few months" meant more than six. He thought about the fire-breathing Miss Far Out, who was no doubt chain smoking in her office, washing down the nicotine with a nice bottle of moonshine. She'd evict him in a minute if he didn't pay the rent when it was due.

"Well, Shelly, I appreciate your time. When you send the package, could you also include any of the reports or data released by the LAPD which you may have in your file? I'd like to have a complete file for myself so that I can address any issue which may arise in the future."

"Oh sure, no problem. The more we share, the more productive we'll be in concluding this matter so we can get Andrew what he is entitled to. I hope he's holding up well under the circumstances."

"As well as can be expected," Zach replied generically, not disclosing that Andrew didn't appear to be suffering from grief over the death of his long-lost brother, the money no doubt easing his pain.

After hanging up, Zach stood up from behind his desk, picked up the things scattered on the floor and did a hulk-like muscle flex, quietly shouting, "yes... yes" The Law Office of Zachary E. Morgan was now firing on all cylinders.

He decided to leave work early, given that he had

no other clients to tend to at the office, and visit Dillion at the Franklin House in Pacific Palisades. The Franklin House was a long term spinal injury care and recovery facility. Dillon was placed there after he was released from the hospital. Zach and Sasha made an effort to see him as often as they could.

Over the years since the shooting, Dillon regained his ability to speak, without any discernable impediment. He also had a computer assistive device which allowed him to browse the internet, send and receive email, watch movies and do the same things others could do with a computer. The device was equipped with eye-gazing software which afforded him the ability to use the movements of his eyes to control a computer mouse.

Initially, Dillon didn't show much interest in the technology, or anything else for that matter. He was unable to adapt to the life of a vegetable and suffered from severe depression. He soon learned that recovering from debilitating injuries required recovery of the mind, not the body. With the help of support groups, he worked through his depression and no longer agonized over his paralysis... and often joked about it. Zach felt that he was slowly returning to the Dillon of old.

"About time, Zach," he said as Zach entered in his room. "What the hell took you so long, did you walk?" Dillon was sitting upright in his bed, his computer monitor in front of him, as his eyes shifted to Zach.

Zach approached the bed and lifted Dillon's hand to assist him with a fist pump, a greeting from their younger days which Zach continued after Dillon's paralysis. "It's called traffic, something you don't have to worry about in here. You look chipper, how the heck have ya been?"

"Been doing great. Working out every day without having to lift a finger, getting in a good swim here and there, seen a few movies and had some great mac and cheese; otherwise, can't complain. How 'bout you?"

"Just peachy. Finally got the law practice going. It's moving along. I was even able to take the day off to see you."

"Nice to hear that," Dillon said with a smile, I knew it was a challenge... congratulations. Maybe someday I can pay ya a visit to your new digs. In fact, I'm looking into resuming my legal studies. Shit, I only had a year of school to go when those bastards shot me.

I'm told that I can pick up where I left off and complete the process online. I don't know what it will lead to, but I've got lots of spare time on my hand I might as well do something with it."

"Good for you Dill. I'll do what I can to help you along. There's a real need for research attorneys out there, and you'd obviously make a good one. It's great to see you on the mend and taking control of your future. You have a lot to offer, my friend."

They spent the next hour discussing Dillon's new goal and catching up with each other. When Dillon began to doze off, Zach quietly left.

He enjoyed the drive home from Pacific Palisades, despite the traffic, and always took the long route down the Pacific Coast Highway. He played the Eagles, louder than normal, with his window down as he absorbed the unparalleled beauty and serenity of the Pacific Ocean and its calming waves.

To his right, down a slight embankment, the mystery of the sea began, spanning thousands of miles. To his left, there was no mystery. Expensive sports cars raced past his old Toyota, the drivers recklessly maneuvering between vehicles, determined to be the first to reach the next red light. Their fancy cars were symbols of status, objects of envy. Zach was not interested in either.

While waiting for the light to turn at a busy intersection, Zach revved his engine, not as a show of force, but to prevent it from stalling. As the light turned green his old car sputtered to reach the next exit toward home.

ELEVEN

DETECTIVE Rogers parked in an alleyway between a gas station and check-cashing business on South Victory Boulevard in Burbank. The area was run down, a good place for a bum like Scooter to sleep it off.

She carefully canvassed the general vicinity where Scooter was found, looking for anything unusual. Transients typically had personal items in backpacks or stolen shopping carts they wheeled around.

A blue milk crate abutting a wall adjacent to a gas station grabbed her attention. In the crate were several items: a baseball cap, a rolled up t-shirt, an empty beer bottle, a folded cardboard please-feed-me sign, a pair of shoes and a large pipe wrench. The shoes and the wrench were heavily stained with a substance resembling blood.

She called for backup and had the area roped off. Investigators processed the scene and removed the crate, using care not to contaminate the evidence.

An analysis of the stains confirmed that the blood was in fact human. Further, a comparison of the blood found on Scooter's clothing at the jail with the stains found on the shoes and wrench, came back as a match.

A warrant was issued for a sample of Scooter's blood. Not surprisingly, the results were negative. It was not his blood on his clothing or the other items.

To satisfy a natural hunch, Detective Rogers pulled the files of active murder investigations and compared the blood of the victims to the blood on Scooter's clothing and belongings. A comparison of blood and other evidence resulted in only one likely match.

On February 3, 2011, Scooter was arrested and charged with first-degree murder for the death of Oliver Randall Pearce. As, he was already in custody for the drunk-in-public offense, Detective Rogers informed him of the new charge in his cell. As expected, he went berserk and responded with a barrage of obscenities. Through his rant, his denial of having murdered anyone was manifest, but ignored. He threatened to get even with those bringing him the news.

Detective Rogers continued to seek tips from the public in hopes of finding further evidence linking Scooter to the crime. A tip from Constance Federoff, an elderly widow living in the same area as Oliver Pearce, placed Scooter at the scene at or about the day of the murder. Mrs. Federoff informed the LAPD that she distinctly saw a man on a scooter, rigged with attached milk crates, racing past her home. Her description of the crates matched the description of the crate found by Detective Rogers.

Another witness, William Parham, a homeless man, provided a statement confirming that Scooter rode around the city on a two-wheeled scooter with a number of crates attached to it for storage. Mr. Parham found the scooter in the alleyway after Scooter was arrested for being drunk and took it for his own use. He later turned it over to the LAPD. The scooter matched the one seen by Constance Federoff.

The LAPD felt that these witnesses, coupled with the blood and other physical evidence, would help secure a conviction. Further, Scooter's statement that the victim "deserved everything he got" and that he would "do it again," when asked about the bloody clothes, was tantamount to a confession and, according to the LAPD, eliminated any reasonable doubt about his guilt.

Detective Cranston praised the work of Detective Rogers and proudly announced at a press conference that the gruesome crime had been solved due to the outstanding investigative efforts of the LAPD. The people of Los Angeles were reassured they could feel safe in their homes knowing the perpetrator was in custody. He felt compelled to urge the district attorney's office to seek the death penalty due to the nature and gravity of the offense.

TWELVE

AFTER a few days as his firm's senior partner, the only calls Zach received at his new office, other than from Shelly Presley, were from a pushy legal software salesman, Sasha, and Miss Far Out, who had to remind him that in addition to the base rent, she expected to receive his share of lease common-area expenses in a timely manner. She wasn't sure whether she previously made that clear to him. She had.

However, things began to improve for the firm within the next two weeks, when advertisements in the local newspapers paid off. Zach was finally able to schedule a few consultations.

He gave up trying to compose his own retainer agreement for Andrew and borrowed a real one from a random law firm's website. After making slight revisions to the compensation portion of the agreement, he sent it to Andrew along with the disposable cell phone. Andrew was instructed to sign and return the agreement and to call Zach every Wednesday at noon.   As it was now Wednesday, Andrew called at precisely noon.

Zach received the file from Presley the day before Andrew called. Not much in the file: a copy of the article relating to the death of Andrew's parents and a report of the people she contacted in her efforts to locate Andrew. She also provided three CDs which contained data from Ollie's computer. A yellow sticky-note was attached indicating "FYI."

The report had no surprises and was otherwise consistent with his conversation with Presley.   Zach undertook a cursory review of the material on the CDs. It was all investment data–irrelevant to Andrew or the estate. He made a mental note to study the information in greater detail later, as Ollie no doubt had a secret for success and Zach would love to learn it.

"Hello Andrew, I'm glad to see you received the things I sent. How've you been?"

"Been okay... just like to get this thing wrapped up quickly so I can put it behind me," as though receiving four million dollars was something dreadful he'd like to forget.

He continued. "So have you spoken to the administrator's office about my money?"

"I have," Zach responded. "There have been a few developments since we last spoke."

"What developments?"

"Well, I'm not sure if you were told, but your brother's killer was arrested. They found him wearing bloody clothes and in possession of what appeared to be the murder weapon. Looks like they'll seek the death penalty."

"Are you shittin' me? No, I didn't hear that!" Andrew shouted. "Why wasn't I told about this sooner? Goddamn son-of-a-bitch. Did they find out why he killed my brother the way he did? I hope the loser rots in hell and I get to watch as they execute his sorry ass." Andrew was excited. He continued talking a mile a minute.

"Calm down, Andrew," Zach interrupted tactfully, "they just arrested him yesterday. It was all over the news."

"Sweet Jesus, happiest day in my life!" Andrew shouted.

Zach continued, "I don't have too many details

about the killer or his motive yet. Apparently, the guy lives on the street; he's a transient. Not sure why he did what he did, but I'll keep you posted as I receive more information. The arraignment is in a few days and I plan to attend."

"Well, I hope you'll attend. You're my attorney aren't you?" Andrew said bluntly, his tone surprising Zach. "You need to tell me everything that goes on with that son-of-a-bitch. Maybe you can get close enough to whisper in his ear that brother Andrew will get painful revenge someday when he least expects it. That'll spook the bastard, ha-ha-ha."

"No can do, Andrew. I won't be able to get anywhere near him at the hearing. There'll be lots of security. But I'll give you a recap of what happens."

Zach moved on. "I also spoke at length with Shelly Presley who, as you know, is handling the estate matter. According to her, the process may take several months since a probate action had to be filed in the superior court to confirm there are no other heirs or creditors claiming an interest in the estate."

"What? I'm the only heir and my brother had plenty of money to pay his bills. Why the hell do they need to go through that bullshit?"

"It's routine. I'll be sending you a self-explanatory form for you to complete, sign and return. And don't forget to send back the signed retainer agreement, if you haven't already done so."

"I'm not one bit happy that this is going to take so long. I'm living in a sleeping bag in a campground and I'm a multi-millionaire. Something's wrong with this picture and I'm paying you to fix it. And, I sent the retainer agreement back to you yesterday, without reading it, so I hope I'm not getting screwed. Please, Mr. Morgan, I hired you to get this done quickly, so do everything you can, even if you need to slip a few bucks to Elvis Presley or whatever her name is."

"No payoffs, Andrew. We're going by the book. You have my word I'll do what I can to wrap this up as soon as possible. Call me next week at noon."

"Whatever," Andrew begrudgingly replied and hung up.

Zach looked at the telephone receiver, hoping future conversations with his demanding client wouldn't be so terse.

It was 12:25 and he felt he deserved the rest of

the day off, which meant he and Sasha could drive together to Amanda's championship soccer game later that afternoon.

In his spare time, which he had a lot of lately, Zach volunteered to assist his daughter's team. He hoped the contacts made as a soccer dad could be converted to legal business for the firm.

Marketing began prior to the game. He distributed his new business cards to parents on both teams, the officiating team, the snack bar helpers, and anyone else who would take them. He also gave out free legal advice to those who asked—and even to those who didn't. Whether his soccer-field lawyering was productive or competent, remained to be seen. If he got two or three clients out of it, it would be worth his while.

Amanda played the position of right forward. She had agility, ball control and speed, but she was the youngest and smallest player on the field. Her team, The Scream, lost only one game, winning nine. They were playing The Incredibles for the under-nine league championship. The Incredibles never lost, beating Amanda's team earlier in the season.

The Scream won the toss and kicked off. The

ball went to Amanda, who crossed into enemy territory before two of her opponents doubled her up, maliciously stealing the ball from her. They proceeded to pass it methodically, weaving in and out of The Scream's defenders. Boom! The Scream's fullback booted the ball hard, clearing it away from the goal all the way to the other side of the field. The Scream players took several shots at the goal, but the ball was punted back into The Scream territory by the aggressive goalie. The Incredibles drilled a few more shots at the net, each missing by inches.

This sequence of possession changes continued over the first three quarters, without a score for either team. As is typical, the defining moments often occur in the waning moments of a soccer game.

As the end of the fourth quarter approached, cheers from the large crowd intensified. The players had their second wind and to them, the game had just begun.

Amanda was at midfield. She passed the ball to her teammate who lobbed it directly in front of The Incredibles' goal. Amanda raced to the ball and fired a shot, hitting the post and ricocheting the ball to her teammate, who instinctively tapped it into the net. The parents erupted. The Scream–1, The Incredibles–0.

Zach watched, choked-up, goose bumps peppered his body.

With less than a minute to go, The Scream attempted unsuccessfully to wrangle the ball away from the opposing forward who raced down the sideline. She launched a missile from the left corner to the edge of the goal. The crowd gasped as The Scream's goalie flew, superman style, to punch the ball away from the net, saving the goal and the game. The cheers were deafening.

Amanda and her teammates hurried off the field, jumping, hugging and bawling their eyes out. They deserved to win–both teams did.

Huddling together, the teary-eyed coach congratulated the girls for winning the tough battle, spoke a few words of inspiration, and confirmed the date and time for the team party. The team mom passed out cupcakes and fruit drinks, which the girls proceed to throw at each other in a victory food fight.

On the way home, Amanda, excited and animated, relived each moment of the game as Sasha and Zach filled in the blanks.

Thoroughly enjoying the afternoon, Zach

imagined a life where he could spend all of his waking moments with his small family. They gave him sanity and purpose. The practice of law distanced him from the pleasures of a simple life and catapulted him into chaos and uncertainty. His dream of a legal career conflicted with his desire to be a devoted and dedicated father and husband. If a balance was ever to be found between these competing interests, he'd have to look hard to find it.

THIRTEEN

ZACH attended Scooter's arraignment, per his promise to Andrew. Such hearings are typically uneventful; the defendant either pleads guilty, not guilty, or no contest to the alleged crime. Although a not-guilty plea was a foregone conclusion, the press filled the courtroom, anxious to get a glimpse of the heinous killer.

Stuart Brooks of the Los Angeles County Public Defender's Office represented Scooter. The prosecutor was a short, skinny, fidgety fellow named Robert Skaggs. Zach wondered how such a slight man could stomach everything that goes along with capital murder cases and not be spooked by the crazed killers seated only a few feet from him.

Scooter was present and looked much like he did when he was arrested, except he wore an orange jumpsuit. As expected, he pled not guilty to all charges. However, his refusal to waive his right to a speedy trial, almost always waived in murder cases, was not anticipated and stunned the prosecutor.

With his deep voice resonating from counsel table, Brooks announced, "Your Honor, let it be known that Mr. Mason not only insists upon a speedy trial, as is his constitutional right, but he waives the preliminary hearing and, for that matter, any and all other hearings and defense motions. He will be prepared to proceed to trial in sixty days or less, provided that the prosecution turns over all discoverable material forthwith. Mr. Mason is not guilty of the offenses to which he is charged and, in fact, he is completely innocent of all such crimes and he wishes to prove his innocence in due haste. Therefore, Your Honor, we respectfully request that this matter be placed on the trial calendar at the court's earliest convenience."

The accused generally has the right to be brought to trial within sixty days of the arraignment and to have a preliminary hearing within ten days of the arraignment. By waiving these procedural rights, the defendant is afforded substantial additional time to prepare his defense. In a capital case, trial in sixty days is unheard of.

Equally of significance was the waiver of

Scooter's right to a preliminary hearing. Ordinarily, a defendant benefits from such hearing as the state puts on a mini-trial, revealing a portion, albeit small, of its strategy. Demanding a speedy trial and waiving the preliminary hearing is either a sign of incredible confidence, or stupidity.

The judge glanced at Skaggs, somewhat amused by Brooks' unusual request, "Counsel?"

Skaggs nervously responded, "The People will be ready for trial whenever Mr. Mason is, Your Honor." Skaggs knew full well that absent a herculean effort by his team, there was no way in hell he'd be ready to convict an accused killer in sixty days.

"Good, we'll set the matter for a status conference in two weeks for the purpose of selecting the trial department and the trial date."

The reporters covering the story scurried out of the courtroom hoping to broadcast their slanted version of the events on news stations before anyone else did.

Brooks relished the few opportunities he had to speak to the press over his seasoned career. He fought for the downtrodden, the societal misfits and considered himself a hero of sorts, deserving of press coverage. It didn't take long for the cameras and microphones to find their way to him in the lobby.

When asked to comment, he reiterated his client's innocence and blasted the LAPD, who, "In its quest to make an arrest for the heinous crime, rushed to judgment by arresting my client, without a smidgen of evidence." He assured the reporters that his client would be ready to decisively disprove the frivolous allegations to a jury when the matter was brought to trial.

Brooks made no effort to explain away the alleged confession, the bloody clothes, the eyewitness, or the weapon found amongst Scooter's belongings.

Based upon the press coverage, Zach thought Scooter was guilty as charged, though he knew nothing of his defense. His bias aside, he was quite impressed with the poise of Brooks and his hardball tactics in demanding a speedy trial.

Before his legal education, Zach believed the accused should be ordered to explain their conduct to authorities when suspected of a crime. If there is truly nothing to hide, then it is a simple matter to clear things up by speaking the truth. The Fifth Amendment protection against self-incrimination was utter nonsense.

Whatever a suspect says should be used against him, without giving him advanced warning, and if the police discover incriminating evidence in his possession without a warrant, that evidence should be used against him too. If this were the rule, the two brothers who killed Abe and paralyzed Dillon would be in prison.

Zach felt that the sluggish legal machine was designed to ignore the victims and protect the guilty with defense attorneys being the enablers. They need extra time to investigate and re-investigate evidence and to hire and consult with one expert after another. To Zach, the layman, the jury's task could be accomplished quickly and competently, but for the lawyers and their silly games.

However, Zach's study of criminal procedure and constitutional law purged him of his early naiveté. He developed a greater understanding as to why lawyers interfere with the simple process of getting to the truth and why it's important to teach the accused to appear confident to the jury, to show positive emotion, to smile once in a while, and to keep his cotton-pickin' mouth shut at all times. If a defendant is guilty, he has the constitutional right, with the proper coaching, to con the jurors into believing he is innocent. This is the basis of

American Jurisprudence, and Zach learned to respect the rules, all of which were premised upon established fundamental rights which could not be infringed, even at the risk of freeing the guilty.

While mindful of the constitutional protections afforded to those like Scooter, Zach was also mindful of the reality that the vast majority of those accused and taken to trial are guilty and should be punished. Scooter was no doubt one of them.

* * * * *

After the arraignment, Zach went back to his office and met with Rick Gainer, his first paying client, and the father of one of the girls on his daughter's soccer team.

Rick was bitten on the hand by his neighbor's dog, a beagle/shepherd mix. The bite mark scarred over, but he was curious as to whether he was entitled to compensation.

"Did it hurt?" Zach asked smiling.

"Oh just a little; no big deal."

"Any problem with the use of your hand?"

"No... it doesn't really bother me. The real problem, Zach, is that my neighbor is a low-life who refuses to keep her property maintained. She hosts loud parties nearly every night and owns at least eleven dogs. They bark, and shit constantly. Her five or so permanent guests have seven teeth between them. I heard that she herself had her teeth knocked out when a police baton, apparently aimed for one of her dogs, struck her dead in the mouth."

"Anyway, I told her a thousand times she needs to get rid of the dogs, stop partying with those goons, and clean up the outside of her home. She doesn't seem to listen; she just stares at me, spins around and walks away without saying a word like she's possessed. Not sure what her problem is, but I'm tired of it and my family is too."

"I thought if I sued her for the dog bite, I'd convince her I'm not going to put up with her disruption anymore and that she needs to shape up or ship out."

Zach mused, "Sounds like a sweetheart. When did the dog bite you?"

Rick thought for a moment. " 'bout four years ago."

"Four years ago?" Zach yelled, laughing. "You waited four years to complain… are you kidding me?" The statute of limitations is only two years. You're way too late Rick."

"Then what the hell do I do about this woman? Can I sue her for being a pain in the ass and a disgrace to the neighborhood? If the jury takes one look at her and her friends they'd lock 'em up."

"And collect what?" Zach asked, "Her dog food money? You need to call the animal control people at the county and make a formal complaint. She's not permitted to have that many dogs in her home. She's also violating odor and noise ordinances. Let the big boys with authority take control of the situation."

"I hear ya, but I've made complaints to them before. No one has the balls to do anything. I'm at the point that if those dogs continue to keep my family up at night, I'll toss them a midnight treat to help them sleep if ya know what I mean."

"That's a negative Rick. Killing someone's pet will cause you far more problems than you have now, trust me. So keep it clean and call animal control again and again and again, if necessary." Zach smiled, hoping

Rick's comment was made in jest.

Rick promised he'd let Zach know of any further developments and they exchanged goodbyes. An easy hundred and fifty bucks.

During the week, Zach had a few other consultations with new clients. Fortunately, none of their problems required that he have anything more than a basic knowledge of the law. He was more a therapist than a lawyer, which, he would soon learn, is a prerequisite to the practice of law.

On Wednesday, Andrew called at noon as instructed. Zach informed him of the developments with Ollie's murder trial. He also broke the news that if Andrew wanted to attend the murder trial, he'd have to find a way to pay for his trip, as he was fairly certain the probate matter would not be resolved prior to the beginning of the expedited trial.

Andrew was not happy. "Mr. Morgan, I made a promise to myself I'd be there to watch that SOB go down. I have no money to travel to California and you know it. Can't I get an advance or a loan on the money I'm owed?"

"I doubt it, but I'll see what I can do. If it's any

consolation, I'll attend a good part of the trial and report back to you." Andrew remained silent, ignoring Zach's thoughtfulness.

Zach continued, "By the way, I received your claim form and the signed retainer agreement and forwarded the form to the administrator's office. Hopefully, they'll make some progress toward concluding the matter."

"Well, like I said before, you were hired to get this done quick, so please do so," Andrew responded tersely, making his point, again.

"I'll do the best I can, Andrew, but these things take time and you have to be patient or you'll drive yourself crazy. That's it for now, so I'll talk to you next week." Zach pushed the END button on his phone before Andrew said another word.

* * * * *

Shelly Presley informed Zach that legal counsel for the administrator would be Nathan Hester.

The two later met in the PA's office on Hill Street. Nathan was a pleasant enough guy, far more knowledgeable than Zach about probate, and everything else for that matter. He had twenty-five years under his belt. Tall and fit, but very calm and soft-spoken, he was probably an athlete with perpetually low blood-pressure. The probate business suited him fine as it didn't require the ruffling of feathers, or the need for Xanax like other areas of practice. It was mundane and paperwork intensive and more importantly, his clients were dead.

He rejected Andrew's request for an advance against the estate. "Since unknown heirs may respond to the probate petition, we don't usually agree to release anything until it's over." Zach figured as much, but had to ask per his client's instructions. Nathan assured Zach he would advise him if there were any claims filed by creditors or potential heirs.

As to the murder trial, Nathan didn't believe it had any bearing on concluding the probate proceeding in a timely manner. He also planned to attend portions of the trial out of curiosity and to extricate himself from the day-to-day bureaucracy in the PA's office. He and Zach looked forward to sharing observations with each other during the long trial.

Over the course of the next several weeks, Zach managed to accumulate a number of clients with relatively small matters. He also filed a few collection lawsuits, courtesy of Randy, and generated some decent fees. Still, he wasn't even close to meeting Sasha's demand, but he had a couple months left to perform his end of the bargain.

The probate matter proceeded as expected. The only heir asserting a right to inherit the estate was Andrew. The sole creditor, Ollie's landlord, submitted a claim for two thousand, one hundred and fifty-seven dollars, which he was forced to pay to clean up the place after the massacre.

Zach informed Andrew of the landlord's claim. Andrew was livid. "That son-of-a-bitch rented a house with no security and he as good as killed my brother himself. Now he wants to get paid for cleaning up the blood? What the hell is this world coming to, Mr. Morgan? Can't we object to that bullshit or sue the SOB for wrongful death?"

"Andrew, considering it's a small part of the

estate and that he is the only creditor, I suggest you don't object and that you move on. Any objection will interrupt the proceedings and delay payment to you."

Andrew paused, "Okay... I guess you're not a fighter, Mr. Morgan. Fine, I'll take your advice, which is what you're getting paid for; however, that asshole's claim is coming out of your percentage, 'cause I sure as hell ain't paying it."

Zach struggled to restrain himself from calling his wealthy client a greedy, disrespectful, good-for-nothing loser. With a grumble, he said, "No problem," and hung up.

FOURTEEN

THE trial of Raymond Mason began promptly on Monday April 4, 2011, in the Los Angeles Criminal Justice Center, the Honorable Judge Carol Waters, presiding.

Brooks, joined by a court-appointed penalty-phase lawyer, and Scooter, were seated on the right side of the defense table; Skaggs, his assistant, and detective Cranston on the left.

Scooter cleaned himself up, big time. Gone was his long, scraggly hair and moustache. He gained about twenty pounds and some muscle tone since Zach last saw him... a perfect looking murder defendant.

He wore a dark suit and tie, which concealed his tattoos, except those on his neck and knuckles. The portion visible on his neck was some sort of two-headed serpent, which appeared to rise from his back to just above his collar and slither around the sides of his neck.

Below each jaw line was a spooky snake-like head with bright red eyes, blood dripping from its fangs. Zach wondered if Brooks considered giving Scooter a turtleneck since the piercing eyes of the violent creature would be staring at jurors every time he looked their way.

The knuckle tattoos weren't offensive. Each knuckle contained a letter, which together spelled the words John Lennon. This might actually please a few of the jurors who grew up in the sixties and seventies. On the other hand, it may provoke more conservative members to send the pothead, flower child to the gallows.

Skaggs looked nervous as hell, but still composed and ready to do battle. His prosecution team worked overtime to prepare the case for trial. He was as thin as a reed, much smaller in stature than Zach remembered from the arraignment. If he pissed off Scooter, Scooter would no doubt pick him up by the neck, break him in half and hurl both pieces of his mangled body at the jury.

Judge Waters, raised in Louisiana before relocating to California with her family fifty or so years ago, was an attractive and classy woman in her early seventies. She commanded respect, in a southern-belle sort of way.

Her voice was soft, a bit nasally, but firm and hadn't quite lost its New Orleans drawl. She purposely slid her small bifocal glasses to the center of her nose so her beady eyes could be seen both above and through the lenses.

Waters was as tough as they come, and had zero tolerance for grandstanding or lawyers wasting her time. During her thirty-seven years on the bench, she handled numerous capital murder trials and considered herself an expert. She insisted that the five times she was reversed on appeal had nothing to do with errors she made. She half-heartedly joked that the appellate judges were incompetent and had their heads up their collective asses on those occasions. Still, she had a very good reputation for solid legal analysis, controlling her courtroom, and allowing the parties to present their cases without much intermeddling.

Anxious to get jury selection underway, Judge Waters began with a speech to those in the courtroom.

"Good morning, ladies and gentlemen. As you know, we will begin the trial of The People versus Raymond Mason. Mr. Mason is charged with, among other things, the first-degree murder of Mr. Oliver

Randall Pearce."

"Let me start out by acknowledging that I'm fully aware of the publicity surrounding this case and that those of you in the audience may have differing opinions or emotions about the guilt or innocence of the defendant. Despite your feelings, I will not tolerate any disruptions in this courtroom. If, during the trial, you feel the need to act in a manner inconsistent with this directive, you can leave the courtroom, go into the restroom or hallway, and take care of your business there. If you're unable to control your emotions, you will be cited for contempt, and I will personally impose the most severe punishment authorized by law for such conduct. I hope I've made myself clear." There was silence in the courtroom as she slowly gazed at the crowd, which collectively felt scolded. She then looked towards the attorneys.

"Counsel, are you ready to proceed with jury selection?"

"We are, Your Honor," Skaggs and Brooks responded simultaneously.

"Good then, would the bailiff please bring in the panel? One other thing, due to the limited space in the courtroom, all observers are requested to leave during the selection process. Once the jury has been impaneled, you are free to return for the trial, provided you can find a seat."

"Bummer," Zach thought. He hoped to gain some pointers from the experienced attorneys as they examined the prospective jurors.

In capital cases, weeding out juror bias can be grueling and time-consuming. But if Brooks had his druthers, he'd simply roll the dice with the first twelve, swear them in and get the festivities under way. Not so with Skaggs.

Brooks always felt compelled to half-heartedly challenge a few members of the jury pool solely to quell any claim of incompetence. When pressed, he favored panel members at the lower end of the economic chain who could sympathize with his homeless client. He'd eliminate some of the mothers if he felt they would feel sorry for the victim and not give his client a fair shake. Perhaps an old grandmother or two might be okay, as they see some good in everyone.

Skaggs, on the other hand, was anal and meticulous. He believed the type of people on the jury determined the outcome of the trial, regardless of the strength of the evidence. During selection, he asked dozens of prying questions to each member of the pool, alienating many of them and boring others to near sleep. Those who did not fit into his algorithm were challenged and sent home. He marched on for hours, oblivious to the effects the monotony had upon the jurors, court staff and legal teams. He spent as much time as he needed satisfying himself that he chose perfectly biased jurors.

Three days later, the seven-men, five-woman jury took the oath. They agreed to impose a sentence of death if the evidence warranted it. Brooks felt a lump in his throat as the jurors, each ultimately approved by him— acknowledged one by one, his and her willingness to kill his client. Scooter displayed no sign of emotion and stared down at the table.

The panel consisted of a dentist, an engineer, two disabled individuals, two homemakers, a city employee, a county employee, three construction workers, and an unemployed writer/actor/singer/producer and director from West Hollywood who settled for a part-time waitress position. The latter member was noticeably deflated when she learned the proceedings would not be televised and she could not give interviews during the trial.

Judge Waters gave the standard admonitions, cautioning the jurors not to speak to anyone regarding the case, read about it or watch television reports. She provided preliminary jury instructions, teaching them the types of evidence they would hear, as well as other matters regarding the conduct of the trial.

"Opening statements will begin on Monday morning at nine o'clock sharp. Don't be late. If we're lucky, we'll have our first witness on the stand by early afternoon." Judge Waters turned to Brooks and Skaggs. "Counsel, I trust you'll edit down your openings to make us lucky." They looked at each other, then nodded to the judge in approval. The court was adjourned.

Skaggs was dismayed as he realized he'd be working the entire weekend editing his six-hour, detailed written statement down to two hours or less. Brooks would do no such editing. His statement would flow spontaneously, concluding when the moment was right, consuming no more than a few moments.

FIFTEEN

ZACH anxiously awaited opening statements at Scooter's trial. With business steadily coming his way, he recognized he wouldn't have time to attend the entire trial, but he owed it to his current and future clients to learn as much as he could about the practice of law by attending when he could.

The courtroom filled to capacity with reporters and spectators. Zach was certain no members of Ollie's family were present, since, other than Andrew, he really had none. Whether Scooter had any well-wishers in the audience was likewise doubtful.

At precisely nine o'clock, Judge Waters took the bench.

"Good morning, counsel, are we prepared to move forward?

Brooks and Skaggs both indicated in the affirmative.

"Great then, bring in the jury and let's get this matter underway."

The jury nervously strolled in the courtroom and took their seats, not quite sure of what was in store for them on the first day of a murder trial.

Once seated, Judge Waters began. "Good morning, ladies and gentlemen. I hope you enjoyed your weekend. This is the part of the trial where the prosecution and the defense will give their opening statements. You will remember from my prior instructions that opening statements are not to be considered evidence. The evidence is what you will hear from the witnesses and see in the form of exhibits. These opening statements will simply give you an idea of what each side believes the evidence will be during the trial."

"With this reminder, Mr. Skaggs, you may proceed."

"Thank you, Your Honor."

Over the years, Skaggs learned that the first few words he spoke to a jury drew out the anxiety lingering in his belly. After a sentence or two, it was game on… the confidence of his preparation took over, the jitters faded to black.

"Good morning, ladies and gentlemen," Skaggs said as he stood behind an oak podium situated approximately ten feet in front of the jury box. A few of the jurors quietly returned the greeting. Others were unsure whether it was okay for them to speak, and opted not to.

"I'm sorry to say that the evidence to be presented to you in this trial will not be pleasant. It will show you the evil side of humanity. It will show you how one vicious and depraved individual brutally stole the life of a young man named Oliver Randall Pearce, known to his family as Ollie."

"Remember, the judge instructed you that what I say... my opinions and my beliefs about this case, are not evidence. I want you to follow the judge's instructions carefully and be fair to the defendant because as he sits here right now, he is an innocent man. If, when it's all said and done, the evidence you see and hear during this trial is not enough to convince you that the defendant is guilty, beyond any reasonable doubt, then I have failed to meet my burden. On the other hand, if the evidence supports a finding that the defendant is guilty of the crimes to which he is charged, then you must convict him, regardless of what I say to you or what Mr. Brooks may say to you. "

"Now, let me briefly describe the specific evidence collected by the Los Angeles Police Department in connection with this crime. Once you observe all of this evidence during trial, I don't believe you will need to hear another word from me, as each one of you will be convinced–beyond any reasonable doubt whatsoever–that the man sitting over there at the defense table," Skaggs pointed, his finger shaking slightly, "that man, Raymond Mason, is guilty of the first degree murder of Oliver Pearce." He paused, collecting his thoughts while glancing at his notes. It was time to educate the jury.

"The evidence will show that Mr. Pearce's body was discovered by the police on October fourteenth, two thousand ten. At the time of discovery, he had been dead for approximately eight days."

"You will hear testimony that he was pummeled repeatedly in the head and with an iron pipe wrench. His skull was shattered, his face unrecognizable."

"You will hear that Mr. Pearce suffered a total of twenty-three stab wounds to his body. While being butchered, his hands were tied behind his back rendering him unable to protect himself."

"Most gruesomely, you will hear that the killer, in a sick, twisted and demented manner, brutally cut off the victim's feet and tossed them in the kitchen sink." Skaggs moved from the podium and slowly approached the jury box, allowing ample silence for this latest disclosure of evidence to resonate. He then spoke softly, apologetically.

"Unfortunately, ladies and gentlemen, we will be compelled to show you photographs depicting the horrendous crime scene and the ghastly things the killer did to this poor young man. The human body has between five and six quarts of blood. That's a lot of blood, and that's approximately how much you will see was splattered and pooled in the victim's small home as he was tortured." Skaggs turned slowly and walked back to the podium. He faced the jury, gripping the sides of the podium with his hands, and continued with passion.

"Mr. Mason was arrested and charged with this crime, and sits here before you because the evidence will show that he, and no one else, committed this crime." Skaggs raised his voice slightly. "When he was arrested, he was wearing clothing stained with the victim's blood.

A pair of shoes found amongst Mr. Mason's personal belongings also had Mr. Pearce's blood on them, and the shoe prints from those shoes matched the shoe prints found at the crime scene. Also found amongst Mr. Mason's personal belongings was a very large, very heavy, pipe wrench, smeared with the victim's blood, which had Mr. Mason's fingerprints all over it. You will hear testimony that this wrench was the weapon of death."

"You will hear that when questioned about the blood stains on his clothing, Mr. Mason not only admitted he perpetrated the crime, but he said he would do it again."

"And, finally, you will hear from a witness who placed Mr. Mason at the scene of the murder."

Skaggs paused again, making sure his audience followed every word. He could see they were mesmerized, right where he wanted them.

"Ladies and gentlemen, there is not much more to this case than what I've just described. Mr. Mason was wearing the bloody clothing, he had the murder weapon, he had the shoes which matched the bloody shoeprints, he confessed to the crime and he was at the crime scene. Once the state presents this evidence to you, I am convinced that you will find the defendant guilty of the crime of first-degree murder. Thank you."

The silence was deafening as Skaggs gazed into the eyes of each juror before taking his seat. They stared back, motionless, stunned by the vulgarity of the crime and suddenly comprehending the importance of their undertaking. Some of them glanced at Scooter and hoped he too would die a horrible death–then and there in the courtroom–without the need for a long, drawn-out trial.

Judge Waters motioned to Brooks, "Does the defense wish to present its opening statement at this time?"

Brooks stood up and addressed the judge as he walked briskly to the podium, giving the impression he was in a state of shock over the outrageous lies just told by Skaggs. "Yes indeed, the defense would very much like to present its opening statement so we can set the record straight right from the start."

"Yes or no would have been sufficient counsel," the judge blurted. "There will be no drama or theatrics in my courtroom. Allow me to make that clear. Is that understood counsel?"

"I apologize, Your Honor," Brooks said, bewildered and acting as though he didn't expect to be scolded. This is a trial tactic employed by some of the more brazen lawyers like Brooks... piss off the judge right from the get-go so the jury will think the prosecutor, the police, the judge, the spectators and the whole world is against him and his poor client–the underdog effect. Anything will help.

"Good morning, ladies and gentlemen." He had no notes on the podium–didn't need them and didn't want them. He spoke candidly from his heart, at least that's what he hoped the jury would believe.

"You heard Mr. Skaggs explain in some detail what he believes the evidence will show. It was a horrific story to say the least, and sadly, some of it is true. In fact, we actually agree with much of what Mr. Skaggs just told you and we won't even challenge most of the things he will present to you during his presentation of the evidence."

"Rather, what I would ask you to do when you reflect upon the evidence is to question what Mr. Skaggs will not present to you as evidence." Brooks emphasized the word "not," startling some of the jurors. He left the podium and approached them, slowly invading their comfort zone. He was the enemy and had to level the playing field. He looked at each of them in random order before he continued with passion.

"There will not be a shred of evidence placing Mr. Mason at the scene of the crime–no fingerprints, no DNA, no hair, no nothing."

"The state will present no evidence that the bloody clothing, the shoes and the alleged murder weapon were worn by–or even in the possession of–Mr. Mason at the time of the murder. Although they were later found in his possession, you will hear my client himself tell you how those items innocently came into his possession after the murder."

"You will hear no confession, contrary to what Mr. Skaggs stated to you. Instead, my client will explain to you how the police improperly twisted his words in an effort to convince you that he confessed to a murder. Mr. Mason will tell you what he said and the context in which he said it. Once he does, you will recognize there was no such confession as the state would like you to believe."

"Mr. Mason admittedly fell upon hard times. When he was arrested, he lived in the streets, surviving off of leftovers found in dumpsters and trash cans. At the time of the murder, he had no record of breaking the law, no rap sheet, and no history of violence–nothing that would even remotely suggest he would gruesomely torture or murder another human being."

"Finally, you will hear no evidence of motive. Mr. Mason did not know the victim and certainly had no motive to kill him. So in addition to all of the other non-evidence, Mr. Skaggs will also leave you guessing why the defendant killed the victim, particularly the way he was killed."

"The man you see in this courtroom," Brooks pointed to Scooter, who grinned slightly at the jurors no doubt spooking some of them, "is not a murderer–not even close."

"As you know, Mr. Mason has the absolute right to remain silent during this trial and you cannot hold it against him if he chooses to exercise that right. But unlike other defendants in criminal cases, he has nothing whatsoever to hide, and you will hear his side of the story–not through me, or Mr. Skaggs, or the numerous witnesses testifying before you in the weeks to come–but from him directly."

"When all of the evidence is in and you're sent back to deliberate, I believe you'll have more questions than answers about the prosecution's rendition of events surrounding the murder of Mr. Pearce. Do not buy into Mr. Skaggs' tall tale which he and the LAPD desperately pieced together to convince the citizens of Los Angeles that they caught a brutal killer. Listen to the evidence and ask yourself why the story is incomplete and why Mr. Skaggs presented no evidence to finish the story for you. If you do this, you will not be able to convict this poor man. Thank you." Brooks smiled, nodded slightly, and retreated to his seat.

Wow, Zach thought, this is going to be a doozy of a battle and the defendant promises to testify on his own behalf to boot. Either Brooks has lost his mind, or he has lots of faith in the credibility of his client.

SIXTEEN

ZACH headed back to his office, too busy to observe the remaining drama in Judge Waters' courtroom. He had clients to tend to and the opening statements filled him with adrenaline, made him proud to be a lawyer... the thrill of competition. He'd catch up on the testimony of the first few witnesses later.

A man was sitting next to his locked office door with a backpack. The man appeared to be a transient, no doubt seeking a handout, but he was slightly better dressed than most bums. He looked to be in his early twenties: tall, slim, with reddish, straight hair, unshaven, but not to the point of overgrowth. He wore baggy jeans, a black t-shirt and a black faded jacket.

Having some sympathy for the cause, Zach politely asked the man if he could relocate to another spot, such as next to Miss Far Out's office.

The man looked up at him, "Are you Mr.

Morgan?"

Surprised, Zach responded, "Yes I am, and you are?"

"I'm Andrew Pearce, your client."

Zach took a few steps back and paused to analyze the situation. "Andrew? What a surprise. So good to see you; I wasn't expecting you." Zach extended his hand and Andrew returned the greeting. "When did you get here?"

Andrew was immediately concerned that the lawyer he entrusted his fortune with didn't have salt-and-pepper hair, a Rolex watch, a neatly pressed bright white shirt and a red tie. Instead, he saw a man not much older than he, wearing a blazer and jeans, no tie, and nothing to suggest he was a seasoned professional.

"After you told me about the trial, I convinced my former foster parents to float me a loan so I could come out here to attend. They gave me enough for a one-way bus ticket and a few days in a cheap hotel. I hope I get my money real soon."

Zach didn't know what "real soon" meant, but he assumed it meant before Andrew's money runs out and he's evicted from the cheap hotel. "Well, that's great

Andrew. It'll certainly be nice to spend some time going over your case and discussing the murder trial with you face-to-face. Unfortunately, I have a few appointments this afternoon... how 'bout you come back here at five-thirty and we'll chat?"

Andrew looked at Zach quizzically, "I don't really have anywhere to go, but I guess that'll work for me. How old are you anyway?" Andrew couldn't hold it in and had to ask. "You look fifteen... are you sure you're up to handling a big case like mine?"

Zach managed a credible retort with a nervous smile. "Andrew, if I didn't know what I was doing, do you think Randy at the bank would've referred me to you? Bankers are big business, they know who the reputable lawyers are, and Randy obviously believes I'm one of them." Zach was selling his client a bill of goods, but to Andrew it made sense.

"Well there's a lot at stake and I don't want anything to mess it up."

"Don't worry," Zach replied, handing him a five-spot, "go get a cup of coffee and meet me back here at five-thirty."

"Okay, thank you, I'll do that. By the way, who's

the chick over there in the manager's office?"

"Uh, that would be Miss Far Out. But don't screw with her, she's a mean, mean woman. If I was a bettin' man, I'd bet she's packin' heat," Zach said chuckling.

"Well, she gave me directions to your office. She also gave me the googlie-eyes and told me to be sure and come back and visit some time. She's a lot older than I am, but I thought she was kinda cute and sleezy, which is the way I like 'em, if you know what I mean." Andrew grinned, picked up his back pack and headed to the manager's office. You've got to be kidding me, Zach thought, briefly reconsidering whether a solo practice dealing face-to-face with clients was actually a preferable alternative to slaving away in his skyscraper office, ripping off insurance companies. "Well, to each his own, Andrew. I'll see you at five-thirty," he said as Andrew strolled away.

Zach's first client scheduled for the day was Beverly Chin, and she had several of them drooping down and around her neck. Beverly just had to have a will prepared by tomorrow at noon because she was flying to Miami and she just knew she was going to die in a fiery

and he'd be fired instantly if he represented a client adverse to the bank. As Mr. Robbins patiently waited for Zach to dispense sound legal advice, sweat began to accumulate across Zach's brow, and the heat one feels when he loses self-confidence in front of a captive audience, rapidly warmed his face and chest. The rules of professional conduct, which dictate the avoidance of conflicts of interest, were something he suddenly forgot.

"Mr. Robbins, I'm going to step outside and make a quick call. I'll be right back." He stood up from behind his desk, giving the impression he had another client in desperate need of emergency legal services, then left his office. The escape allowed him to collect his thoughts and avoid looking like an incompetent ass to his new client.

He went into the lobby where he took a deep breath, fanned his flaming hot face and dialed Randy.

"Randy, hey, it's me Zach. Hope all is well. Hey listen, I have a client in my office who was just sued by Commercial First. I think I have a conflict, but I thought I would discuss it with you real quick."

"Think you have a conflict? Randy chuckled. "You do have a conflict. You can't sue people for us and then represent our customers against us... geez Zach, are you freakin' kiddin' me?"

"Yeah, that's what I figured," Zach said, cowering. "But what if he wants to pay the claim? I mean, he seems to be willing to pay if he gets some kind of a discount. Not sure if this is proper, but if you let me know what the bank will settle for, I'll see if I can work a deal; if I can't, I'll send him on his way."

"Zach, seriously, tell me yer pullin' my leg. This is a textbook case on how to lose your license before you even have a chance to use it." Randy spoke with a condescending tone as though a law professor.

"But you're a big boy now, and I guess if you can save us legal expense by settling litigation against this guy, I sure as hell won't turn your ass into the bar. Your other client might, but I won't. Give me the customer's info and I'll call you back shortly."

Zach complied, then returned to his now impatient client.

"I'm sorry for the interruption, Mr. Robbins. Let's see, where were we? Okay, now you realize you'll have to file a response to this lawsuit within thirty days after you were served, don't you? Do you recall when you received these papers?" Zach mentioned nothing about his conversation with Randy.

"About ten days ago. I would prefer not to pay a lawyer to file a response. I want to get this settled before it gets out of hand."

"What are you willing to pay to make this go away?" Zach responded. "The claim is thirty-six thousand but with interest and legal fees, it's probably closer to forty-five thousand."

"I'd pay fifteen within ten days. If those bastards won't take the deal, I'll file bankruptcy."

Zach's phone suddenly vibrated; Bach's, Fur Elise accompanied the vibration. "I'm sorry Mr. Robbins, I'll be right back." He stumbled out of his office door, the music from his phone gradually increasing in volume. Robbins was beginning to think he was the butt of a hidden camera joke. He didn't think the joke was one bit funny.

It was Randy and he cut to the chase. "Tell Mr. Robbins we'll take twenty-seven grand. This is quite a discount and he should take this offer before it's off the table, which is in fifteen minutes."

Zach responded, "He'll pay twenty-five grand.

I'm advised if you don't accept this, he'll file bankruptcy."
Zach was now negotiating adverse to his client, the bank,
a clear conflict of interest. He also made an offer much
higher than the fifteen thousand authorized by his other
client, Robbins–at least two ethical violations in eight
seconds, and counting.

Randy paused. "Okay, let's split the baby and
make it twenty-six grand and we've got a deal."

Zach told Randy he'd call back shortly. He went
back into his office where his frustrated client appeared
to be packing up his things to leave.

"Sorry about that, Mr. Robbins. So what if I can
get the bank to take twenty-six thousand?"

"Fat chance based upon what I've seen from you
so far. But if you were able to accomplish that, I'd say,
you're one hell of a lawyer, and I'd probably give ya a
bonus."

"Well, I just got off the phone with the bank, and
they'll actually take twenty-six." Zach, the hero, smiled,
"But don't worry about the bonus–it's all in a day's work.
Deliver a cashier's check to Randy Blake at the bank
within ten days and this case will be history," he said
proudly.

"That's it? Seriously?" Robbins asked, surprised the settlement of a lawsuit could be so easy. "You're fantastic. Between you and me, I would have paid the entire forty-five, today if they pushed it. I just wanted to see how low they'd go. They must have shitty lawyers who've never learned to call a bluff," Robbins said laughing.

Zach absorbed the comment, shuddering at the thought that he just screwed his big-bank client by falling for his new client's bankruptcy story. Ethical violation number three.

He advised Randy of the deal after Robbins left, mentioning nothing of the bluff or the bank's shitty lawyers, of which, he was one.

SEVENTEEN

ANDREW walked into Zach's lobby at five-thirty, moments after Zach finished revising Beverly's plagiarized will.

"Hi Andrew. It's sure a pleasure to finally have an opportunity to meet you." They moved into Zach's office as he spoke. Andrew said "Hi," but nothing else.

Zach got right to the point. "I know waiting is the hardest part, but we're getting close. No further claims were filed in the probate action and the administrator's office is in the process of finalizing the paperwork for the judge to sign. After this happens, the money will be paid."

"What's the ETA?" Andrew asked.

"Not sure, but I have to believe this will all be done within the next thirty days or so."

"Damn it, I guess that means I'll be livin' on the streets for a few weeks, as I only have seven or eight days' worth of hotel money."

"We'll see what happens and take it day by day. For now, why don't you tell me about yourself?" Zach was truly interested in learning about his client and the difficult life he had. When they spoke by telephone, he didn't delve into the painful details. With Andrew now in his presence, compassion seemed to be in order.

"To tell you the truth, Mr. Morgan, I'm not too comfortable discussing my shitty life, but since you're my lawyer 'n' all, I guess I should fill ya in." Andrew looked down, saddened by the subject.

"When I was about five, my mom got sick and died. It was quick. She was there one minute, gone the next. A few years later, my dad was killed in a fire in our barn. My brother, Ollie, then flew the coup and I was left alone. It was all kinda fucked up."

"Wow, sounds horrible. I'm sorry to hear that," Zach said.

"I was shipped from one foster home to another throughout the state. Most of them were okay, but I never felt like I had a home. The parents changed, the kids changed, my schools changed, it was a revolving door."

I think most of the fosters felt I was trouble. But they really had it wrong. I wasn't a model kid, but I wasn't that bad either. I hated to go to school and I'd sneak cigarettes and a few beers here and there. Hell, all kids do those things."

"A couple of the homes I lived in had other kids who were orphaned or discarded by their parents. A few fosters took their anger out on the kids, including me, and beat us silly. When I was twelve, one of them shot two of my foster brothers dead with a shotgun after they refused to stop clowning around while he was tryin' to watch Wheel of Fortune. Crazy shit, man." Andrew was still staring down, shaking his head as he relived his experiences.

"I moved around a lot and never got a handle on who my family was, or if I even had a family. Ollie took off as soon as he turned eighteen and did his own thing; looks like he did pretty well." Zach nodded in agreement.

"When I was thirteen or fourteen, I was arrested for throwing batteries at a police car, kind of a dare by my friends. The batteries missed, but there was hell to pay to my fosters. I think their names were Jack and Ella. They beat the livin' shit out of me and I had to go to the

ER with several broken ribs and busted teeth." Zach now had an explanation for Andrew's random missing teeth.

"Nothin' new. I had the pulp knocked out of me more than a few times. I never understood why they thought that breaking my bones and making me bleed was perfectly okay, but that the stupid little things I did to deserve it were not."

"What about high school, did you finish?" Zach asked.

"Yeah. It was not on my list of priorities, but somehow I managed to get through it and graduate, thanks to my last fosters, Stan and Becky Johnson. They're the ones who gave me the money to come here. Turns out, Stan was a cousin of my father, so I guess they weren't technically fosters. They took me in and helped me get my head on straight. They even got me to take a few community college courses, but the college scene didn't cut it for me."

"After I turned eighteen, I hit the road, just like Ollie. I lived in homeless camps, under bridges, in back alleys and in abandoned homes and cars... anywhere that had some degree of security. It was tough livin' on the streets, scavenging for food and clothes, and tryin' to stay warm. But I liked the freedom of having no one to answer to."

"A few years ago, I hitchhiked to Austin. Nice place. I've been livin' in the campground ever since. They provide the necessities, which they receive from charity. I try to help out by talkin' to some of the younger kids about the importance of finishing school, blah, blah, blah. They don't listen. They'll turn out just like me."

"When I get my money, I'll send some to them 'cause they can sure use it," Andrew said, deep in thought.

"That's quite a story." Zach said somberly, "Seems like you've had it pretty rough. So where was Ollie during this time? I mean, he was loaded, why didn't he help you out?"

"I lost touch with Ollie. I had no idea he made it big. I think he wanted a new life after what happened to our dad and he got out of Dodge as soon as he could. I can't blame him. He didn't want me tagging along to bother him. I got a few calls from him after he left, but they stopped and I haven't seen or heard from him for probably ten years or so."

"What about your parents, how were they before

they died?"

"Don't remember much. I try to forget my whole childhood thing." Andrew became noticeably distraught and made it clear he was done with his autobiography.

Zach considered his own life as a boy. He didn't have much, but he had the support of a family–parents he would see every day and a secure place he'd call his home. Being handed off from one strange family to another was unthinkable.

Like Andrew, Zach enjoyed the thrill of pissing off his parents and other figures of authority. However, he couldn't imagine being tortured by those who raised him. A stern lecture by his mom and dad was the extent of his discipline and it usually convinced him to clean up his act, at least temporarily. He knew they would take a bullet to protect their children and would never lay a hand on them.

Zach realized that Andrew deserves every penny he would receive from his brother's estate.

"We have a big day tomorrow. The opening statements were this morning. Ray Mason has declared his innocence and his lawyer has made it clear he will testify."

"I can't wait to look that SOB in the eyes. Give me a few minutes with him alone and I'll end the trial before it starts," Andrew said with a smirk.

"Well, go get some sleep. I'll see you over at the courthouse at nine o'clock. Since you're family of the victim, I'm sure they'll have a seat for you, but you may want to arrive early because the courtroom will fill up pretty fast."

Andrew nodded in agreement and said goodbye. As he left the building, he stopped by Miss Far Out's office. She was gone for the day.

EIGHTEEN

BEFORE trial, Zach ran into Nathan Hester, who filled him in as to the events the day before. Per Nathan, the state's first two witnesses were the deputies who initially responded to the scene, each of whom gave the jury graphic details of what they discovered in Ollie's home.

Brooks had only one obligatory question on cross-examination, which he asked both deputies: "Did you personally observe any evidence which suggested to you that Ray Mason was ever in the victim's home?" Both witnesses responded in the negative as expected.

Zach found a seat behind Skaggs and his team. Detective Cranston was called to the stand at nine o'clock. Andrew was nowhere in sight.

After spending at least an hour and a half walking the detective through the preliminaries and showing the jury several gruesome photographs of the crime scene,

Skaggs moved to the heart of Cranston's testimony.

"Detective, I am going to show you state's exhibit thirty-five and ask if you recognize this item?" Skaggs placed the exhibit contained in an evidence bag on the witness stand. Cranston struggled to stretch latex gloves over his large hands before handling the exhibit, glancing over to the jury as he popped them on snugly.

He looked at the contents of the bag and responded, following the script Skaggs laid out for him a few days before the trial. "Yes, it's the pair of pants we found on Mr. Mason's person at the time he was arrested for being drunk-in-public."

"I'll also show you state's exhibit thirty-six. Could you tell the jury whether you are familiar with this item and, if so, what it is?"

"Yes, this is the jacket the defendant was wearing when he was picked up."

"What about exhibit thirty-seven, what is this?" Skaggs asked, trying to convey to the jury that he was learning what all of these things were at the same time they were.

"Exhibit thirty-seven is the pair of shoes we found in a milk crate located in the proximity where the defendant was found drunk or on drugs and passed out."

Brooks jumped to his feet, "Your Honor, I object to the conclusion that my client was under the influence of drugs or that he was passed out. We've heard no testimony of drug use and no testimony that Detective Cranston was even present when Mr. Mason was arrested. Therefore, the detective has no idea whether my client was high, drunk or whether he was in la la land. It's pure speculation, it's hearsay, it assumes facts not in evidence, and it calls for a medical opinion. While the fine detective may be able to put a story together in an effort to convict an innocent man, he sure ain't no doctor and has no expertise in these matters. The court must therefore strike this outrageous and inflammatory testimony." Brooks finally shut up. He succeeded in breaking up the momentum.

It took less than a day for courtroom observers to recognize that Judge Waters' reaction to the lawyers was eloquently predictable. She'd lean back in her chair during testimony, as though relaxing with a glass of cabernet watching television. When agitated, she would casually sit up. When ready to pounce, she'd place her chin in her palms as both elbows provided support, glare at the offending attorney through her bifocals and lash out. It made no difference whether what she had to say was best said out of the presence of the jury. Let the court of appeals scrutinize her comments later. She'd make her position known then and there.

As Brooks began his long-winded objection, Judge Waters assumed the full chin-in-palms position. When he concluded his diatribe, she went in for the kill. "Counsel, do not make speaking objections in my courtroom! If you want to argue, you are to request a sidebar to discuss the matter outside of the earshot of the jury. You will not make nonsensical speeches each time you feel the need to object. You are to simply object to the question, state the grounds for the objection in one or two words, and patiently await my ruling. I hope I'm clear on this because I will not repeat it, and if it happens again, you will be writing a very big check... or worse, understood?"

Brooks looked at her expressionless, like a little boy being scolded. "Yes, Your Honor." Judge Waters owned the courtroom.

"That said... objection sustained. The jury will disregard the testimony which referred to Mr. Mason as having been under the influence of drugs or alcohol, or having been passed out."

"Thank you, Your Honor," Brooks mumbled before taking his seat. The entire exchange was a waste of time and he knew it since the arresting officers would give their personal account of the comatose condition Scooter was in when they picked him up. Nonetheless, his underdog defense got a small boost by the judge's hostility.

Skaggs continued. "Detective, can you identify state's exhibit number thirty-eight?"

"Yes I can. This is the pipe wrench we found in the defendant's milk crate where we found the shoes."

"Did you observe any blood on any of these exhibits at the time you first saw them?"

"Yes, all of them were stained with what I believed to be blood."

"Did you confirm whether it was in fact blood on these items?"

"Yes, we sent the items to our lab for testing and they tested positive for human blood."

Brooks could object on the grounds the testimony regarding the bloodstains was based upon what others told the witness and therefore constituted hearsay. His strategy, however, was not to quarrel with the majority of the state's evidence, only prove it had no connection to his client.

"Whose blood was found on these exhibits?" Skaggs paused for effect, pointing to the exhibits lined up in front of Cranston.

"We determined that the blood on all of these items came from Oliver Pearce."

"Are you certain of that?"

"As certain as I am that it'll be dark at midnight," he said, looking at the jury, smiling.

"Okay. At some point did you attempt to obtain fingerprints off of the wrench marked as exhibit thirty-eight?"

"Yes we did. We lifted prints which matched the fingerprints of the defendant."

"Do you recognize exhibit thirty-nine?"

"Yes, it's the milk crate discovered in the proximity where Mr. Mason lay drunk."

"What the heck, Your Honor? Drunk? Same objection." Brooks blurted.

Judge Waters sat up, "Detective, if you didn't see

the defendant drunk, don't testify that he was drunk. Objection sustained. The jury will disregard the drunk comment. As for you, Mr. Brooks, I consider use of the word, 'heck,' in my courtroom to be as offensive as the word or words you actually intended to use, so be very careful. You are testing my patience, which is not good at this early stage of the trial."

Most of the jurors chuckled at the detective's obvious and successful effort to push Brooks' buttons and they paid no attention to the objection or the judge's ruling.

"Did you find any prints on the milk crate, Detective Cranston?"

"We were able to obtain a few unknown prints from the crate; however, we found lots of prints which belonged to Mr. Mason."

"Just a few more questions, Detective. Did you find any shoeprints at the murder scene?"

"Yes we did. It appeared the perpetrator tracked blood throughout the home at the time of the killing. The shoe-print data was thereafter sent to the lab for analysis."

"Did you match the shoeprints to any shoes?"

"Yes. They were identical in every respect to the soles of the shoes found in the defendant's crate." Cranston picked up the shoes, displaying them to the jury as he answered the question.

"Thank you, Detective, the state has no further questions of this witness at this time."

Brooks avoided the long walk to the podium, deciding instead to stand next to his lonely client while he examined Cranston.

"Detective, did you personally observe any evidence which suggested, in any way, shape, or form, that Mr. Mason was in Mr. Pearce's home at the time of the murder, or at any time before or afterwards." Brooks looked at the jury before he finished the compound question, smiling as though his brilliant query would abruptly end the trial with an acquittal.

"Well, that's a very good question, Counsel. As a matter of fact, the answer is yes." Cranston was prepared for the predictable question, which Brooks asked the two previous witnesses, and continued with confidence. "As the lead detective handling this case, I personally observed: one, the clothing worn by your client which was covered with the victim's blood; two, the shoes in your client's possession which were covered with the victim's blood; three, the shoeprints from those shoes, which matched the bloody shoeprints found in the victim's home; four, the murder weapon which was not only smeared with the victim's blood but which also had your client's fingerprints all over it; and five, the statement by Constance Federoff who observed your client near the victim's home on the day of the murder. So yes, to answer your question, there was extensive evidence which I personally observed which reflected that Mr. Mason was indeed inside the victim's home at— and no doubt before—the time Mr. Pearce was tortured to death. I hoped that answered your question counselor."

Even Zach knew you should never ask a question you don't know the answer to unless you're desperate and in need of a Hail Mary. With his answer, Detective Cranston stole the soapbox from the experienced public defender and used it to give a persuasive closing argument to the jury.

Brooks recognized his blunder and tried to recover. "May we approach?" he shouted as he walked to the bench, assuming the judge would approve. Skaggs arrived with a grin as Brooks whispered angrily,

"Objection, Your Honor, move to strike. This testimony is unduly prejudicial and is based upon hearsay and it's further non-responsive to my question. The court should sanction Mr. Skaggs and this witness for this little ploy and a mistrial would also be entirely appropriate."

"Overruled," Judge Waters responded. "You opened the door by asking the open-ended question and Detective Cranston gave you his answer. If it's prejudicial, too bad. Move on."

Brooks wanted to grab the bloody wrench off of the evidence table and test it out on Cranston for setting him up and making him look like a moron. For his part, Scooter searched for a weapon of his own to use on Brooks for helping Skaggs and Cranston put him to death. Unfortunately, neither the tissue box, nor the water pitcher sitting on the defense table, would cause injury. He could only stare at his lawyer, making it very clear that one more screw up like that and he'd sink his teeth into his jugular.

"Okay, fair enough, Detective. Let's cut to the chase. Do you know if Mr. Mason actually purchased the clothing he was wearing before he allegedly killed Mr. Pearce?"

"No idea."

"Did you find evidence, like a receipt, showing that he purchased the shoes before the murder?"

"Nope, we didn't."

"Do you know where he purchased the wrench before he used it to allegedly kill the victim?"

"I don't know that he did purchase the wrench, Counselor."

"No you don't, do you Detective?"

"Nope, never said I did."

"It's true, is it not, Detective Cranston, that Mr. Mason could have found the wrench and the clothing in a trashcan after the murder and after they were already stained with the victim's blood, isn't that true?"

Cranston smiled and gently shook his head at the far-fetched suggestion. "That's not the way I view it, Counsel, not at all."

"It's fair to say, Detective, that you found no direct evidence establishing that my client was in the victim's home, that he stabbed the victim repeatedly, or that he bashed in his head and chopped up his body, did you?"

After he asked the question, Brooks realized it

was similar to the last dumbass question. He panicked and looked down at his blank legal pad, pretending to the jury that his question was strategically calculated. Please, oh please, just fucking say no, Brooks said to himself, not wanting to hear Cranston do another summation with the judge's full approval.

"Well, I believe the things I just told you about make it clear to me he was there… would you like me to repeat them Mr. Brooks?"

"No thank you, sir, he said with hostility.

Now tell us, Detective, did you find Mr. Mason's fingerprints in the victim's home?"

"No, we did not. The perp obviously wore gloves."

"Gloves? … What? … Gloves? Are you serious, Detective? Is it your testimony that Mr. Mason butchered Mr. Pearce and was stupid enough to ride his little scooter around town wearing clothes and shoes dripping with the victim's blood, holding the bloody wrench, but he was smart enough to wear gloves during the massacre to avoid getting caught? Is that your testimony, sir?"

"I've seen violent criminals do stranger things

than that, Mr. Brooks. Would you like me to give you a few examples?"

Brooks shouted, "No thank you, Detective. I get to ask the questions, not you."

"Did you find any of Mr. Mason's hair at the scene?"

"No."

"Not a single fingerprint or strand of his hair from Mr. Mason?"

"No."

"What about evidence that Mr. Mason even knew the victim… any evidence of that?"

"No, but we do know from a witness– Constance Federoff–that Mr. Mason was in the area of Mr. Pearce's home."

"Sir, I didn't ask you if Mr. Mason was near the victim's home, I asked you if there was any evidence that Mr. Mason actually knew the victim. Yes or no will suffice."

"Well, if he was near his home, he may have known the victim, so the answer would be yes."

"C'mon Detective, you're guessing aren't you? I've been in the area of Mr. Pearce's home, does that mean I knew him?"

"Don't know, Counsel," Cranston said smugly.

"I get it, Detective. You find it very difficult to acknowledge to the jury that you have zero evidence that Mr. Mason and Mr. Pearce knew each other, don't you?"

"Objection, Skaggs interjected, he's arguing with the witness."

"Sustained… move on, Counsel."

"Now, Detective Cranston, with all of the work you put into this investigation, you surely came up with a motive for the murder. So please tell the ladies and gentlemen of the jury why Mr. Mason would want to kill Mr. Pearce?"

"We are not aware of a motive. But as you know, Counselor, lots of people are killed by people who have no obvious motive."

"Just answer my question, Detective," Brooks said impatiently. "Actually, allow me to answer it for you… the answer is no, you have no motive, isn't that true?"

"There is one, we just don't know it yet, so yes, technically that's correct."

"Did you find Mr. Mason's DNA at the scene?"

"No, we did not."

"Did you locate any witnesses who at any time observed Mr. Mason at Mr. Pearce's home?"

"At the victim's home? Not to my knowledge, but Constance Federoff observed him in the area of the victim's home."

"Not to your knowledge? Well, you would be the one to know if you did. You're the lead detective, aren't you?" Brooks did the finger quotation marks when saying the word, lead.

"No, there were no eyewitnesses we could find."

"When you arrived on scene, cash and valuables belonging to Mr. Pearce were in plain view for anyone to see, isn't that correct, Detective?"

"Yes, some, but most of what he owned, appeared to be in banks."

"Did Mr. Mason, my homeless, penniless client, take any money?"

"We don't know, but there was a few hundred dollars cash on the counter in the victim's home."

"So... you have no fingerprints, no hair, no DNA, no motive, no known relationship between Mr. Mason and Mr. Pearce, no eyewitnesses placing him in the home, no evidence that Mason owned the clothing, shoes, or wrench at the time of the murder, and no evidence that he took money sitting right in front of him after he mutilated the victim? Is that all true, Detective Cranston? Oh never mind, no need to answer that. I think we all have a clear picture now. Your Honor, I'm done with this witness," Brooks shouted, slamming down his yellow notepad on the defense table, feigning frustration over the prosecution's witch-hunt.

"Oh wait, I'm sorry, I do have one more question, Detective," Brooks said calmly, imitating Columbo as he pointed to his temple.

"Objection!" Skaggs tried to bark, but instead squeaked timidly. Zach wondered why Skaggs waited so long to try to shut the man up.

Judge Waters ignored the objection, as if a referee holding back the penalty flag so the boys could keep playing.

"You testified that Mr. Mason's clothing was stained with the victim's blood. My question is, did you test the clothing for anyone else's blood?"

"I believe the clothing, the shoes and the wrench were tested for your client's blood, but the tests came back negative. Given the evidence we had, along with the defendant's confession, we did not see a reason to test every inch of the clothing or shoes for anyone else's blood. However, as to the wrench, all blood on that piece of evidence came from the victim."

"Thank you. So I take it the answer is no, correct? You did not test the clothing for blood from another person?"

"No, we did not test the clothing for any other blood."

"You just mentioned a confession. Were you present during this supposed confession?"

"No."

"So you have no idea what exactly was said by my client, do you?"

"Only what's in the report, and the way I read it, it's a pretty clear confession."

"Confession to what, Detective Cranston? What in your mind did my client confess to?" Brooks demanded.

"Murder, Counselor. He confessed to murder."

"That's what you think, Detective, and that's why we have a jury here. Fortunately, they will hear every word of this so-called confession and make their own decision, free of your opinion." Brooks shook his head in disgust and sat down. "I have nothing further of this witness."

Judge Waters recessed for lunch, admonishing the jurors not to discuss the matter with one another before she dismissed them. She then took the opportunity to rip into Brooks for his argumentative style of examining the witness. Brooks knew he was walking on the thinnest of eggshells and that before the trial concluded, he'd be dipping into his savings account.

Although Zach sensed Brooks was grasping at straws in a desperate attempt to save his client's life, he was impressed by the lawyer's passion for the cause. One thing was clear, Scooter wasn't going down without a fight.

Where the hell is Andrew? Zach wondered, but surmised that he arrived too late to find a seat. Before he left the courtroom, Zach informed the bailiff that the victim's brother would be present for the proceedings and he'd like to have a seat reserved for him. The bailiff, a pleasant, goliath of a man, assured Zach that Andrew would have a seat during future sessions.

NINETEEN

ZACH met Sasha for lunch before heading back to the office. They were able to enjoy such pleasantries a few times a week since he started his own practice. He never had the luxury of having lunch, or dinner for that matter, with his wife while at FF&W.

He filled her in on the details of the trial and other matters involving his clients. Sasha felt happy for him and proud of his short-term accomplishments. Zach was doing what he wanted to do and with relentless enthusiasm and energy. In retrospect, she realized that she did the right thing in supporting her husband's decision to venture on his own. She may even extend the six-month deadline to help him out a little, but she wouldn't tell him that.

After he stopped talking, Sasha took a bite of her arugula salad, washed it down with a few sips of green tea, and quietly announced… "I'm pregnant."

Zach stared at her in silence as if trying to translate what she said into something understandable. He finally responded, "What?"

"I'm pregnant, Zach, ya know, having a baby."

He took in her words as he was overcome with a smorgasbord of emotions: happiness, sadness, love, worry, pleasure, fear, and every other feeling which renders a person unable to speak effectively. He stumbled, "Are you serious? How did that happen? I mean, I know how it happened, but when did you find out and why didn't you tell me?"

"Zach... calm down, honey. I just found out this morning. I took a pregnancy test, actually three of them. No question about it. We're going to have another baby."

"Oh my god, Sasha, I love you. This is unexpected, but I am so very happy. I can't believe this. Did you tell Amanda?"

"Not yet. I figured we should both tell her tonight."

"Awesome, wow, I'm in shock. I'm the luckiest man alive. Thank you, Sasha, for sharing your life with me. You're unbelievable."

The two managed to embrace across the small

table while remaining partially seated. Their tears commingled as their faces joined, their eyes gazing into each other's. "It doesn't get any better than this my love," Zach whispered to his wife. They were in their own little universe, oblivious to the other diners who watched with curiosity, wondering what could have triggered the outpouring of affection.

Zach wiped the salad dressing off of his tie and Sasha's make-up off of his white shirt. He and Sasha walked arm and arm to her car. He gave her another long hug, followed it with a kiss, and told her he couldn't wait to get home to break the news to Amanda.

* * * * *

Zach no longer wondered where Andrew was during the trial. He witnessed his young, homeless client playing tonsil hockey with Miss Far Out through the window to her office. Wow, that's disturbing, Zach thought as he walked to his office, unable to comprehend what quality either of them had which would induce instant attraction toward the other.

He tried to put the visual of the two of them out

of his mind and retrieved his messages from his answering service. He had several of them, which meant he'd be busy most of the afternoon. For the first time in his short career, he was relieved he had no new appointments.

His initial call was to Rick Gainer, the client with the pain-in-the-ass neighbor.

"Hi Rick, this is Zach returning your call. What's up?"

Rick was distressed. "Damn Zach, 'bout time you got back to me. I'll tell you what's up. That woman and her loser friends filed papers to have a restraining order issued against me. They claim I poisoned three of her dogs. I love dogs and I would never do that. Besides, the cops came out and found no evidence I did anything wrong, no poison, no nothing. They almost arrested her for spitting on one of the deputies." Rick was speaking a mile a minute.

"Whoa, slow down Rick. Tell me what happened so I can understand it." Zach reached for a yellow pad on his desk in case Rick said something worth memorializing.

"Okay, okay… last night those damn dogs were

on a rampage, barking and howling their heads off, having a freakin' dog party or something. I got fed up and went to what's-her-name's house and told her to shut them animals up or she and those dogs would be sorry. The big, fat goons with her then threatened to do to me whatever I threatened to do to her dogs. I believed they meant what they said, so I went home with my tail between my legs, no pun intended. I was going to call animal control today to make a complaint, like you suggested before."

"So, early this morning I hear banging on my door, and sure enough it's the whacko lady with two cops demanding to speak to me. She said three of her dogs were found frothing at their mouths and collapsed, dead as can be. She told them I threatened to kill them and that I carried out my threat by giving them poison."

"And what did you tell them?"

"I told them I did threaten to kill every single one of those damn dogs." You moron, Zach said to himself rolling his eyes. "But I also told them I was very mad when I said it and that I would never, ever actually do it. I was only trying to convince her to shut them up so my family could sleep. I told them they could search my house for poison if they wanted and that I'd even take a lie detector test. They took me up on the search and went through the house... found nothing."

"One of the deputies then told her there was no physical evidence linking me to the murder of her dogs and that they couldn't do anything without evidence. They told her if she believed I was a threat to her or her other dogs, she could file papers and ask a judge to give her a restraining order against me."

"Then the shit hit the fan. She went bat shit crazy at the cops because they didn't arrest me on the spot. She cried and shouted and nasty shit was spewing out of her mouth as she shook her head back and forth. I'll be damned, her spit splattered on one of the deputies. He went into orbit and cuffed her and threw her in the squad car. I just watched and listened to her and the deputy argue about whether she intended to spit on him, or whether it was an accident. The deputy told her she was under arrest for assaulting a police officer. She began to scream bloody murder. It was actually pretty damn funny if you ask me."

"Sounds like a hoot. Did they take her away?"

"Eff no, I think they realized she's a meth-head

lunatic who can't control her temper, and they let her go."

"So, about noon today I was served with documents she filed with the court. The papers say I need to be in court first thing tomorrow morning because she wants a restraining order to stop me from harassing her and her guests, and to stop me from killing her dogs. This is bullshit, Zach. I would never kill a dog or even give one a whack on the ass. I might say I would, but I wouldn't actually do it. You believe me, don't you?"

"Of course I do, Rick." Zach had no such belief. "But you need to control your words. Think about it… you go to her house threatening to kill her dogs and the dogs are found dead the next morning. The finger will be pointed at you every time."

"So what do you think happened, Rick?"

"Personally, I think one of the other neighbors did it, but I'm not saying a word since that crazy lady needs be taught a lesson."

"Do I actually have to go to this hearing tomorrow morning?"

"No, but if you don't, she'll win by default and if you violate the order, you'll be arrested and held in contempt." Zach studied up on restraining orders during his down time.

"Tell me what I should do then," Rick asked in desperation.

"I can handle the hearing for you in the morning, but my hourly rate is two hundred dollars and it could get expensive. You might want to go by yourself to keep costs down. It's really no big deal. Let the judge know there's no evidence you had anything to do with the slaying of the dogs. If you're lucky, the judge won't give her the restraining order and the case will be over then and there. On the other hand, the judge may issue the order as a precaution and you'll have to go back to court for another hearing. If that happens, you should hire me to go with you."

"Well, I can't afford an attorney right now. I'll just wing it tomorrow and see what happens. Maybe she'll piss off the judge and get arrested in court."

"Whatever, Rick. Let me know how it goes and good luck being your own lawyer."

"Thanks for the insight. I'll keep ya posted."

Zach called several other clients and a few opposing attorneys. Randy's collection cases were building up and many of the defendants hired bankruptcy attorneys to help them get Zach off their backs. He did what he could to work with them, even tried to negotiate deals to help them avoid bankruptcy. Randy's marching orders were to recover as much as possible, using Zach's best judgment under the circumstances.

Once he completed his calls, he headed home to Sasha and Amanda. He was excited about Sasha's news, and anxious to share it with Amanda.

As he left, he saw Andrew and Miss Far Out getting into her car, no doubt heading to a bar to get hammered or to her place to do the unthinkable. Andrew waived and Zach obliged by waiving and smiling back. Miss Far Out didn't waive, didn't smile, and hurried into the car, refusing to acknowledge Zach's presence.

Zach and Sasha picked up where they left off with an extended hug. Dinner was on the table. Tonight it was her favorite, crab legs with twice-baked potatoes. Amanda was already seated, rocking back and forth in her chair.

"Hey sweetie, how was your day?" Zach asked, giving her a peck on top of her head.

"Pretty good, except I hate every guy in my school. They're all so stupid and they stink. Especially

179

this guy named Alfonso who is really hot, but he's creepy and he thinks every girl in school likes him, which they don't." Sasha and Zach smiled at each other. Amanda's negative assessment of Alfonso meant she had a major crush on him.

"Oh well, little lady, without boys there'd be no men, and without men there'd be no women, right honey?" Zach glanced over to Sasha seeking support for his words of wisdom.

"More like, without men, there'd be much happier women." Sasha said, laughing far more than warranted by her retort.

"Whatever. You guys don't even understand." Amanda responded, shaking her head in frustration.

As they were seated around the small table, Sasha told Amanda she and her father had some exciting news to share with her. Amanda looked back and forth at each of them, smirking.

"Duh, I already know. You're pregnant, Mom. If you want to keep things like this a secret, maybe you should hide the test results in a place other than on the sink in the bathroom."

Zach and Sasha glanced at each other, shocked

by the unexpected response. They paused, then burst into laughter.

After the little non-secret was exposed, Amanda let her mom and dad know she was ecstatic about having a baby brother or sister to boss around.

TWENTY

ZACH skipped the morning session of Scooter's trial as he decided his firm had grown to the point of requiring the assistance of a part-time secretary, four hours per day, Monday through Friday. He had three women to interview, two fresh out of high school, and the third out of high school for thirty-eight years.

Unfortunately, the younger prospects spoke a language not conducive to the practice of law. "Well, Mr. Morgan, I'm like totally into the law thing. I've always told my mom and dad that someday I would want to go to law school. My parents were like, that would be great and they like, got me to do this interview. I was like, totally stoked."

The third candidate was Ginger. "Gin ja," as she called herself, was a late fifty-ish, cheerful African American. She had a muumuu dress sized-body with big, white teeth and she instantly impressed Zach with her smile and sense of humor.

Ginger gained experience answering telephones, taking messages, and greeting customers during her employment at *Dr. Arnold's Crooked to Straight Chiropractic Clinic*. Most of the clinic's work was performed at the request of personal injury attorneys who were thrilled with Dr. Arnold's treatment, his diagnosis, and the prognosis given to their clients. He and the attorneys formed very profitable alliances ripping off insurance companies. Zach wondered if FF&W defended any of those cases.

Dr. Arnold lost his license and became known around town as a chiroquacktor after several of his patients sued him for exacerbating their injuries. It seems the doctor didn't always take x-rays before adjusting spines, necks and shoulders–although he charged for the procedures. Shortly before the time Ginger was let go, the clinic received at least six lawsuits from the doctor's crippled patients.

Ginger would be a perfect fit for Zach's practice and he told her so. He placed a small desk in the space behind the reception counter and called it her office. The desk came equipped with a two-line telephone, an outdated computer and a color printer, sans the expensive color ink cartridge.

She had little experience typing, but she let him know she'd work on her "typin' " skills every day until she became "most excellent at typin' letters 'n' such." She liked to finish her sentences with the words, "an' such." Occasionally, she'd make the sound, "mmm hmm," as though she was convincing herself it was okay to say what she just said.

Ginger's hours would be eight o'clock until noon. Her compensation was minimum wage, fine by her since she was in it to escape her lazy, cranky, retired husband. The money was only a perk.

After spending the morning showing her the ropes, Zach gave Ginger off an hour early, made a few calls, and headed back to the trial.

He ran into Nathan, who likewise missed some of the earlier proceedings. Another colleague filled in the blanks: "Nothing much in terms of fireworks; Skaggs rehabilitated Cranston, then Brooks reminded the jury there was no direct evidence linking his client to the crime scene. They went back and forth for an hour or so and finally Judge Waters cut them both off as the testimony became cumulative. Skaggs next put on the two deputies who arrested Mason when he was passed out. Brooks objected, but the judge let them testify that, in their opinion, Mason was drunk as a skunk to the point of being unconscious. This afternoon, the medical examiner will testify after the lady who saw Mason near the victim's home."

Updated, Zach went into the courtroom. To his surprise, Andrew was sitting in his reserved seat. To his further surprise, Andrew's new girlfriend, Miss Far Out, sat next to him. Shit, he thought, as he approached them, politely saying hello. He tactfully took Andrew aside to explain the proceedings and recap the prior testimony. Zach could see Miss Far Out from the corner of his eye glaring at him as though he was the murderous defendant on trial. When he finished with Andrew, Zach found a vacant seat in the rear of the courtroom, declining to sit near the toxic woman.

Judge Waters took the bench, and ordered the bailiff to bring in the jury.

Skaggs announced, "The People call Mrs. Constance Federoff."

All heads turned to the courtroom door as it

opened and an elderly woman dawdled in, assisted with a walker. She had gray, thinning hair, contrasted with visible streaks of white, and wore just enough makeup. No doubt a pretty woman in her day, trying to age with grace. She slowly made it to the witness stand, placed her walker beside her and used it to balance her body as she lowered herself into the chair. She politely declined the bailiff's offer to help her. Her pale hands were shaking, perhaps from nerves, but most likely from a tremor condition. Once seated, she was asked to raise her right hand, which she did, and the clerk read the oath, to which she responded affirmatively.

Skaggs began. "Good afternoon Mrs. Federoff, I hope you didn't have a difficult time making it here today."

"No, not too bad, but I don't make it to the city much and after all the traffic getting here, I don't plan to ever come back, that's for sure." For her age, she spoke rather quickly, in a clear voice.

"Well, we're glad you made it safely. As you are aware, we're here to discuss your knowledge of certain events pertaining to the murder of Mr. Oliver Pearce. Let me ask you first, did you know Mr. Pearce?"

"No, sir, I did not. But I heard what happened to that poor fella." She shook her head slowly. "It's just terrible what's going on in our world today."

"Yes, I agree, it sure is. Did you live near Mr. Pearce?"

"Yes, approximately a block away. The reason I know this is because I saw all of the police at his house when they found him."

"Thank you. Now, at some point, did you contact the police in connection with the crime?" Skaggs spoke softly, calmly, like they were having tea in her living room.

"I called them after they said they arrested someone for killing that poor young man. The newspeople said the person arrested was pushing a scooter with things attached to it at the time of the murder. I thought I had information which might be important. Them newspeople on the television always tell us to call a tip line if we can help with crimes, so that's exactly what I did." She looked over to the jury as she explained her actions. "Now I didn't expect a reward mind you, I was just doing my civic duty."

"Thank you for doing that. So when you called

the tip line, what did you say?"

"I told them I seen this man a week or so before they found the dead man in his house. He was pushing this contraption, not a shopping cart, but a strange contraption with baskets hanging all over it. He was pushing it with his foot like it was one of them scooters and I thought maybe it was the scooter they were talking about on the TV. Now, I didn't say I seen the man do anything wrong mind you, I just told them what I saw, and that was that." She again glanced over to the jury, wanting to make it clear that she wasn't taking sides in the battle.

"Okay, Mrs. Federoff, did you get a good look at the man pushing the scooter?"

"No, sir, I didn't. My eyes ain't as good as they used to be. I didn't see his face."

"No problem. But you did get a good look at the scooter he was pushing, didn't you?"

"Oh yes. It was an odd thing to have in our neighborhood. Every so often, we get a homeless person wandering around with a shopping cart looking for a handout. But this man went flyin' by my house on the sidewalk pushing this scooter which had all of these things attached to it. I didn't get a good look at what he was carrying in those baskets, but if I remember correctly, the baskets were blue and the scooter was a dark color. It looked like the baskets were filled up with junk. I only saw him for a few seconds, but it was unusual so that's why I called the police."

"I'm going to show you the People's exhibit number fifty and ask you if this is an accurate photograph of the scooter you saw?"

She slowly put on her reading glasses which dangled from a chain hanging around her neck. "Yes, this is it, this is what I saw."

"I'm next going to show you the People's exhibit thirty-nine, and ask you if this is the type of basket you saw attached to the scooter?"

As soon as Skaggs picked up the exhibit and before he could place it in front of her, Mrs. Federoff confidently answered, "Yep, that's it, that's what I saw on that scooter, that's exactly what it was."

"You sure about that?"

"Yes, sir, I am."

"Okay. Now, when you saw this gentleman, was he going in the direction of Mr. Pearce's home or was he going in the opposite direction?"

"Oh, he was going in the opposite direction for sure. I happened to be on my porch and looked up and saw him zoom by."

"Great. Thank you, Mrs. Federoff. I have no further questions." Skaggs smiled and took his seat.

Brooks assumed his position at the podium. "Mrs. Federoff, how old are you?"

"I'm eighty-six years old, raised during the Great Depression."

"Well, you don't look a minute over seventy." She didn't respond to the complement, causing Brooks to feel uneasy for making it.

"Now, can you please look over at my client, Mr. Ray Mason, and tell the ladies and gentlemen of this jury whether he was the man you saw riding on that scooter?" Brooks turned and pointed to his client.

She gazed over at Scooter, sized him up, then looked back at Brooks. "I'm sorry, I don't recognize that man at all. I didn't see the person on the scooter clearly. I suppose it could have been him, but I couldn't tell you one way or the other."

"Thank you. And isn't it true that you didn't see

if that person on the scooter was wearing bloody clothes, did you?"

"No. Like I said, I really didn't see anything but a man zooming by my house on a scooter with them baskets on it. I thought it was strange so I called the tip line. There's really nothing more to the story than that."

"You testified that you saw this person heading away from the victim's home, correct?"

"Oh yes, he zoomed by, going in the other direction."

"But you have no idea whether that person was ever at the victim's home, do you?"

"No, sir, I don't."

"Okay, just to be clear then, you don't recognize Mr. Mason as the person operating the scooter and you don't know whether he was at the victim's home, correct?"

"Yes, both questions are correct."

"Now, isn't it true that you saw this crate or basket on TV before you called the tip line?" Brooks picked up the crate from the evidence table.

"Yes, they showed a picture of the basket on the television news program."

"And isn't it true that the only way you remember the basket on the scooter is because you saw the basket on TV?"

"Oh no, no. I remembered that scooter and the baskets hanging off of it real clear from when it zoomed by my house. It stood out in my mind due to the fact that it was a very weird looking thing the person was riding."

"Thank you, I have no further questions." Brooks realized he never should have asked her a thing since she simply reiterated, and set in stone, her damaging testimony. She was the only witness placing Scooter near the scene, and he helped make it crystal clear to the jury that she saw exactly what she believed she saw.

Skaggs had no follow-up. He glanced over at Brooks, giving him a quick smile as the court excused his star witness.

Mrs. Federoff stood slowly, steadied herself on her walker and ambled past the jury, making a point to smile at each juror. They responded in kind. Once she was behind Skaggs, Skaggs addressed the judge, "Your Honor, the state calls Dr. Benjamin Reynolds."

Dr. Reynolds was a respectable looking older

gentleman. Salt-and-pepper gray hair, physically fit, and nicely dressed. He was medical examiner for the county of Los Angeles.

Skaggs directed him through the preliminaries… where he studied, his work history, the number of autopsies he performed and his courtroom experience. He was a pro at testifying, very articulate and concise.

"Doctor, are you familiar with Mr. Oliver Pearce?"

"Yes, I am. I was assigned to perform the autopsy on Mr. Pearce."

"Good then, let's get right to the point. In the course of the autopsy, did you notice any injuries to Mr. Pearce's body?"

"Oh yes, lots. The victim in this case was severely brutalized. He suffered major blunt-force trauma to the head, numerous penetrations by a sharp object to the torso, ligature wounds to the neck, and his feet were crudely amputated."

"Okay, let's start with the injuries to the head, could you describe them for the jury?"

"Certainly. The victim appeared to have been struck several times on the back of the head and face with a heavy object. In my evaluation of the skull and jaw, I would estimate he was hit at least ten times with this object." The doctor was trained to turn to the jurors as he answered each question, a trial tactic too scripted for many lawyers, but encouraged by many others.

"Did you come to any conclusion as to whether these blows to the head were fatal?"

"Given the condition of the body, a number of things could have been fatal, most particularly, the loss of blood. That said, in my opinion, the shattered skull and the injuries caused by the trauma to the brain would have been inconsistent with life. However, my examination reflected that he received many, if not most, of his other injuries while he was still alive and before he was inflicted with a fatal blow to the head... a very painful ordeal this young man had to endure. Sadly, he was tortured."

As Brooks had no objection to any of the evidence relating to the cause and manner of death, it was unnecessary for Skaggs to show all of the autopsy photographs. However, in the interest of making the record, and in hopes of inflaming the passions of the jurors, Skaggs published the horrific pictures, one by one, on the large projection screen as he and the doctor gave the jury a lesson on the things that happen to a human body whilst being butchered by a madman. Brooks' pretrial efforts to exclude the evidence failed miserably. Judge Waters believed each and every photograph was probative and that, as macabre as the pictures may be, the jury needed to view them.

After presenting the slide show, Skaggs moved on. "Doctor, did you have the occasion to analyze the wrench which is marked as state's exhibit thirty-eight?" Skaggs handed him the exhibit.

"Yes, I did."

"And could you ascertain whether the injuries on Mr. Pearce's skull were consistent with having been caused by this wrench?"

"Oh yes. I reviewed the contours of the wrench and matched them to the injuries to the head. In fact, in one instance, it appeared that the perpetrator may have lost his grip on the wrench, causing it to turn slightly. The adjustment device on the wrench was then imprinted on the skull—a perfect match."

"Thank you, Doctor," Skaggs said after pausing.

"Now, Dr. Reynolds, you testified that the victim had penetration wounds on his torso, could you describe what you observed?"

"Sure. There were approximately twenty-three wounds from a very sharp object, like a razorblade or scalpel. I found the nature of the wounds quite interesting in that the depths of the penetrations were very uneven, from a few inches to superficial. I concluded that the perpetrator appeared to slice the victim using a random vertical and horizontal motion, like this." Dr. Reynolds moved his right arm like an orchestra conductor as he imitated the killer.

Skaggs placed the gory photographs of the stab wounds back on the screen, eliciting further details about the injuries. During this hour-long process, Dr. Reynolds provided the jury with the length, width and depth of each and every wound he observed.

"Doctor, could you next describe the ligature wounds around the neck which you observed?"

"The neck had what appeared to be linear marks the size of a ten- to twelve-gauge wire or rope. However, I don't believe the pressure applied by the rope or wire was sufficient to cause death by asphyxiation. Although not itself determinative, the u-shaped hyoid bone in the neck was not fractured, which we often see in strangulation deaths. In my opinion, the victim may have been subdued by the loss of oxygen, but did not die from it."

"Is it your testimony that the victim could have passed out from the lack of oxygen and was then tortured?" Skaggs prompted the witness to provide the rehearsed testimony.

"Very likely, yes. Given the circumstances, I believe he was rendered unconscious during strangulation and then bound or tied by the perpetrator. Upon regaining consciousness, I believe the remaining injuries were inflicted upon him."

"Finally, Doctor, you testified that Mr. Pearce's feet were, using your words, 'crudely amputated,' what do you mean?"

"Quite simply, the perpetrator chopped the feet off above the ankles with what I believe to be the butcher knife found at the scene. The knife was rather dull, but sharp enough to penetrate skin and chop through bone. We discovered small pieces of bone in several places on the victim's body. This suggests that the perpetrator made a number of strikes with the dull blade to cut through the skin and bone, much like one would expect to see when chopping firewood. As he continued to chop through the bone, it splintered, and these splinters were found distributed on the body."

Several jurors stared at Scooter with disgust. Others could only look down, desperately attempting to conceal assorted emotions as they imagined the psychopath doing the same thing to someone in his or her own family.

Relentless, Skaggs next treated the courtroom to more graphic photographs, blown up so the jury could see the nerve endings dangling from each leg and foot. Skaggs was indifferent as he put on the show, oblivious to the impact upon the jurors, none of whom had ever seen this side of humanity. His confidence in his presentation, and his lack of emotion, could have been interpreted by some as a fetish for blood and guts. Zach wouldn't have been one bit surprised if Skaggs tossed out bags of popcorn and boxes of Dots to the jurors as they watched the horror movie he directed and produced.

After this grand finale, Skaggs finally concluded. "Thank you, Doctor, I have nothing further."

Brooks politely stood, thanked the doctor for his time, and informed him, Judge Waters, and the jury that he had no questions. He wanted that man off the stand, out of the courtroom, and hopefully out of L.A. as quickly as possible.

Skaggs next called William Parham, who was escorted into the courtroom by the bailiff.

The jurors collectively laughed when he raised his left hand, thinking it was his right hand, as he swore to tell the truth, the whole truth, and nothing but the truth.

If Dr. Reynolds was a model witness, Parham was his antithesis. He clearly fell victim to the blistering California heat, a fact revealed by his brown, leathery skin. With matted hair and teeth the color of raw shrimp, he took the stand, wearing stained jeans and a blue button-up, torn near the collar. He blinked his eyes repeatedly, no doubt a nervous tick.

Skaggs asked him his name and the city of his residence, but hoped that the specific details of Parham's living arrangements would not be revealed to the jury. They were, as Parham volunteered that he lived on the streets of L.A., in no particular place.

"Mr. Parham, you were subpoenaed to testify in this case, correct?"

"Yes, sir."

"And you actually came forward on your own to give the police some information regarding Mr. Ray Mason, correct?"

He waited for his blinking eyes to stop as a cue to respond. "If you're referring to Scooter," he pointed at the defendant, "yep. I found his little skateboard thingy by the gas station. The police were askin' questions about him so I gone up to one of the officers and told her what I knew."

"What did you know that you felt was important to tell the officer?"

"Just that the skateboard was sitting there all by itself one day so I began to use it. I knew it belonged to Scooter 'cause he fixed it up real good. It had kinda like a handlebar to steer it and storage spaces on it. He always rode it around, but I figured he was done-in or somethin' and he didn't need it no more. So I took it."

"Done-in? What do you mean by that?"

"I mean killt by someone or busted, one or the other." He squinted as though blinded by an interrogation light. His tick was causing him to struggle to focus upon the prosecutor who stood in front of him.

"Did the skateboard you took have any milk

crates attached to it?"

"It maybe had four or five or six, but one fell off when it tipped over as I was taking it."

"Where did you take it from, do you recall?"

He looked up, giving this question some thought. "It was near the gas station over there on Victory Boulevard."

"Is that where you found the skateboard?"

"Yes, sir."

"Did you observe whether there was anything in the crate that fell off which you left behind?"

"Looked like some shirts and a big ol' wrench and some sneakers, to the best of my remembrance. Might have been able to use the sneakers, but I just wanted to get the hell outta there, and didn't have time to pick 'em up."

"You testified you previously saw Mr. Mason, or Scooter, driving around on the skateboard with those crates attached, is that correct?"

"Yes sir, all the dang time."

"Thank you, Mr. Parham. Pass the witness, Your Honor."

Brooks jumped to his feet and shouted "Are you

telling this jury you stole my client's belongings, Mr. Parham, is that what you're saying?"

Scared by Brooks' unexpected aggression and his loud, deep voice, Parham looked around for help. Finding none, he put his head down on the witness stand and began to sob. "Yes, I stoled it, but I thought Scooter was a goner 'cause he never left his stuff anywhere before. I'm sorry. Please, ladies and gentlemen of the jury, please don't make me go back to jail, please. I can't go there no more." He couldn't contain himself. His eyes blinked rapidly as he cried like a baby, praying to the dear lord and the jury for forgiveness. Zach, and everyone else, including Brooks, felt sorry for the pathetic witness.

"Settle down Mr. Parham. Do you think you're on trial here today?" Brooks calmly asked after he allowed the jury plenty of time to take note of the hopeless witness.

"I was told the jury would listen to my story and decide what to do to me. He said if I said the wrong things, I would go to jail for rippin' off the skateboard." Parham looked over to Scooter, "I'm sorry, Scooter, I didn't know." Scooter grinned, but his eyes adequately warned Parham that he would be paid back once he was acquitted and released.

"Who told you that you would go to jail if you said the wrong things, Mr. Parham?"

"That skinny little man sittin' right there." He pointed at Skaggs, the jury laughed in unison.

"Oh he did, did he? Are you certain it was him?"

"Yes, sir, I'm one-hundred percent sure."

"Well, thank you, Mr. Parham, you've been very helpful. I have no further questions. And, by the way, you are not on trial here today. When you're finished testifying, I can assure you that you can walk right past that skinny man," motioning to Skaggs, "and right out the courtroom door, and no one will bother you, okay?"

"Okay, thank you, sir." Parham said, relieved, wiping the tears from his face.

Skaggs didn't even try to rehabilitate his witness, as it would have served no purpose. The testimony was not critical since Scooter didn't dispute that he put the items in the crate which was left behind. On the other hand, Brooks was handed a small bonus and would argue that the prosecutor employed fear tactics to get witnesses to say what he wanted them to say to get a conviction.

After Parham left, Judge Waters announced that

the court would be in recess. Brooks thought she was going to crucify Skaggs for what he told Parham, and maybe she was. However, as the jury began to exit the courtroom, Andrew stood up, slowly walked over to Scooter and cold-cocked him in the face, instantly knocking him out. Miss Far Out jumped onto Andrew's back, put him in a chokehold, wrestled him to the ground and instructed him to chill the hell out. The bailiffs scrambled to quell the chaos and render first aid to Scooter, who quickly regained consciousness. His blood was splattered all over the defense table and Brooks' white shirt.

Andrew was immediately taken into custody. Judge Waters adjourned the trial to the following morning and gave a long admonishment to the jury, which essentially prohibited them from considering the knockout punch as evidence of guilt or innocence. She scheduled a hearing for the next afternoon to decide contempt charges. She would forbid Andrew from entering the courtroom during the remainder of the trial.

TWENTY-ONE

ZACH knew Andrew was unstable, but never thought he would do something so drastic. On the way back from the trial, he decided that the first call he would make when he returned to his office would be to Nathan. He had to implore upon him to put the pedal to the metal in the probate proceeding so he could be paid and then promptly fire his volatile client. He wanted no more of Andrew.

Walking past Miss Far Out's office, he could see her crying in the lobby. Under the circumstances, he felt he should attempt to console her.

"Is there anything I can do?" Zach quietly offered as he peered into her office door, keeping his compassion to an absolute minimum.

"No." She said sternly. "It's all your fault. If you would have gotten him his money earlier, none of this would have happened. He probably wouldn't have gone to the stupid trial in the first place."

Zach considered her nastiness and responded in kind. "You've known him what... four days and you think you know what he would've done if he received a few million dollars earlier? For all you know, he would have put out a hit and had that killer iced in jail."

"He would not. He's a very caring man who was obviously distraught in the presence of his brother's murderer. I would've done the same thing if it were someone in my family and I had to look at those disgusting pictures of the body."

"Maybe, but it doesn't make it right. And as to getting Andrew his money quicker, no can do. It's not up to me and Andrew is fully aware of the process, you are not."

"I know more than you think I know," she said as she looked at Zach, black mascara streaking down her face. "Are you going to help him get out of jail?"

"I was not retained to assist him with an assault and battery, or a contempt case. I'll try to speak with him tomorrow, but he may be held in jail for a few days or more."

"For kicking the shit out of his brother's killer?

What the hell? The guy's gonna be sentenced to death. A sore lip and broken nose can't possibly be something he's concerned about."

"If you were paying attention to the trial," Zach interrupted, "you would have noticed that the defendant is claiming he's innocent, and until the jury finds him guilty, he is innocent. Therefore, knocking him out in the courtroom is no different than knocking you out in your office," wishful thinking on Zach's part. "It's a crime to punch people, especially when they're defenseless."

"Whatever," she said curtly, assuming a crossed-arms, spoiled-brat position as though arguing with her father. "I love him, and he wants to marry me on the beach in Newport as soon as he gets his money."

She continued, "You need to do whatever is necessary to get him out of jail. If you want to jack up your already excessive lawyer's fee, fine, but I need him out now, understood?"

Zach had had enough. "With all due respect ma'am, you may possess the power of a cougar and use that power to connive my client out of his riches, but that's between you and him. However, you will never tell me what to do. I do not represent you; I will never represent you; and, but for me having to walk past your sorry ass to get to my office, I wouldn't care to ever look at you. So put that in your crack pipe and smoke it." He abruptly left her office, slamming the door, but instantly realized that biting his tongue would have been more consistent with professional standards.

It took him a few minutes to calm down before he picked up his phone and called Nathan.

"Hi Nathan… where to begin? I assume you saw my client sucker-punch Mason, did you not?"

"Are you kidding me? I enjoyed every bit of it. I was hoping he'd give Brooks a piece of the action too."

"Yeah, me too," Zach responded, not necessarily agreeing, but wanting to be one of the guys.

"Hey, I'm touchin' bases with you again to get a better idea of the timing for bringing the probate matter to a close. Andrew's future, at least near term, is uncertain, given his antics today. He'll no doubt need some cash for bail and to retain counsel."

"Well let's see," Nathan said, trying to be helpful. "The petition was filed last October; the time for filing creditor's claims has expired; and no one has filed any papers challenging the petition. I prepared a draft of the final accounting and distribution plan, which I expect to complete and file within the next week or two. Once it's filed, it should be approved by the judge and we'll be in a position to distribute the funds, less statutory fees. So I'm thinking maybe three weeks to thirty days, tops."

"Perfect, I'll pass this information on to Andrew. Thanks Nathan, I'll see you tomorrow."

Soon after finishing his call with Nathan, Miss Far Out stormed through his small lobby and into his office. "Listen to me you shyster, no one ever talks to me like you did and gets the last word. Let this be fair warning that if you ever speak to me unkindly again, you will be evicted from this building, do you comprehend that you piece-of-shit lawyer?"

Zach, sitting at his desk, was quick to react as though he planned for these types of incidents. He had a choice of two items to pull out from his desk drawer. One, a Glock .40; the other, a dictation recorder. As killing the woman may jeopardize the receipt of the hefty fee from her boyfriend, he opted for the recorder. He grabbed it, calmly stood up, put it in front of her quivering red lips, and pressed the record button.

"Miss Far Out, you are being recorded, could you

please repeat what you just said to me about being evicted from my office 'cause I'd really like to show your boss and the owner of this building how great the customer service is around here?"

She stared at him ready to attack, but repeated nothing and darted out of his office.

TWENTY-TWO

WHEN Ginger arrived the next morning, Zach gave her a summary of his run-in with the property manager. He told her to be on the lookout and not to take any crap from her. "As long as the rent is paid on time, she has no business bothering us."

"Oh don't you worry, Mista Morgan, I'll teach her a lesson if she tries to mess wit' you or me and that's a promise. When I worked at Dr. Arnold's, we always had people come in angry wantin' to start somethin'. All I would do is stand up out of my chair so they could see my big-ass body, and I looked into their little eyes tellin' them to bring it on and such. Ain't none of them messed with me after that... mmm hmm." Ginger waived her hands around as she described the menacing way she protected Dr. Arnold. They both laughed.

"Good, but try not to get into it when clients are around, if you can avoid it."

"Oh don't worry, I'll be tactful, don't you worry, Mista Morgan." Zach sure liked his new hire.

"Wonderful. A few new clients will be coming in this morning. You can greet them and ask them to fill out this information sheet. They also need to pay the consultation fee up front. Once they're ready, let me know and I'll come out and show them into my office. You can answer the phone and take messages. If a call is from a client or prospective client, try to get as detailed a message as possible, and if they just need to talk your ear off, let them. One thing I learned in my short career is that the average client just needs to be comforted with conversation."

"If the message is from an opposing attorney, try to be nice, but if he or she is rude to you, you have my permission to be rude back... in a professional way of course. These are the basic ground rules around here. Not much else you need to know at this point."

"Oh yeah, one other thing... you can call me Zach."

Ginger looked at him quizzically, "Okay, will do. But how do I professionally tell someone to go to hell? 'cause I don't wanna offend anyone and such."

"Good question," Zach laughed. "Use your judgment, Ginger. But if you find yourself at a loss for words, feel free to tell him or her to go to hell the good ol' fashioned way. If another person offends you, you can offend back. Think of yourself as a chameleon... change colors to match your surroundings." He laughed again.

Ginger settled into her desk and readied herself for her new role. Within minutes, she fielded her first call. It was collect from the jail, on behalf of Andrew Pearce. "Shoot," she whispered as she put the phone down having received no prior instruction as to handle collect calls. She went to the doorway of Zach's office, not crossing the threshold. "There's a Mista Andrew Pearce on the phone, calling collect, should I put him through?"

"Oh yes, I'll speak to him every time he calls. Thank you, Ginger."

Ginger returned to her desk and put the call through.

"Hi Andrew," Zach said. Before you speak, you need to understand that we are likely being recorded. How are you?"

"Shitty. When can you get me outta here?"

"Not sure. I'll check to see what, if any, charges have been filed and what the bail is later this morning. I'll also try to arrange a visit with you. But, as you know, I have not been retained... " Andrew cut him off.

"Yeah, whatever man, well I would appreciate you doing your best to help me out. Could you stop by Julie's office and tell her I'm okay and you'll be taking care of me?"

"Who's Julie?" Zach asked.

"You're freakin' neighbor man. What do you mean who's Julie? You rented your office from her, she's your landlord and she's my lady."

"Sorry, didn't remember that being her first name. In any event, she and I aren't on speaking terms, so you'll have to tell her yourself if and when you get out."

Andrew hung up.

Zach looked at the dead receiver and cursed his client.

A few moments passed as Zach contemplated how to handle Andrew. Experience would have given him answers. Having none, he'd just take his lumps and put up with him for another month or so.

Ginger broke his train of thought when she handed him a client-intake sheet signed by Brian Perri. After a cursory review of the form, Zach went to greet his new client.

"Good morning, Mr. Perri, pleasure to meet you," Zach said with a smile, extending his hand. Mr. Perri grinned slightly as he slowly lifted his right arm and offered his limp hand, obviously not in the mood for pleasantries. Zach walked behind him, directing him to his office. "So how are you this morning?"

"Shitty," he said as he situated himself in the chair in front of Zach.

"Well, that's not the first time I heard that today," Zach said chuckling, "but it can't be all that bad, can it?" Mr. Perri stared at him, hoping the lawyer would cut out the small talk.

"So how can I help you?"

"Should I start from the beginning or do you want me to get to the point?" Zach hoped he'd start somewhere in the middle so he didn't have to listen to all of the minutia, but he kindly told Perri he had plenty of time and he could start from the beginning if he wanted to.

"About two months ago I was driving down San Vicente, like I did every day, when a delivery truck coming the opposite direction swerved to miss a car in front of it. After the truck swerved, he was headed right towards me. I slammed on my brakes, and the car behind me hit me like a freakin' train, which caused me to hit the delivery truck. It was a produce truck carrying a load of peanuts. My car and the car that hit me were totaled. I was knocked out cold, so I didn't see what happened after we collided. They transported me to the hospital."

"Last week, I received a letter from a law firm threatening to sue me, claiming the whole kit and caboodle was my fault since I should have avoided hittin' the truck. Can you believe it? My fault?" He handed the letter to Zach. "I don't know what to do... my wife and I are worried sick."

Zach read the letter. "Looks like they represent the truck driver and want you to pay for the truck, the contents in the truck and the injuries to the driver. This is nonsense. You said you hit the breaks to avoid colliding with the truck barreling toward you, right?"

"Yes, otherwise, I could have been killed."

Zach continued reading. "Hmm, it says you were

cited for a cell phone violation. Were you on your cell phone at the time?"

"Yes, but what difference does that make? It had nothing to do with what happened."

"They'll claim you could've avoided the accident had you been more attentive. To be honest with you, they may have a point if they can show the phone was in use at the precise time of the accident."

"What was the extent of your injuries?" Zach asked.

"I broke my jaw, several ribs and my collarbone. Still feel like hell."

"Okay, I don't see a big problem. Here's what I want you to do. Bring me your auto insurance policy and your medical records. If you have the police report, I'll need that too. Don't speak to anyone other than my secretary, Ginger, or myself. I'll look into making a claim against the other drivers based upon your injuries. Your insurance will cover your defense."

Perri impatiently shook his head side to side as he said, "No, no no, I have no insurance. If I did, I wouldn't be here, Mr. Morgan."

"Are you serious, you were driving without

coverage? I'm surprised you weren't cited for that too. You have a real problem, Mr. Perri. You're what, fifty, sixty years old? At your age, you should have lots of insurance to protect you and your family against things like this."

Perri stared at Zach, considered his comments and paused briefly. His face gradually reddened. "Mr. Morgan, I didn't pay you to tell me the same damn thing my wife has been yelling at me for every single minute over the past week. You're supposed to help me get out of this, not make me feel worse by suggesting I'm an idiot."

"No, Mr. Perri, I didn't mean that at all. I'm sorry if you took it the wrong way," Zach said before being interrupted.

"How long you been practicing law anyway?" Perri asked rudely.

"I used to work in a very big firm that defended these types of cases."

"Didn't answer my question, son. I asked how long you been doin' this?"

"Since last December, why?"

"I thought so... well you better start learning

how to treat a client with respect. I knew there was a reason I don't like lawyers." Perri abruptly grabbed the letter out of Zach's hand, stormed past Ginger's desk and left the office without saying another word.

Zach stared into space, baffled, brooding over whether he could be disciplined by the bar for suggesting to a client that he was an idiot.

Ginger sensed the commotion and slowly approached his office. "You okay, Zachary?"

"Just peachy," he said, simulating a grin.

"Good, 'cause here's your next client," she said showing her big toothy smile as she handed him another intake sheet. Zach didn't want another client, ever. Sasha was right. He didn't know what the hell he was doing.

"Also, a guy named Mista Gainer called to tell you the crazy neighbor didn't get the restrainin' order against him for killing her dogs and such. He said the judge took one look at her an' threw her outta his courtroom. Can the judge do that, Zachary?"

"A judge can do anything a judge wants to do, Ginger," Zach said quietly, still troubled by Mr. Perri.

TWENTY-THREE

AFTER lunch, Zach went to the 77th Street Regional Jail on South Broadway in an effort to speak with Andrew. However, while he was paying the parking meter, he noticed Andrew and Miss Far Out across the street, hugging, kissing and laughing like teenagers.

They didn't see him, and he did his best to keep it that way. He quietly maneuvered his way back to his car, thankful that Andrew no longer required his services to help bail him out of jail.

He proceeded to Scooter's trial, which was already underway, and found the only empty seat, located in the rear of the courtroom. As he walked in, Judge Waters glared at him, recognizing him as the lawyer for the victim's brother who nearly caused her to declare a mistrial. Zach was in no mood for her and looked away, declining her invitation to make eye contact.

Several people from the press also took note of

Zach. They would later hound him for an exclusive about his poor client who couldn't control his emotions as he sat in the same room with the killer of his brother, forced to endure picture after picture chronicling the massacre. Zach would love to come clean and tell them that his so-called distraught client is living it up, planning a wedding and dreaming about how he will spend the murder victim's millions. But Zach will say no such thing. The exclusive story will consist of two words: "No comment."

Scooter looked surprisingly good for having been the recipient of Andrew's right hook. His eye was swollen, and he had a bandage on his nose. Zach didn't know the details of his injuries, but he was glad there were no wires holding his jaws together.

The lawyers spent the morning session arguing Brooks' motion for a mistrial. According to Brooks, the assault upon his client in open court by the victim's brother, witnessed by some—if not all—of the jurors, was highly prejudicial to the defendant, who is now forced to testify with a swollen, bruised and bandaged face.

Skaggs viewed it differently. He argued that the attack would garner sympathy for the defendant and he should therefore be glad he got belted. When he takes the stand, the jury will see him as a battered victim, not a perpetrator. Further, he argued, the court adequately admonished the jury not to consider the assault in their deliberations, so they'll surely forget about it.

Judge Waters denied the motion for a mistrial. She ruled that the jurors should not be underestimated in their ability to dole out impartial justice, that they were properly admonished, and that it must be assumed they would heed the admonishment.

Skaggs' next witness was a forensic blood specialist, Dr. Peggy Rhine. She would authenticate and expand upon the prior testimony of Detective Cranston relating to the blood evidence found on Scooter's clothing, the shoes and the wrench.

As is his practice, Skaggs spent substantial time qualifying the witnesses and allowing her to brag about her achievements in the field of forensic science, particularly blood science, as she called it.

Once qualified, her testimony was short. She confirmed that the blood on Scooter's clothing, the shoes and the wrench matched the victim's blood. She also stated that the lab tests she performed on the shoes confirmed not only a blood match, but that the shoeprints were identical to the prints found in the blood at the scene.

It was Brooks' turn.

"Now Dr. Rhine, when you tested the clothing for blood from someone other than the victim, or Mr. Mason, what did you find?" Brooks knew perfectly well that she performed no such test for blood from sources other than Ollie or Scooter. His question for purely for effect.

Skaggs, objected, "Assumes facts not in evidence. As Mr. Brooks is aware, there has been no testimony that this witness, or any other witness, tested the clothing for blood from anyone other than the victim or the defendant."

Before Judge Waters could rule on the objection, Brooks quickly interjected, "Oh, I'm sorry, is that a true story, Dr. Rhine? Is it true that you did not in fact test for blood from others?"

"Yes, that's true."

"Well, I stand corrected. I apologize, Your Honor, for not paying closer attention. I guess I'm surprised there were no such tests performed. I just thought it would be important to know whether there was someone else's blood on the clothing. But I guess the prosecution didn't think so. Therefore, I have no further questions." Brooks wanted to make this point loud and clear, but he would pay the price.

"Counsel, you've been warned about making speeches, yet you've done it again. We'll take this issue up later." Judge Waters glared at Brooks. She was not happy.

Skaggs next called Deputy Cramer, the jailhouse officer who discovered the blood on Scooter's clothing, and who heard the purported confession.

"Deputy, please tell us exactly what Mr. Mason told you after you confronted him regarding the bloody clothes he was wearing?"

"It's in my notes here," Cramer looked down at his report. "He said, and I quote, 'You can lock me up, pig, but that SOB deserved what he got and I'd do it again, and I'll let you have it too if you come back here to my cell you jackass.' "

"Did you understand his comments to refer to the murder of Mr. Pearce?"

Brooks popped out of his chair, "Objection,

Your Honor. Among other things, and I can list them all if the court so desires, this calls for the witness to engage in the worst kind of speculation. How on earth does this witness know what was in the defendant's mind, or who exactly the defendant was referring to when he made that statement while he was drunk?"

"Counsel, I've said it before, and I meant it then and I mean it now—no preaching!   Keep it short and simple... or else. Objection sustained."

Skaggs continued, "But you did understand by his statement that the witness would hurt you too, correct?"

"Objection, leading."

"Overruled, move on Counsel."

"I certainly thought he'd try to hurt me. He wouldn't have succeeded, but he may have tried," the deputy said as he grinned to the jurors.

"Thank you. I have nothing further."

Brooks stood behind his client and asked, "Deputy Cramer, did Mr. Mason ever tell you he killed anyone?"

"No, but he implied it."

"Move to strike."

"Granted. The jury will disregard everything after the word, no. Sir, please tell us only what you know based upon your personal knowledge," Judge Waters ordered.

Brooks continued, "You have no idea who Mr. Mason was referring to or what he meant when he made that statement to you, do you, Deputy?"

"I have a really good hunch, but no."

"Well, people shouldn't be sent to death row on a hunch, now should they, Deputy?" Not expecting an answer to the rhetorical question, Brooks concluded, "Thank you, I'm finished with this witness, Your Honor."

Cramer responded anyway, "I'm not the jury, Counsel, ask them." He motioned to the jury.

"Deputy, Deputy, Deputy," Brooks said softly shaking his head, "Fortunately we have very smart people on the jury who know the difference between an unsupported hunch, like yours, and real evidence. Your Honor, move to strike, and then I have no further questions of this man."

Judge Waters stared down Brooks. "The jury shall disregard the witness's last comment and shall also disregard Mr. Brooks' speech made in response to said comment."

After a few short follow-up witnesses and near the end of the afternoon, Skaggs confidently announced, "The state rests, Your Honor."

The jury was admonished and released. Judge Waters then turned to Brooks and demanded that he give the clerk a check for five hundred dollars, payable to the court. She also warned him that the next time he disobeys a court directive or argues with a witness, the fine will triple and he'd be doing weekend duty picking up garbage on the side of the freeway. Brooks smirked as he wrote the check, oblivious to the judge's threats. His job was to obtain an acquittal, even at the expense of professional etiquette.

The court had one final matter to tend to... Andrew's contempt proceeding. Zach was caught off guard. He thought, incorrectly, that the contempt hearing was no longer on the court's calendar since Andrew was released from jail.

Judge Waters announced, "People versus Andrew Pearce."

Zach stood, not knowing what to do, petrified.

He hadn't spoken to Andrew since he abruptly hung up on him, and he had no idea where he and his bridezilla were.

In a dramatic fashion, the double doors to the courtroom were pushed opened by the bailiff. Andrew, Miss Far Out, and another individual, whom appeared to be an attorney, entered. They approached counsel table, leaving Zach utterly confused as to his role in the packed courtroom. Should he sit back down in the audience, or is he ethically obligated to join his client and provide additional support to the new defense team? If he'd had a choice, he'd prefer to run like hell out of the courtroom, down the thousand flights of stairs and through the streets of L.A., right back to where he belongs, in the safety of the tiny cubbyhole office he had at FF&W.

Zach soon recognized that his expertise was not needed. He decided his best course of action was to calmly and nonchalantly sit his ass down and give the appearance that he fully expected another attorney to be representing his client during the contempt proceeding.

"Good afternoon, Your Honor, June Gregory for the defendant, Andrew Pearce, who is present in court." She spoke with a slight New York accent.

Judge Waters began. "Mr. Pearce, what you did yesterday in this courtroom was despicable. Taking matters into your own hands is never a good idea, but when you do it in a court of law, it is contempt. I know all of this is difficult for you, given your relationship with the victim, and I am sympathetic with that, but your actions cannot and will not be tolerated in my courtroom. Because of what you did, we were very close to starting this trial all over again. This would have caused a waste of scarce judicial resources at a tremendous expense to our taxpayers."

Save it, Lady, Andrew thought, I couldn't care less about you, your courtroom, or your fuckin' taxpayers.

"Fortunately, I believe we minimized the impact your conduct had on the jury. However, your actions nonetheless fit the definition of criminal contempt. That said, we'll handle this in one of two ways: You can plead guilty right now and I'll impose a sentence; or you can plead not guilty and we'll set the matter for further proceedings. Would you like to take a moment to speak with your counsel before you tell me how you wish to proceed?"

Andrew responded, "No ma'am, we already spoke about this and she advised me you would say exactly what you just said. She also said you're a tough SOB and that I should ask you what my sentence will be before I plead guilty."

The audience erupted into restrained laughter. Judge Waters did not. Her piercing eyes turned to Miss Gregory, who forced a smile in an effort to trivialize her client's comment, while holding back the instant rush of bubble guts which nearly caused her to shit her pants.

"Lucky for you, Counselor, I consider your observation of me to be complimentary. Thank you," Judge Waters said after a short reflection.

She turned to Andrew. "The sentence will be a fine of five thousand dollars, payable to the county of Los Angeles, within ninety days. You will also be required to reimburse the county for all the medical expense it incurred in providing treatment to Mr. Mason for the injuries you inflicted upon him. And, you will be prohibited from attending the remainder of this trial."

"However, I will allow you to attend any sentencing of Mr. Mason if he is found guilty. In such case, my bailiff will watch you closely. If you do anything like what you did yesterday, you will go to jail for a very long time. Do you understand the sentence, and would you like to plead?"

"Yes ma'am, I guess I'll plead guilty and take the deal, but I don't think I should have to pay his medical bills since he's gonna be executed and it was a waste of money to treat him in the first place. But fine, I'll do it your way to get it over with."

"Good decision. Let the record reflect that Mr. Pearce has pled guilty to the charge of contempt and that he agrees to the sentence I just recited. The court is adjourned."

Zach hung around to speak with Andrew and June in the hallway of the courthouse. Andrew had nothing to say and let his new lawyer deal with Zach while he waited with Miss Far Out on a bench.

After introducing himself, Zach kindly asked June, "So can you tell me what's going on with Andrew?"

"Your guess is as good as mine. I was contacted by Julie, who manages the building I'm in."

Oh, that's just beautiful, Zach thought. He and June are actually neighbors in their office building and she no doubt has heard lots of slanderous statements made about him by Miss Far Out.

"She requested I assist her in getting her fiancé out of jail since, according to her, his current lawyer is incompetent," June said, smiling.

"So I made a few calls, met him at the jail, and got him released. Julie posted bail for him in the amount of ten grand. When Andrew was released, he asked if I'd assist him with this contempt matter. I agreed, and here we are. Not much more than that."

"Did he ask you to assist him with his brother's estate?" Zach inquired with his fingers crossed, hoping he didn't lose his job.

"No. As far as I'm concerned, my representation of him terminated after he pled guilty to the contempt charge. I was paid five hundred bucks for my services, and I'm done. To tell you the truth, I don't want anything to do with him or her."

"Why not?"

"Because Julie is a crazy lady. She's not a nice person and is full of drama. I've known her a few years and I cringe when I see her around the building. As for Andrew, I obviously don't know much about him, other than his prior minor criminal record. He seemed like a nice guy, until he threw me under the bus with Judge Waters just now."

"Yeah. That was somethin'. Well, if you don't already know, I'm Andrew's other attorney, whom Julie described to you so eloquently. I represent him in the probate matter and I don't think he wants to speak with me right now, due to a heated disagreement I had with Julie. Can you do me a favor and simply let Andrew know it's in his best interest to call me as soon as possible. I'd like to walk over there and tell him that myself right now, but I'm not sure what reaction I'd get from him, or her." Zach and June turned their heads in unison toward Andrew and Miss Far Out as they sat on the bench.

"Well, for the record, I didn't believe a word Julie said about you. I'm sure she'll have choice words about me now that my job is complete. Anyway, I'll pass on your request; great meeting you. I'll see you around."

"Thank you. By the way, I guess you and I are neighbors. I'm in suite two-twenty-five. If you need anything, let me know," Zach said, as he walked away without acknowledging Andrew, who was now fondling his sidekick in the courthouse hallway.

TWENTY-FOUR

TROUBLED by his deteriorating relationship with Andrew and the risk it may have on his fee, Zach was restless and unable to sleep. Rather than spend hours attempting to control his uncontrollable brain synapses, he undertook some late night research to confirm whether his fee would be protected if he was fired by his client. Miss Far Out had a lot of influence over Andrew, and Zach believed it was only a matter of time before she advised Andrew to do exactly that.

Fortunately, the law was on Zach's side thanks to the top-notch retainer agreement he cut and pasted from the websites of competent practitioners.

Nothing he did in the course of his representation of Andrew thus far constituted a breach of the retainer agreement. Worst case, he'd have to sue Andrew and tie up the administration of the estate until Andrew conceded. He was happy with the strength of his legal position, versus that of his unpredictable client.

Still wide awake, he decided to look at the CDs previously given to him by Miss Presley of the public administrator's office. The CDs outlined Ollie's financial strategies, which helped him accumulate his fortune. According to Nathan, Zach's fee would be paid within thirty days, barring any dispute with Andrew. Therefore, he would be in need of some good investment advice for the mound of cash he would soon receive.

He spent the next few hours trying to understand the way the stock market works. He had no experience and never invested in anything other than the small savings account he and Sasha held together.

Ollie's strategy was way over Zach's head. Of the dozen or so articles and other files Zach glanced through, he found nothing useful for the average know-nothing investor. But he did learn that he could easily open an investment account with an online brokerage and within seconds buy and sell stocks and mutual funds on his own. He figured it would be a good idea to open an account once he received his fee. He'd also study up on some of the big companies he heard of on business TV channels and buy a few shares of each of them. He would soon do his part to advance American capitalism.

On the second CD, he found numerous financial statements and other records issued by various companies, all components of the Dow Jones and NASDAQ. The information contained in these documents could have been written in a foreign language as far as Zach was concerned. He understood none of it.

One file entitled, "CR," would not open without a password. Zach assumed it was a ticker symbol for a stock. He was intrigued that the file was protected by a password, which led him to believe that the mother-of-all investment secrets was hidden inside.

He tried a few obvious words and numbers: Oliver, Pearce, OliverRandall, OliverPearce, RandallPearce, Randall, ORP, Ollie, OlliePearce, Ollie's social security number, birth date, address and anything that came to mind, all to no avail. He'd work on this later, as he finally felt the need to sleep.

* * * * *

It was Friday morning, and having overslept, Zach arrived at the office after Ginger. She joked and told him he'd be fired the next time it happened.

He received a message from Andrew, which simply requested a call back. Zach complied.

"Hi Andrew, how are things?"

"Fine, but let me cut to the chase. Julie tells me you screamed at her and treated her like a woman shouldn't be treated. I won't have any of that. She and I are going to be married and no man, whether it's a lawyer, doctor, priest or even the president of the United States will ever speak to her with an evil tongue. You may not like her, but I do."

"Anything else Andrew?" Zach calmly stated after musing over Andrew's hypocritical evil tongue reference.

"Yeah, what the hell's going on with my money? It's been forever already, and I'm starting to get concerned that maybe you're in way over your head. Are you? 'cause I can have you replaced at the drop of a hat."

"Thank you for the kind words Andrew. First of all, I'm told the process should be complete within the next three to four weeks. The PA's office is finalizing the accounting and will be submitting it to the court for the judge's signature. It may be sooner, but the estimate is three to four weeks. It's out of my hands now so you just have to wait."

"Second, you shouldn't threaten to fire me. It's not conducive to a good attorney-client relationship. If you want me out, you will still be required to pay my fee. If you refuse to do so, I will immediately sue you and attach your inheritance. This will create a delay and I'm sure you don't want any further delays. Also, if you want to replace me, you'll wind up paying me and the poor lawyer you replace me with. My suggestion to you is that you and your soon-to-be bride treat me with respect because I am the only person you know who has any interest in helping you."

"Geez man, no need to get uptight and shit. I'm just trying to expedite matters," Andrew said defensively.

"Well, expedite them without being an asshole." Zach said, slamming down the phone.

As he hung up, Zach heard Ginger yelling, "Ain't nobody talk to me like that, no way, you white bitch. I'll jump ova this counter and break your skinny white ass into pieces and then let Mista Morgan finish ya off with his big ass cannon in his desk. Now, you got sumpin to say, you say it nicely. If you don't, then go on and git outta here... bitch."

Zach raced into the lobby to find Ginger and Miss Far Out having it out. Andrew no doubt told her to strategically barge in the office to double-team him while he and Andrew were doing battle on the phone. Fortunately, Zach's highly trained new employee thwarted the offensive.

"Ladies, ladies, relax. What's the problem?"

"Well, she done come in here like she owned the place demanding she talk to you right now and such. I recognized her as being the bitch from hell you told me about and I told her no way Jose. Ginger's neck slid back and forth as she waived her index finger in the air. "She got in my face, which was huge-ass mistake, part one. She done made huge-ass mistake part two when she said I ought to put a license plate on my rear end 'cause it's the size of a veedoubleya."

"You told me, Zachary, I ain't have to put up with that kind of misbehavin' so I let her have it." Ginger struggled to catch her breath.

"It's okay, Ginger. You did right. Now, Miss Far Out, I will not tell you this again. Get out of my office and don't ever come back. If you do, I will have you arrested for trespass. I will also make sure you are fired after I sue your boss and the owner of this building all because of your harassment. They won't be one bit happy about that. Whatever you need to say, put it in writing and fax it, email it, or stick it in the mailbox. I will no longer tolerate your childish and disruptive conduct. And don't ever talk to my employee like that again. If you chose to do so, it will be at your own risk because I won't stop Ginger here from ripping that pony tail off your little head and shoving it up your ass."

Daggers from Miss Far Out's eyes shot at Zach and his bodyguard as she felt helplessly outnumbered. "Fine then," she abruptly responded, "I won't give you this invitation to the wedding." She spun around and marched out with her arms crossed, invitation in hand.

Zach and Ginger stared at the door, then each other in disbelief. "Oh lordy, wha' da hell's wrong with that woman, Zachary?"

"Sorry about that, Ginger. You should know that Andrew Pearce and Miss Far Out are not stable. I think they must be eatin' some potent mushrooms or something because I've never seen such erratic behavior in people. To think after all that has happened over the past few days they have the audacity to invite me to their wedding... it's scary crazy." Zach shook his head, grinning.

They took deep breaths, then readied themselves to get back to work. As he walked toward his office, Ginger asked, "Zachary, I hate to change the subject, but I got this girlfriend who asked if we handle wrongful death cases. Her husband and son were electrocuted last month when a power line done fell in their back yard. It was so sad to all of us and we been tryin' to help her and her three little boys. She and I were talkin' yesterday and she thinks the power company should be responsible 'cause the wire done fell off the pole and kilt them. Is this something you can help out my friend wit', Zachary? She ain't got no money, but I'd be happy to help work on her case with you for free."

"Are you kidding?" Zach asked, not yet able to recognize when Ginger crossed the line between being serious and joking. "Did this really happen?" If Ginger landed him a client like this, she would be promoted to office manager, chief paralegal, executive secretary and head of PR for the firm.

"Hell yes I'm serious, Zachary. I see her every

day and do my very best to help wit' food and such for her boys. Sad, sad, sad... mmm hmm."

Given the tragedy, Zach didn't want to appear too excited. "Wow Ginger, that's horrible. I'll tell you what, get on the phone with her right now and let her know we're on our way to her house to meet with her. I don't normally do house calls, but for you, I'll do it."

"Oh thank you, Zachary, I knew the good Lord put you here in my life for a reason."

Ginger called her friend and told her she and her boss would be there in about a half-hour.

Zach walked Ginger to his small car and helped her get situated in the passenger seat. Tough fit, but she made it.

During the trip, he couldn't help but notice the white-knuckled death grip Ginger had on the sides of her seat. As he drove, she stared straight ahead, her eyes wide open. She didn't say a single word, other than a quick "turn right," or "turn left," as she directed him to their destination. Someday he'd ask her what that was all about.

They reached her friend's house located in a peaceful, modest neighborhood. Ginger lived a few houses over. Zach could see that she and her retired, so-called lazy husband, had done pretty well for themselves. Maybe Ginger was too hard on him.

Ginger walked in without knocking. Daphne Stevens was sitting on the sofa, tears welled up in her eyes as she anticipated the meeting and reliving the tragedy to Zach.

Ginger made the introductions. Before taking a seat on the sofa next to Daphne, Zach noticed several family photos on the end tables. Her three boys appeared to range in age from three to ten. Dad was a handsome man, Daphne an attractive woman. Together they looked like a happy couple with their young family. Excellent picture to present to a jury, he thought.

Zach began, "Ginger told me about the tragic accident involving your husband and son, and I am so sorry. I can't imagine what you and your family must be going through right now and you have my deepest sympathies and condolences." He spoke gently, sincerely.

"Ginger asked me if I could help you through this terrible ordeal. Rest assured, Daphne, I will do everything in my power to see that you and your boys are taken care of."

"Thank you, Mr. Morgan," she said, tears beginning to fall.

Zach continued after brief pause, allowing Daphne to grieve. "Has anyone from the utility company contacted you since the accident?"

Daphne wiped tears from her eyes and face. Sniffling, she responded, "No, but I got a few calls from someone who said he was with an insurance company. He wanted to come out and talk to me and meet with my boys. He said he would try to get me some money to pay funeral expenses and he would need me to sign papers before he gave me the money."

"What did you tell him?"

"I told him I already paid for the funeral since John, that's my husband, had a small policy that covered the arrangements. The man then said he'd be breaking company policy, but he felt bad for what happened so he would give the funeral money directly to me to use as I see fit. He wanted to come by last week to have the papers signed, but I put him off 'cause I don't know what to do. I miss John and Jacob so much. John would know what to do. My boys cry for their daddy and brother every day."

"I'm so sorry, Daphne," Zach was nearly in tears himself, "but that man is not looking out for your best interests. If you let him, he would have given you only a few dollars, which is far, far less than what you and your boys are entitled to. He would have made you sign a release, releasing the company from all further claims you have against them. Promise me you will not talk to him again. He's the enemy."

"Okay, Mr. Morgan," she said pausing, "but what in the world am I supposed to do now? We have very little money to live on and my next house payment is due in two weeks. I can't lose this house, it's everything John worked for."

"You and your boys need to sue the utility company that did this to you. They'll be forced to pay substantial amounts of money so you'll be provided for. I will see that this happens, you have my word." Zach meant it.

"Thank you, Mr. Morgan. Ginger here has been a godsend and she speaks highly of you. I know the two of you will do the right thing for me and I'm so grateful you took the time to come here to meet with me in my home."

"I consider it an honor, Daphne, and please call me Zach."

"So why don't you tell me, as best you can, what happened to John and Jacob?"

"I'll try, but it might be a little hard for me." She hesitated before continuing.

"John was doing yard work out in the backyard. He always worked outside on Saturday mornings. He loved the cool air and early morning breeze." Daphne paused and began to whimper as she looked down. "I heard a loud pop and ran outside to see what happened. John was lying on the lawn with a big cable on top of him. Smoke was coming off of him and he was having a seizure or something, and it was so so so terrible." She began crying, barely in control, wiping her eyes and nose with a tissue. Ginger joined with tears of her own.

"I tried to help him when he was shaking, but my boys ran out and I had to keep them away from the cable 'cause I didn't know if it could electrocute them. But my oldest boy, Jacob, tried to help his daddy and grabbed the cable to move it. He got electrocuted and fell to the ground on the cable." Daphne was stricken with grief and appeared unable to continue.

After a moment of sobbing, she managed to go on.

"The fireman showed up and they pulled them away from the cable. But I could tell they were dead. I couldn't believe that my boy and John were dead. They were here one minute and gone the next." Daphne finally broke down and Ginger rushed to her aid, hugging her like a child, rocking back and forth.

She finished, "My boys and me watched their brother and daddy die right in front of us and I can't get it out of my mind. My boys loved their daddy and Jacob, and nothing will help them get through this. We had a wonderful family, Mr. Morgan."

Zach struggled to find words, but none could ease the pain of his new client. "I am sorry for what you experienced," he said softly, moving closer to her on the sofa, hugging her gently. "Like I said, I'll do whatever I can to help you through this. No person should have to endure what you and your sons experienced."

Zach and Ginger did their best to console Daphne, but understandably, they couldn't. She had to gain composure on her own terms, if that was possible.

The three of them spent the next hour or so discussing the legal process and a retainer agreement, which Zach conveniently brought along with him. His fee would be twenty-five percent if he settled the case without having to sue, and thirty-three percent if litigation was necessary. In his novice opinion, the case was worth millions.

Daphne was comforted knowing that her future was in Zach's hands. He was warm, caring and trustworthy. He promised to let her know as soon as there were any developments.

After handling a few other matters at the office, Zach met Sasha for lunch. He repeated Daphne's sad story, bringing Sasha to tears. She couldn't fathom what she would do under similar circumstances.

Moving to a less edgy subject, he asked Sasha if she had any luck guessing the password for the secret investment file on Ollie's CD. He put her in charge of figuring it out, and even enlisted Amanda's help, offering her ten bucks if she solved the mystery.

"Nope," she said smiling, "not yet, but I'm trying. I'll get back on it as soon as I get home. I'm actually going through a list of common passwords people use which I found on the Internet. I must admit, I'm intrigued and anxious myself to see what secret is in the file. This Ollie fella knew what he was doing when it came to making money."

"No problemo," Zach smiled. "We have time. Don't get consumed with it." They then hugged, kissed and said their goodbyes for the afternoon. Zach was off to court to observe Scooter's defense case in chief.

TWENTY-FIVE

BROOKS and Skaggs spent a few moments arguing over the admissibility of blood evidence and expert testimony. Apparently, Brooks hired an expert who planned to testify that, in addition to Ollie's blood on Scooter's clothing, there was blood from an unknown person.

Skaggs argued that it was irrelevant whether there was unrelated blood, as it would add nothing material to the case. The victim's blood was found on Scooter's clothing and his other belongings, including the murder weapon... end of story.

For his part, Brooks opined that the blood from another individual was more recent than the victim's and would prove beyond any reasonable doubt that his client did not commit the crime. He insisted he would logically put all the pieces together for the jury and that the court must allow him an opportunity to do so to avoid reversible error.

Judge Waters—not about to be reversed on appeal—concluded, rightfully so, that the defendant should be permitted to introduce any evidence, even if only marginally relevant, which may establish his innocence. She was not entirely clear on what the defense theory was, but she decided to err on the side of caution and allow the evidence. She warned Brooks that if he headed down the road to nowhere, she would not hesitate to strike all of the evidence from the record and admonish the jury to disregard the nonsense.

Brooks then called Dr. John Bristol, who acknowledged that the jacket worn by the defendant did in fact contain the blood of the victim. According to the doctor, it also contained a modest amount of blood from another person, the identity of whom was undetermined. The testing by Dr. Bristol suggested that the third person's blood was stained into the clothing long after the victim's blood.

However, upon cross-examination, Dr. Bristol admitted he could be wrong as to the timing and sequence of the staining. When Skaggs grilled him even further, he admitted he was most likely wrong and that the unknown person's blood could have stained the clothing before the victim's blood.

On re-direct, Brooks managed to get his star witness to reverse himself again, which did far more damage to his credibility than good. Brooks was not happy with his highly paid expert's sudden waffling on this major issue. Scooter's defense strategy took a nosedive.

After Dr. Bristol's debacle, the court recessed for a short break. No one knew for sure who would be testifying next for the defense.

Zach fumbled for his cell phone in his briefcase to confirm he turned it off earlier. It would surely become the property of the judge should it happen to make a peep during the trial. He would also face contempt for violating her strict rules regarding cell phones and other electronic devices which were posted on several signs prominently displayed in her department.

Before turning it off, he read a text from Sasha. *"Z - the secret password, believe it or not, is actually the word PASSWORD, ha ha ha. Looks like the financial genius wasn't very original. Can't understand what the document says though. C ya 2 nite. Luv ya :)."* He grinned while pressing the off button.

Judge Waters took the bench and the jurors sauntered to their seats.

"The defense calls Mr. Ray Mason," Brooks announced confidently.

Zach was more than surprised. He glanced back at Nathan whose eyes revealed similar astonishment. They both expected Scooter to testify, but neither of them imagined it would be this soon into the defense case.

Scooter wore the same suit he wore the first day of trial. He looked rested and refreshed, but for the slightly blackened eye and the bandage on his nose. He half-heartedly smiled at the jury as he took the stand. Brooks assumed his position at the podium.

"Mr. Mason, you're the defendant in this case, correct?"

"Yes I am. That's why I'm here, I guess."

"And you're accused of brutally murdering Mr. Oliver Pearce?"

"That's what they say."

"You realize you don't have to testify to defend yourself, don't you?"

"So I've been told, but I ain't studied no constitution. That's why I hired you," he said smugly, grinning as he turned his head to the jury, hoping to generate a laugh. He didn't.

"Even though you have the right to remain silent, you've decided to speak to the jury, isn't that true?"

"Yep, guess so."

Scooter appeared indignant to his lawyer and cavalier to the process. First impressions speak volumes, and unless Scooter showed he appreciated the seriousness of what was transpiring, his sales pitch to the jury might wind up being a catastrophic and deadly flop.

The alienation persisted as Brooks walked his client through his background, including his time living on the streets of Los Angeles. After about a half hour or so of Scooter isolating himself from the jury, Brooks decided to cut to the chase.

"Okay. Mr. Mason, where were you on October sixth, two thousand ten, which, from the testimony we've heard, is the day Mr. Pearce was likely murdered in his home?"

"I'm not sure where I was but I was prolly hustling money. I mean, I wasn't at his house, if that's what yer askin' 'cause I ain't never been to his house. I didn't even know the man or where he lived."

"Did you ever meet Mr. Pearce?"

"No."

"Were you ever in Burbank?"

"Mightta been there once or twice in my lifetime. I try to stay away from that rich-bitch neck of the woods 'cause nobody pays nothin' to people like me over there, so why would I ever want to go there?"

"Mr. Mason, I appreciate you trying to be helpful, but could you please just listen to the question and answer only the question I ask you?"

"Sorry. I'll try, but this here's stressin' me out."

"I know it is, but do your best."

"So, it's your testimony that you were never at the victim's home and you were only in the city of Burbank once or twice?"

"Objection, leading, asked and answered, and compound question," Skaggs complained, barely audible.

"Overruled."

Bewildered, Scooter looked at the judge, then

Skaggs, and then Brooks for direction as to what to do next.

"You can answer the question, Mr. Mason," Judge Waters said impatiently.

"Oh. What was it again?" Scooter was squirming in his seat.

"Is it your testimony that you were never at the victim's home?"

"That is correct, yes. But Mr. Brooks, kin you come here a sec, I got something to ask you?"

"I'm sorry, Mr. Mason, we can't talk right now. Once we take a break, we'll be able to talk amongst ourselves in private."

"Now, can you describe this skateboard or scooter we've heard others testify about?"

"No can do, not right now, 'cause I hafta take a real serious piss. I'm 'bout to explode. When I get nervous, my bladder fills up quick. That's why I wanted to talk to ya." The unexpected comment nearly sent Brooks into full cardiac arrest. The jury and the spectators tried their best to contain the urge to howl, but pockets of laughter disrupted the proceedings.

"Your Honor, may we take a short recess to

accommodate the witness?" Brooks looked at Judge Waters, hoping to see compassion and understanding. Instead, her beady eyes told Brooks it was his obligation, as the attorney of record for the defendant, to make sure the defendant relieves himself prior to the beginning of each session so as to avoid these types of outbursts. The next time the defendant needed to urinate in the middle of his testimony, Brooks knew he'd be writing another check.

"The court will be in recess for five minutes. If anyone else hears nature calling, please take care of business now." Frustrated, she left the bench. The bailiffs escorted Scooter to the restroom.

Fifteen minutes later, Judge Waters announced to the attorneys and the jury that she had an unforeseen personal emergency and she would need to adjourn the trial until Monday morning. She apologized and assured the jurors there would be no further interruptions.

The hypocrisy was not overlooked by Brooks who glared at her while she retreated to her chambers behind the bench. Why is it acceptable for her to close down the courtroom for an entire afternoon for personal issues, the nature of which she doesn't bother to disclose, but when a witness needs a short break to take a leak, she goes berserk? He considered shooting the thick rubber band he was about to place around his file at her ass just to gauge her reaction, but laughed to himself as he also considered the consequences of the assault. Such random and bizarre thoughts often popped out of nowhere during his stressful murder trials, no doubt a defense mechanism helping him cope.

Zach was pleased the judge shortened the session. He'd head back to the office and get some work done.

First on his list was the drafting of a demand to DesignElec, the utility company responsible for the electrocution deaths of John and Jacob Stevens.

Initial demand letters should be firm, but not overly aggressive, as their purpose is to open, not close, the lines of negotiation. But Zach wanted this one to be downright nasty. Daphne's pain had a profound impact upon him, and the thought of the weasel from the insurance company maneuvering to get her to sign a release for pennies, made him want to go straight to war, skipping all diplomatic resolution efforts.

The letter was short, sweet and to the point. It

let them know that if they didn't agree to pay the sum of eight million dollars as compensation for his clients' loss, they would be sued. They had ten days to comply with the demand; if they refused, the lawsuit would be filed on the eleventh day.

From his experience at FF&W, Zach knew the demand was only a pipe dream. But he guesstimated that two million dollars each for Daphne and her children was nonetheless within reason. Daphne would be satisfied if she received only a small portion of what he demanded. Compensation could not bring back her family and, but for taking care of necessities, it meant little to her.

He returned a few calls, reviewed his bleak but improving financial condition, and decided to go spend the remainder of the afternoon with his wife and daughter.

On the way to his car, Zach approached Miss Far Out's office and noticed the door open. The florescent lights in the lobby, which usually flicker all day long, were off. He thought it was odd, even for an odd woman. He entered the small lobby, quietly called for Miss Far Out, but saw nothing, heard nothing. Her office was behind the lobby. She was a one-woman show, all that was needed to manage the center.

He approached, then cautiously entered. Miss Far Out was sitting upright in her chair, a bullet wound was perfectly centered between her eyes. For good measure, the killer also put one through her heart. The taste of bitter vomit surged to Zach's throat, but he somehow managed to keep it down. He ran out of the building to the safety of his car, not knowing if the killer was still around. He dialed 9-1-1 and, uncharacteristically out of control, screamed for help.

TWENTY-SIX

THE police requested that Zach stay put while they conducted their investigation. He complied.

The building was roped off and squad cars were everywhere, as was the investigation team.

In the midst of the chaos, June ran into Zach who described to her what had occurred. She was horrified, not so much that Miss Far Out was the victim, but that there was a shooting in the otherwise quiet office building.

As he waited in the hallway outside of Miss Far Out's office, Zach overheard the investigators give their preliminary opinion of how the crime transpired. The shooting appeared to be motivated by robbery, as Miss Far Out's purse was missing, and a small safe was open and empty. The general consensus was that the assailant walked in and took her by surprise, firing the lethal shots before Miss Far Out could comprehend what was

261

happening.

Zach advised the investigators that he didn't hear any gunfire, but that he probably would have if he was in his office when the shots were fired. He told them he returned to his office approximately two hours prior to the time he found her body and that he didn't pay close attention to her office when he passed it to get to his office. The lights may have been on and she could have been sitting at her desk, alive and well at that time. He didn't know.

A detective asked why his attention was piqued while he was on his way out of his office, but not on his way in. Good point, Zach thought, wondering if his lack of alertness now made him a prime suspect. He responded that he was in a hurry to get to his office and wasn't paying attention. This was the truth, and it appeared to satisfy the detective for the time being.

He hoped the detective didn't force him to lie by asking him how his relationship was with the victim. Telling the truth would have promptly ended the investigation, caused him to be cuffed, read his rights, taken to jail, and subsequently executed for the crime.

The investigation wrapped up about four hours

later, but the detectives promised to return the next day. They urged the tenants to be on the lookout for anything suspicious and to lock the doors to their offices.

Sasha and Amanda were sound asleep when Zach returned home. Wired, he needed a serious drink or two, or three. Sleep was not on the menu for at least a couple of hours.

As a distraction from the recent events, he glanced through the mail, the newspaper, and Amanda's report card. The one "D" she received, in spelling, surprised him. He'd have to discuss it with her in the morning. The other grades, all A's and B's prompted a smile as did the teacher's comment: *"Amanda is very inteligent. But she needs spend more time to practising her spelling flashcards."*

He shook his head with a grin, relieved that Amanda's teacher, and not Amanda, needed to study harder.

After two shots of tequila, Zach went to his computer to look at the secret CR file Sasha cracked. She was right; the document in the file was unintelligible. It consisted of symbols, shapes and random characters situated on three pages, clearly not the get-rich-quick secret Zach hoped for.

The gibberish was written in tiny print. Zach blocked the text with the mouse and increased the font size. He noticed that the font type identified on his screen was Typographic Symbols. That's odd, he thought. He then changed the font type to Arial. The monitor suddenly displayed something legible.

After reading the document, he poured himself two more shots. He read it again, then poured himself another three. Now drunk, he passed out face down on his keyboard.

He awoke a few hours later, the sun peeking in the kitchen window. Sasha and Amanda, still asleep, had no knowledge of his late night binging. His head was throbbing hard as he thought of the murder of Miss Far Out and the vision of her bloody body.

His attention turned back to the CR file, which he read again to make certain his intoxicated imagination wasn't screwing with him. The document appeared to have been written by Ollie. It was dreadful.

THE CANDLE ROOM

I was born on December 4, 1979, in Columbia, South Carolina.

Daddy and Mommy were drug dealing losers before I was conceived, during the pregnancy, and after I was born. They never wanted me in their lives, and had no problem letting me know that I was a mistake caused by a miscalculation.

As a kid, I was a tub of lard and ugly as sin, facts Mommy and Daddy reminded me of daily. "Get out of my face and go bounce to your room Fat Boy," Daddy would yell when I bothered him. Fat Boy was my nickname around the house.

My diet consisted of junk food and lots of soda to wash the nutritious food down. The pickles and wilted lettuce on the leftover ten for a buck hamburgers were my only source of vegetables. Mommy stocked the home with things that she and Daddy devoured while getting drunk and snorting white shit up their noses day and night without giving a damn that I was in their presence. It didn't take long for me to develop a craving for junk food and, after a while, the cravings became uncontrollable.

My brother, Andrew, was born on January 16, 1987. I always wondered why Mommy had another kid, since she never wanted me.

The four of us lived in a little home in a wooded area outside of Columbia. Junk cars and broken machines and equipment surrounded the home. Daddy promised Mommy that he would restore and sell them at a great profit, but never did. Instead, he collected more and made more promises.

There was a busted up wood barn behind the house. Bonnie, our horse, lived in the barn. I liked to hang out with Bonnie. She was my only friend.

When I was about 11, Mommy became real sick. She said it was because she had too many parties. She was weak and coughing and would just lay on the couch day after day. She lost a lot of weight and eventually dwindled away to nothing.

After she became sick, she apologized to me for not being a good mother. She said she didn't want me to live like she did and told me to get an education and stay away from drugs and alcohol.

I forgave Mommy and didn't want her to die. I wanted us to start fresh and wanted to have a normal relationship with her, but it was too late.

One day after school, Daddy told me an ambulance took Mommy to the hospital and that she wouldn't be coming home anymore. He said I'd have to die and go to hell if I ever wanted to see her again. I hated my daddy.

Years before Mommy died, when I was about six or seven, Daddy pretended he loved me—at least sometimes. He began to request my presence in the candle room... a corner of the barn which he set up nicely with bales of hay, blankets and lots of candles. He framed the area with two old, splintering red and white barber's poles, some bent up sheet metal, and stacks of used bricks. This secluded the candle room from the rest of the barn.

Daddy called it the candle room because he always had candles burning. He said they gave him peace and helped him find his soul. Daddy made it very clear it was his sacred place and we were never to disturb him there.

Daddy was acting very strange when he invited me to his little sanctuary for the first time. He hugged me tightly, which Daddy never did before. He told me he loved me, that he was proud of me and that he wanted the best for me. I was happy and I smiled, as no one ever told me such things. I don't remember smiling much around Mommy or Daddy, but I remember smiling at that moment, feeling that things had changed.

Then Daddy began to undress as he stared directly into my eyes. He stood before me, naked. I turned my head to look away, not comprehending what was happening, but he gently twisted it back, made me focus.

Daddy asked me to undress too. I did, but I didn't understand why. He was being nice to me for a change and I wanted to please Daddy.

For years, Daddy and I met in the candle room and each time I had to do bad things which became more and more painful and grotesque. Daddy was oddly at peace as he tortured me. He seemed to be comforted by the candlelight and the grace in which the flames danced about the room.

But those flames cast shadows of monsters on the walls which only I could see. Monsters staring at me, moving toward me as I was abused by Daddy. I was frightened of the monsters, but I was more terrified of Daddy. I hoped the scary monsters would rip me away from him and swallow me so that I would never see him again.

When he was finished with his sick business, Daddy would blow out each candle, one by one and the monsters would disappear.

I endured this ritual over and over again, each time hoping and praying that Daddy would find his soul and stop. He didn't. I cried, but without tears, too afraid to express the horror. Mommy would never hear me cry.

Daddy made it clear to me that what we did in our special place was to be kept a secret. If I ever told anyone, including Mommy, I would be locked in the trunk of one of the old junk cars to rot in hell and no one would ever find me. This scared me, so I complied, afraid of the consequences.

When Mommy was sick, Daddy no longer ordered me to the candle room. I thought Daddy felt bad for his sins and decided to stop. He didn't.

One night, I approached the dimly lit barn looking for Andrew. Through a small opening in a boarded-up window, I witnessed the very things that caused me to become emotionless, to lose the desire to associate with others, the desire to experience happiness, and the purpose of life. My brother—not me—was now Daddy's prey.

I watched with twisted and conflicted feelings as Daddy humiliated Andrew. On the one hand, I wanted to burst in and charge the son of a bitch with a pickaxe pummeling him beyond recognition. On the other hand, I was hurt by the realization that Daddy now chose Andrew over me. I was no longer even worthy of being victimized.

The abuse of my brother continued for several years. Andrew never mentioned it to me, probably because Daddy also warned him about rotting in the trunk. But Andrew knew I was aware because he saw me, more than once, watching through the window, no doubt hoping his big brother would come to the rescue and save him from Daddy and the monsters trying to reach him.

Mommy died without ever knowing what Daddy did to us in the candle room. Andrew and I never said a word about it to each other.

After Mommy died, Daddy kept a large stash of drug money in a big holiday popcorn can hidden underneath blankets in his bedroom closet. The amount of money in the can fluctuated depending upon the drug deals going down, but it never seemed to fall below a hundred grand. From the day I stumbled upon it, I kept a close watch on the amount of cash in that can.

Shortly before my eighteenth birthday, I studied the workings of the kerosene heater which Daddy used to warm the barn. Daddy was creative when it came to filling the heater with kerosene. He drilled a hole through the heater's fuel cap and fed a small hose though the cap. The other end of the hose ran through a window in the barn and to a special pump placed outside the window submerged in a large barrel of kerosene. When turned on, the pump would force kerosene from the barrel through the hose and into the heater's fuel tank.

This contraption saved Daddy the hassle of having to take the heater outside every time it needed a refill. This contraption would be used as my murder weapon.

Twelve days after my eighteenth birthday, which no one observed—no card, no gift, not even a pat on the back for becoming an adult—I poked several small holes in the hose to the barn heater, such that when the pump was turned on, the kerosene would shoot out of the holes, around the heater, onto the hay and ignite as it made contact with Daddy's treasured candles. I drained down the kerosene in the heater so Daddy would turn the pump on full bore.

On December 16, 1997, my plan worked perfectly. Daddy was in the barn when he activated the pump, spewing kerosene everywhere and igniting the hay with a fury. The heater exploded, obliterating the candle room, the barn, poor Bonnie and Daddy. I didn't want to hurt Bonnie, but she was old and sick and needed to be put out of her misery. We were all put out of our misery that day.

I never told Andrew what I did. All that mattered was that

that child molesting bastard we called Daddy finally found his good for nothing soul.

Soon after his death, I took the money from his popcorn can and headed west. I wanted nothing to do with the life I had known.

I realize that my act of retribution would never erase the harm caused by the twisted abuse perpetrated upon my brother and I, but ending Daddy's life was a necessary evil which I was compelled to carry out, in order to carry on.

TWENTY-SEVEN

ZACH'S head was spinning. Miss Far Out's murder, Ollie's mind-blowing autobiography, and the tequila took their toll. He decided to drive to the office before Sasha and Amanda woke up. He needed cool air.

The building was still cordoned off with crime scene tape and a deputy was stationed in front of Miss Far Out's office. Zach identified himself and was allowed access to his office.

He stared into space, pondering what to do with Ollie's memo. The fact that Ollie killed his father over a decade ago didn't seem material to any issue of current significance. It had no impact on the probate case and it didn't seem to have any bearing on Scooter's murder trial. Besides, it was possible that the crime lab reviewed the memo and already discounted its relevance. After all, the lab had Ollie's CDs and likely combed through the material.

On the other hand, he and/or Andrew would surely have been told of the contents of the explosive memo if the lab discovered it.

Zach concluded that due to the volume of financial documents on Ollie's computer, the fact that the killer was already arrested, thus eliminating the need to meticulously review all of said documents, the fact that Ollie's sordid family history was never mentioned in the press or by investigators, he was the only one to have read the little story.

Zach could either keep it secret, or disclose it to those who would want to know about it, such as Andrew. But Andrew was likely devastated by the killing of Miss Far Out, and the last thing he'd want to hear was that Ollie murdered his father, even if his father deserved it. Zach decided to tell no one about the memo, at least for now.

The following Monday, Zach let Ginger run the office solo and headed to court for the early session. Before he left, he gave her the DesignElec demand letter to type along with a few other tasks. He told her to take messages, and if she finished early, she could leave to avoid being bothered by the ongoing police activity.

Ginger looked at him, perplexed. "Hell no. I'll take my good ol' time. I'd rather be here, gunfire an' all, than go home to my lazy and borin' husband," she laughed, sort of.

She asked him what she should do if the detectives decided to question her about Miss Far Out since they might find out she came close to ripping her in half a few days ago.

"Very simple... cooperate with them. But if they arrest you, you're on your own," he said jokingly, as he walked out the door.

When he arrived in the courtroom, Andrew's non-appearance, although expected, reminded him of instructions he forgot to give Ginger. He quietly escaped into the hallway to give her a call.

"Ginger, I forgot to tell you, lock the door and don't open it for anyone other than law enforcement. Andrew may decide to come to the office to discuss the death of Miss Far Out. I don't want you to let him in or talk to him, as he will likely be too emotional and erratic. I'll call him and try to speak with him sometime this morning."

"You got it, Zachary. But he already called this

mornin' and left a message for you to call him. He said the po-leece are askin' him questions and such. He said he ain't done nothing wrong and that he loved that woman. Do you want me to call him back to tell him you'll be gone today?"

"You've got to be kidding me... police? No, no, don't talk to him. I'll call him later."

"I'm sorry to upset you, Zachary. I won't talk to him no more."

"No, no Ginger it's not you, it's the nature of the beast in this business."

Distracted, Zach went back into the courtroom as the trial was about to start. The drama caused by his first client was beginning to consume him. He took a deep breath. No big deal, he thought. Standard procedure for the police to question the boyfriend of the victim. His stomach was in knots from the events over the past couple of days.

Scooter was already on the stand waiting to testify as the jurors streamed into the box. He was dressed down a bit, long- sleeved white shirt, dark slacks, no jacket.

Judge Waters began the proceedings by

apologizing for the interruption caused by her little emergency on Friday and reiterated that there would be no further delays. She then motioned to Brooks to begin.

Brooks resumed his position at the podium.

"Mr. Mason, when we left off, I had asked you to describe the skateboard Mr. Parham testified about. Could you do that now for the jury?"

"It ain't no skateboard, it's a scooter. That's why they call me Scooter. I built it from the ground up. Found some wheels, a little board, a fence pipe, some ol' bicycle handlebars, and some nuts and bolts and designed 'er myself. I'm pretty darn proud of that thing. I guess that son-of-a-bitch..." Mason put his hand to his mouth, "excuse me... Parham took it from me. When this is all over, he best be givin' it back."

"Mr. Mason, I know this is difficult, but please try to focus on what I'm asking you, okay?"

"I'm tryin'."

"Now, why did you decide to build the scooter?"

"To git around town and collect me some things."

"What do you mean collect you some things?"

"I live on the street and I need to find things to eat and to wear 'cause it gets colder than hell out there. I attached some ol' milk crates to the scooter to put stuff I find in the trash. The scooter lets me git around town wit' all my stuff so people like that loser Parham don't steal my shit if I leave it behind."

"I see. What kind of items do you look for to put in your crates?"

"Whatever I kin find; food mostly. It don't matter if it's half eatin', has hairy mold growin' on it, it's rotten, or it smells like death, I take it and store it in my scooter. When I'm starvin' it's better for me to eat a puked out hamburger I scooped up behind a bar, than nothin' at all." Scooter displayed no shame as he described his grocery shopping routine.

"I'm sorry to hear that, Mr. Mason," Brooks interjected, wishing his client would shut the hell up and get to the point that they rehearsed ad nauseam before the trial.

"What other things do you put in your scooter?"

"My werkin' signs I use to try to collect some money. I also put clothes in there, books, a radio I used to have, some shoes, some tools, and anythin' I kin find that maybe I kin sell."

"Your source of income is panhandling, correct?"

"Well I call it werkin'—not beggin'—and people give me tips for werkin'."

"When was the last time you had twenty dollars or more in your pocket?"

"Ha-ha, now that's a real good question, Mr. Brooks… 'bout time you got to a good one. Musta been five, six years ago when I found a fifty dollar bill outside a China market. I thought I hit it big until I tried to spend it in the store and the Chinaman grabbed it from me, sayin' it was phony and he was gonna call the pigs. I think that slant-eyed, son-of-a-bitch just stole it for himself 'cause it sure as hell looked real to me."

Judge Waters quickly interrupted, "Mr. Mason, I've been very patient thus far, but will you please watch your language. Some of us, including myself, may find your comments very offensive. You can tell your story without using that type of language, understood?"

"Sorry. Yes, ma'am."

"Mr. Mason, where do you get your clothes?" Brooks was desperately trying to reel Scooter in and keep him on point.

"Mr. Brooks, everythin' I have comes from trash cans and dumpsters. I ain't got nothin' that don't, 'cept these clothes I'm wearin' right now, thanks to you givin' 'em to me."

"You're most certainly welcome," Brooks said with a smile, glancing at the jury.

"Mr. Mason, I'm going to show you a few exhibits and ask you some questions. I want you to listen carefully to each question and just answer it. You don't need to go into a long explanation unless I ask you to do so, do you understand?"

"Yes, sir."

"Great. Now, directing your attention to what is marked as the prosecution's exhibit thirty-five," Brooks handed him the exhibit, "do you recognize this item?"

"Yes I do, these are my pants."

"And where did you get these pants, Mr. Mason?"

"I have no clue exactly where, but they was in a dumpster."

"How do you know that?"

" 'cause I jus' told you man, everything I have

come from the trash cans. Also, I remember finding them and some other things with that wrench over there." Scooter pointed at the wrench on the exhibit table. "I remember thinkin' the wrench was worth somethin' and I found these other things with it in the same place. They might have all been in a bag in a dumpster."

"And you don't know specifically where you found these items?"

"I tried and tried to remember, but I can't. I prolly pick through twenty, thirty dumpsters and trash cans every day. I just can't remember, Mr. Brooks."

"But you do remember finding these pants in a trash dumpster, correct?"

"Yep, and the wrench, and my jacket, and them shoes right there." He motioned to his worldly possessions arranged on the table.

"Mr. Mason, the prosecution alleges that you were wearing these clothes and shoes on the day Mr. Pearce was murdered and that you murdered him, is this true?"

"No, ain't none o' that true, no way. I ain't killed nobody, never."

"It is also alleged you used this wrench here to strike Mr. Pearce over the head, is that true?"

"No, it ain't true, I ain't ever even met Mr. Pearce, why would I wanna kill him?"

"Mr. Skaggs further claims you used this big ol' knife," Brooks picked it up from the evidence table and held it in the air as though ready to decapitate a turkey, "to dismember Mr. Pearce's feet, is that a true story, Mr. Mason?"

"No, that ain't no true story. I ain't never even seen that knife until Mr. Skaggy pulled it out during this here trial." He looked at Skaggs rudely as he pronounced his name wrong. A few members of the audience laughed. The jurors didn't see the humor.

"Mr. Mason, did you kill Mr. Pearce?" Brooks asked slowly.

"No way man, no fuckin' way."

"Why then is his blood all over the clothes you were wearing."

"Musta been on them clothes already when I pulled that stuff outta the dumpster." He looked at Skaggs and yelled, "You got it all wrong, Mister. I ain't done nothin' wrong 'cept drank too much."

"Why was Mr. Pearce's blood on the wrench and shoes you had in your crate?"

"Hell if I know. I sure as hell ain't killed nobody."

"Mr. Mason, you heard testimony from Dr. Bristol wherein he said there may have been blood on your clothes from someone other than the victim, did you hear that testimony?"

"Yes sir, I did."

"Can you tell the jury why your clothes had blood on them from a person other than Mr. Pearce?"

"Cause I kicked the shit outta that asshole Brady who was messin' with Momma." Mason spoke with passion. This subject got him angry.

"What? Wait a second... who is Brady and who is Momma?" Brooks interrupted, knowing full well what the answers were. "Slow down, Mr. Mason, and tell us what happened," Brooks said calmly.

"Objection, irrelevant, calls for a narrative," Skaggs yelled.

"No it isn't, and no it doesn't. Overruled." Judge Waters shouted back, somewhat intrigued by the direction of the line of questioning. "But Mr. Mason, I must again insist that you watch your language."

"Tell us what happened," Brooks asked again.

"Well... Momma ain't really my momma, but she's up there in years, old enough to be my momma. She only has one leg, and it looks real bad; it's all red and black. She's been livin' on the streets longer than I kin remember. She's like a momma 'cause she helps me out and gives advice and she cares about me like I'm her own blood and flesh."

"She used to be real good gettin' around with crutches, but she kin hardly walk no more causa her leg. She spends her days over at the park, and me and my friends bring her food 'n' stuff. We also help move her quick-like when the pigs come by to try and arrest us for loiterin'."

"I toll her she should go on and git arrested since she can get her nasty leg takin' care of in jail. But no, no, no, Momma ain't never goin' to no jail, no way."

"Anyways, Momma, she loves to read lots of books 'n' stuff. I ain't no real reader myself."

Never would've guessed, Zach thought.

"I always bring her books I find in the trash. It's funny 'cause even if a book is torn in half and missin' pages, Momma still wants it 'cause she says she makes up the missin' parts in her mind. It's wut keeps her young and thinkin'."

Skaggs, jumped to his feet, "Your Honor, may we approach?"

"Fine." Judge Waters said, annoyed by the interruption.

Brooks and his assistant, and Skaggs and his two assistants walked briskly to the bench. The court reporter repositioned herself to transcribe the discussion.

"Your Honor, what on earth does this Momma lady have to do with the murder of Mr. Pearce? The witness is off on a tangent. The jury couldn't care less what books Momma reads or whether her leg is decaying with gangrene. We're wasting time." Skaggs whispered angrily, veins bulging from his petite forehead.

"I guess he's got a point, Mr. Brooks. Where ya goin' with this?"

"Your Honor, I didn't realize the defendant was going to discuss Momma's life story." Brooks was fibbing. He specifically told Mason to talk about Momma as much as he could until the judge shut him down. He figured the jury would like Momma and they would learn that Mason was a caring, adopted son who was trying to assist the poor, crippled, homeless woman, not a cold-blooded, sadistic killer.

"I'll try to get to the point."

"Great, do that," Judge Waters said, and the discussion ended. The combatants went back to their bunkers, each smiling, letting the jury know that his argument was the most persuasive.

"Mr. Mason, could you tell the jury how blood got on your clothing?"

"I was tryin' to until Skaggy over there interrupted me."

"Objection, move to strike!" Skaggs screamed as he stood up.

"Sustained and granted. The jury is instructed to disregard that last comment. Sir, you are testing my patience," Judge Waters said, teeth clenched.

Brooks continued, "Mr. Mason, we're trying to get to the reasons why you had blood on your clothing from someone other than the victim. Could you just focus on that question?" Brooks knew that if his client didn't get to the point quickly, the judge would terminate this very important line of examination.

"Y'all crackin' me up now. I'm tryin' to tell you, but y'all just keep cutting me off. Lemme finish, will ya, once and for all?" Scooter was lecturing the lawyers as he shook his head back and forth.

"That Brady sumbitch went and stoled Momma's books and she was tryin' to stop him. She was screamin' and cryin' and tryin' to get up, but she couldn't. I walked around the corner and seen it happenin'. So I ran over and tackled him like I was a football player and I beat the livin' shit outta him. I think I busted out a few of his teeth. He got up and run off. I told him if I ever see him again I'd kill him. Ain't nobody ever take nothin' from Momma or cause her problems, ever."

Judge Waters rolled her eyes, but gave up trying to censor the proceedings; offensive language is all he knows.

"Did this Brady fella get any blood on your clothes?"

"Hell yeah he did. He bled on my jacket, my shirt, my pants, the grass, my fists, he done bled everywhere, 'cause I really let him have it preddy good."

Scooter smiled proudly as he described the righteous beating to the jury.

"Now, Mr. Mason, the prosecution alleges that you confessed to killing Mr. Pearce, that you said he deserved it, and that you said you would do it again. Did you ever make any such statements?"

"I ain't confessed to killin' nobody. That pig that said I confessed is a got damn liar. He asked me where the blood on my clothes came from. I never said I killt Mr. Pearce or anyone else. I was referrin' to the ass whippin' I gave Brady, not Mr. Pearce, as I ain't ever even seen Mr. Pearce. Brady deserved the whippin' for stealin' from Momma and when I kicked his ass, Brady got blood all over me and that's what was on my clothes, Brady's blood, not that dead man's blood." Scooter emphasized Brady's name each time he said it.

"I didn't even know Mr. Pearce's blood was on my clothes when I talked to that pig in the jail. How da hell was I supposed to know that?"

"And, like I told the pig in jail, if I see that sumbitch Brady around Momma again, I just might kill his ass. Then Skaggy would have the right man for once."

Skaggs erupted, "Your Honor, this is ridiculous.

Could the court please admonish the witness to address me by my proper name and to refrain from his continued use of his highly offensive language?"

Skaggs wanted to distract the jury from Scooter's plausible explanation for the confession. Although not the most articulate defendant who's ever testified on his own behalf, Scooter's story could create reasonable doubt and Skaggs knew it.

"The witness is again instructed to be more respectful to the prosecution and those of us in the courtroom." Judge Waters had no impact upon Scooter. She was simply making a record of her admonitions. He controlled her and her warnings were pointless.

"Judge, I ain't never said I kilt Mr. Pearce. If I did kill him, I sure as hell would have made it worth my while by takin' all that cash he had sittin' there in his house. I ain't that stupid to leave money behind, hell no. Me 'n' Momma coulda used it ta buy some brew and some bandages 'n' ointment for her leg."

Brooks was thrilled with the performance by his client. His offensive language, the serpent eyes of his tattoo and his hippy knuckles were forgiven. He glanced at the jury and smiled as he returned his gaze to his client.

"Thank you, Mr. Mason, I have no further questions at this time."

Judge Waters preempted Skaggs' cross-examination. "It's about eleven-thirty, I think this is a good time to break for lunch. My clerk reminds me we missed our morning break, so let's take a longer lunch. We'll resume at one-thirty." She admonished the jury and left the bench.

Impressive, Zach thought of Brooks, though he wasn't sure how the jury would react to Brooks' client. On the one hand, Scooter appeared to be genuine and oddly credible in presenting his bizarre story. On the other hand, the jurors probably didn't like him, and if they didn't like him, they may not believe a single word he said.

Zach left the courtroom. He immediately called Ginger to inquire about the happenings at the office.

"I made two new appointments for you tomorrow morning. I hope that's okay Zachary 'cause I know yer busy 'n' such."

"Great, thank you for holding down the fort, you're doing a wonderful job."

He called Andrew, who picked up after the first ring. "Andrew, where are you and what the hell's going on with the police?"

"What's goin' on is the cops think I had something to do with Julie's death and they tried to interrogate me here at her apartment. I told them I ain't talkin' to nobody unless I have a lawyer present. They didn't like that one bit. I expect they'll pick me up and take me to the station to rough me up and try to get me to spill my guts. Are you in?"

"What do you mean am I in?" Zach replied, surprised by the lack of emotion Andrew expressed over the loss of his soul mate.

"You gonna represent me?"

"Represent you? Zach paused.

"Hold on, Andrew. First of all, let me tell you that I'm very sorry about what happened to Julie, I really am. I know the two of you were close and it must be difficult for you right now, especially given the circumstances of her death."

"Second, I can represent you if you want me to, but if you happen to be charged with her murder, which I'm not suggesting you will be, it'll cost you a fortune. I'd need to bring another lawyer on board who has experience in murder cases. More importantly, it wasn't too long ago that you didn't want anything to do with me. I'm not so sure you have any respect for our attorney-client relationship."

"I knew your fee would be the first thing you asked about. Geez, don't you care about what I'm going through here? First my brother, then my woman and all you seem to think about is how much money you'll get from me."

"No, Andrew, that's not true at all. I feel for you, I really do." Zach meant this, especially after he read Ollie's little story.

"These things require lots of time and attention. I'll be living, eating and dreaming about you twenty-four-seven. The cost will be substantial. Also, you and I have to be on good working terms, which we are not."

"Okay, Mr. Morgan, here is what I propose just to shut you up. Believe it or not, I trust you and I like you even if I act like an prick sometimes. I was even going to see if you'd be my best man."

Unbelievable, Zach thought, sadly. Andrew has lots of misfiring neurons in his troubled brain. As he listened, Zach cursed all child molesters for the catastrophic mental illnesses they cause to their small victims.

"When the estate thing closes, you'll get the fifteen percent we already agreed to. I'll throw another ten percent on top of that just to keep you working on my case. If those SOB's charge me with murder, which they sure as hell better not, I'll pay you another twenty-five percent to represent me—this totals fifty percent, which, by my calculations, equals roughly two mill. So... ya in, yes or no?"

Hell yes I'm in, Zach wanted to shout, but kept it professional. "Fine, in addition to my fee, you'll have to pay the costs of any experts needed to defend you if you're charged. But don't assume you'll be charged simply because you've been questioned. It's standard protocol for boyfriends and husbands to be questioned first. Therefore, you're probably putting the cart way before the horse."

"I hear you. But these guys were real assholes and they all but said I was going to jail, which is a crock of shit. I ain't done nothing, but it looks like I need to spend a fortune to protect myself."

"Understood," Zach replied pensively. "I'll do what I can to help you. Don't talk to anyone about any of this."

"Great. When can we meet to discuss our strategy?" Andrew asked, as though making plans for a tailgate party at a Dodger game. He either never learned to show emotion, or he had none to show.

"The trial of Mason is coming to a close. I'll be in court all afternoon. How 'bout we meet at my office at five-thirty this afternoon? I'll also bring you up to date on the trial."

"I'll be there," Andrew said as he hung up.

TWENTY-EIGHT

TRIAL resumed at precisely one-thirty. Skaggs was ready to pounce Scooter on cross. He got right to the point.

"Mr. Mason, let me understand this. Is it your testimony that you just happened to find bloody clothes, bloody shoes and a heavy bloody pipe wrench in a trash dumpster and that, rather than call the police to report what you found, you put the clothes on and rode away on your little scooter, is that your testimony?"

"I guess so," Scooter said as he stared at Skaggs, "but the blood was dried up, so it ain't like there was wet blood 'n' shit drippin' all over the place when I found them. To tell you the truth, I didn't even know it was blood until ya'll told me it was blood."

"I see," Skaggs replied, acting intrigued. "And you just happened to carry around that wrench for several months because you wanted to sell it?"

"I thought I could, but there ain't no buyers for it."

"Right. And those bloody shoes, you just happened to find those in the dumpster too, is that what your testimony is?"

"Yep."

"What size shoe do you wear, Mr. Mason?"

"Whatever size I can find, Mr. Skaggy."

"Objection, Your Honor."

Judge Waters was resting her chin in her palms. "Mr. Mason, I have already cautioned you about being disrespectful in my courtroom. If you continue to ignore my caution, you will not be happy. Are we clear on this, because this will be your final warning?"

"Yes ma'am, clear as mud." Judge Waters looked to the heavens and tossed her pen on the bench, exasperated.

Skaggs continued. "What size shoe do you wear, Mr. Mason?"

"Last time I checked, about a twelve."

"Pretty big feet, wouldn't ya say, I mean bigger than most people, right?"

"I guess, but I ain't in the habit of checkin'

people's shoe sizes, you?" Zach wondered why Judge Waters didn't just instruct the bailiff to shoot the smartass and get the trial over with.

"What size are these shoes, Mr. Mason?" Skaggs asked as he slammed the bloody shoes on the witness stand for Mason to look at.

Mason picked up the shoes and took his sweet time looking for a size label inside the shoe. "Well I'll be damned... they're a twelve. Dang, I shoulda worn 'em, but I ain't never even tried 'em on."

"So the shoes are the same size as what you normally wear, correct?"

" 'peers so."

"And you agree that the killer also had a size twelve foot?"

"If he wore these here shoes, I would guess so, but it don't mean they fit him. He coulda had a size ten foot. I ain't no detective, but just because someone has a size twelve shoe, it don't mean he has a size twelve foot."

Scooter grinned at the jury, feeling confident he just busted the case wide open with his analysis.

"I see. Isn't it true, Mr. Mason, that you

somehow convinced Mr. Pearce to allow you into his residence and that, once he let you in, you brutally tortured and killed him, isn't that true?"

"Hell no, that ain't true, Skaggy, that ain't true at all."

"Why did you butcher Mr. Pearce?"

"I didn't. I didn't even know the sumbitch."

"Well, you forgot to tell the jury this morning when you testified that one of the things you gave to Momma shortly after the crime was a newspaper article detailing the murder of Mr. Pearce, didn't you?"

This was news to Brooks. His face quickly became flush as he suddenly felt the urge to evacuate his bowels.

"Don't know nothin' about that."

"Now why on earth would you have such an article, Mr. Mason?" Skaggs was holding up page two of the L.A. Times published on October 15, 2010, one day after the body was discovered.

"Sir, I don't have no idea what yer talkin' 'bout. I give Momma lots of newspapers. She likes to read about crimes that happen around here."

"Sure you do. Okay, whatever you say."

"Now this Brady fella, you say you beat him to a pulp after he tried to steal Momma's possessions, right?"

"Yes I did, and like I said before, I'd do it again. He's a punk."

"Isn't it true that you told Brady you killed a man and after you told him that you showed him this article to brag about it and to confirm what you did, isn't that what happened, Mr. Mason?" Skaggs spoke louder than he had the entire trial as he ripped into the witness.

"I ain't killed nobody, and if you say that one more time, you'll be the first."

Judge Waters pounded her gavel... "Court will be in recess until three-fifteen."

The jury was escorted out of the courtroom. The judge was fuming. There would be hell to pay.

"Counsel, I need to see both of you in chambers, stat."

Skaggs, Brooks, and their respective entourages scurried past the bench. The door to Judge Waters' chambers slammed shut after they entered.

Her office smelled musty. Dark wood paneling adorned the walls and ceiling. A long cherry wood conference table covered with neatly stacked documents consumed most of the room. There were several family photos, awards and other knick-knacks randomly placed in a built-in bookshelf. The ego wall behind her desk proudly advertised her educational, professional and community accomplishments—quite impressive and intimidating, which was Judge Waters' intent.

The judge took a seat behind her desk. The others never managed to sit before she erupted.

"I'm not sure what the hell your client is trying to pull here, Counsel, but I'm not putting up with it. If he's on a suicide mission, he's about to be successful. I can tell you this though, he will not sabotage this trial and appeal a guilty verdict claiming I was too hard on him in front of the jury. He chose to testify and he's doing his best to hang himself and disrupt these proceedings in the process. I can't control what he says, but I can place his ass in another room and have him watch his fate unfold on a video screen if he keeps up his antics."

Brooks listened as he was scolded yet again. He stared into her eyes as she ranted, but he said nothing, appearing indifferent rather than restrained. His uncontrollable client took its toll on him and he was tired. He wanted the trial over... win, lose or draw, he didn't care.

She continued. "I assume you've cautioned him against engaging in this type of conduct, especially in front of the jury which will decide whether he lives or dies, haven't you?"

"I have, Your Honor," Brooks spoke softly, "but he is who he is. This is the way he speaks on the street and he's highly offended that Mr. Skaggs brought this case against him. He's very bitter and emotional."

"Save it, Counsel. I couldn't care less what his problem is. If he says one more thing I consider to be out of order, the trial will be adjourned and we'll move him to another room, hopefully in the dirty, moldy basement of this building, understood?"

"Yes, Your Honor. I'll do my best to properly advise him."

"Well you'd better."

Judge Waters and the attorneys left her chambers and went back into the courtroom, at which time the judge recited on the record a toned-down summary of the discussion which took place in chambers.

Brooks quietly advised Scooter that the judge had it out for him and that if he didn't control his hatred toward Skaggs, he would be thrown out of the courtroom and the jury would most certainly fry his ass. Scooter apologized and agreed he'd try to be nice.

The jury was brought back and Skaggs resumed his cross.

"Mr. Mason, you admitted to Brady you killed a man, didn't you?"

"He's a good-for-nothin' liar, if that's what he said."

"And Brady took the newspaper article and threatened to go to the police to rat on you, didn't he?"

"Rat on me for what?"

"And you beat him up and threatened to kill him if he went to the police, didn't you?"

"Yes, I beat him, but he ain't never threatened to go to no police 'cause I ain't done nothin'."

Skaggs could have gone much further, but he made his point and the witness was unpredictable; best to stop now rather than allow Scooter an opportunity to undue all the damage he did to himself.

"No further questions, Your Honor."

As is typical during a capital trial, attorneys have investigators ready to quickly find evidence which may be necessary to address any surprise testimony presented by the opposition. Brooks previously disclosed the names of Brady and Flora Sampson, aka Momma, as possible witnesses, but Skaggs never bothered to interview them before trial. After Scooter brought the subject up during the morning session, the state's investigators went on an all-out hunt for Momma and Brady during the lunch hour.

Brady was found first. He was panhandling outside a mini-mart a few blocks from Wright Park, a run-down ball field close to Scooter's old stomping grounds. He was not well liked so his fellow transients readily pointed him out to the investigators. When confronted, Brady informed investigators he used to be Scooter's friend but that Scooter became violent toward him. They had a physical altercation after Scooter told him he killed someone and showed him the newspaper article, which led him to believe the person he killed was Mr. Pearce. Brady said Momma kept the article with her things, but he didn't know if she still had it. He agreed to testify, but only if he was protected after trial. The investigators assured him Scooter would be going to prison for a very long time.

Momma was found soon thereafter, lying on a blanket in Wright Park. Her leg was covered with a tightly wound pillow case. She was pleasant to the investigators, but refused to talk negatively about Scooter. She didn't recall a bloody confrontation between Scooter and Brady, but she was quick to admit that she didn't have a great memory.

The article relating to Ollie's murder, along with a dozen or so similar articles, was found a few yards away from where she was lying, mixed in with a small stack of books and old newspapers. Momma said she was finished with the books and since they were so nice, the investigators could take them if they wanted to read them. She didn't want to give them her collection of newspaper articles. She told them she likes to keep tabs on crimes and she tears out and saves the more interesting stories.

To help gain her trust, one of the investigators went back to his squad car to retrieve a thriller novel he had finished reading and gave it to Momma. He convinced her to let him borrow her newspaper collection, assuring her he'd bring it right back. He also gave her some fries left over from lunch and a bottle of water. She thanked him, smiled, and cracked open her new novel as she propped herself up against the stinky restroom building located in the park. The investigators never mentioned the significance of the article detailing Ollie's murder.

On re-direct, Brooks had Scooter testify that he couldn't read newspapers well and didn't understand anything but basic English; that Brady is a liar, and that he never admitted killing anyone to Brady, or to anyone else for that matter; that Momma had lots of newspapers and was fascinated with gory murder stories; and that he never wore the bloody shoes even though they were his size.

Brooks never asked any of his clients, including Scooter, to disclose to him whether they committed the crime to which they were charged. He always had his suspicions, but chose not to hear the truth directly from the source. It was more productive for him to perform his duties as an officer of the court while in a state of denial. Being kept in the dark allowed him to do everything he could to defend his clients with a straight face. At this particular moment though, Brooks believed his client was guilty and there was little else he could do to save him.

After Skaggs advised that he had no re-cross, Brooks announced, "The defense rests."

The court adjourned until the next morning.

TWENTY-NINE

ANDREW was waiting outside when Zach arrived at his office at five-fifteen, fifteen minutes early. He was unshaven and reeked of booze and smoke.

"Hi Andrew, let's go inside," Zach said, not looking at Andrew as he unlocked the door. "Have a seat in the lobby, and I'll be with you in a minute."

"Well don't make me wait long," Andrew responded with a frown, noticeably irritated that he wasn't given priority service.

Zach went to his office to check his messages from Ginger. Before talking to Andrew, he would put out other fires to punish Andrew for being early. Although he sympathized with Andrew, given the anguish and tragedy in his life, he'd prefer to avoid him as much as possible.

Fortunately, Ginger did a good job handling office affairs and there didn't appear to be anything life threatening, except a new client who needed to immediately sue his plumber for seventy-six dollars, before the plumber filed bankruptcy. Zach would tell Ginger to pass on that client.

"Okay, Andrew, let me start first by updating you regarding Mason's trial. There's a very good chance he'll be convicted and if the jury hates him as much as I think it does, he will likely be given the death penalty. He says he didn't know anything about your brother and the reason his clothes and other items were covered in your brother's blood was because he found them in a dumpster that way."

Andrew interrupted, "Yeah right, like that'll fly, what a jackass."

"Unfortunately for him, the police found a witness who testified that Mason essentially confessed to the murder. It's hard to predict where the jury is with all this, but if I was a bettin' man, I think he's gonna hang. I can't imagine that the jury has any sympathy for him, especially after he took the stand and acted like a punk."

"Good, he'll get what he deserves." Andrew was more subdued than usual, probably because of the booze and other mind-altering substances.

"I expect the trial to conclude within the next day or so. If he's convicted, the DA's office will want you to provide a statement during the sentencing phase."

"Fine, whatever man. I just want all this over with. And now this shit with Julie... things couldn't get any more fucked up for me right now."

"Yeah, no kiddin'. What a horrible tragedy, all for a few bucks."

"When was the last time you saw her?" Zach asked.

"The morning of the day she was shot. We stayed at her place the night before. I made breakfast for her. She went to her office and I decided to hang out at the house and watch TV and take a nap. The next thing I know, cops were banging on the door. I opened it up for them, 'cause I got nothin' to hide, and they asked who I was. I told them, and they barged in. One of the cops informed me Julie was shot and killed. I 'bout died on the spot. We were gonna get married in a week and now she's gone," he paused, staring down.

"The cops started askin' me questions, which I refused to answer. They tried to get me to confess to killing Julie, but I didn't say a word, except I told them I wanted you present and wouldn't talk without you. They were pissed as hell, but I stood my ground. They finally left, but I'm pretty sure they'll be back real soon."

"What makes you so sure?"

"They were talking between themselves, loud enough so I could hear them. They said that the killer is always the husband or boyfriend, and that it'll just be a matter of time before they figure it all out and throw my ass in jail."

"Well Andrew, if you did nothing wrong, you have nothing to worry about. As I understand it, the murder was part of a robbery. Since you're soon to be a rich man, you have no motive to rob anyone. Sometimes the police jump the gun and try to intimidate potential suspects and that's what they did with you. I wouldn't worry about it. You're grieving and you need to take time to go through the process."

"Geez, you're actually a stand-up guy," he said as he glanced up to look at Zach. "I'm sorry for always being an asshole to you. I know you're only looking out for my best interest."

Zach took the compliment lightly. "I'm your lawyer and you're paying me well, at least I hope so. I'll do everything I can to properly represent you and advise you. You should never question that, Andrew. Now, go home and get some sleep, you look and smell like death."

"I will. Let me know when the jury convicts that SOB."

"Will do." Zach said, as he escorted his client out the door.

Given Andrew's life thus far, Zach predicted that his large inheritance would be blown in less than a year or two. If he's still alive, Andrew would likely wind up a victim of his circumstances: penniless, abusing drugs and alcohol and back in his little campground in Texas. Sad story all the way around.

Zach called Patty Sanders, a prospective client who left a message inquiring as to whether he handled family-law matters. Although he hadn't as of yet, he'd consider it.

She made it clear that her husband was a lying, cheating drunk who was physically and mentally abusive and is addicted to gambling. Until recently, he was winning lots of money, which she spent lavishly. His sins were overlooked as long as he was bringing in the dough, but he fell into a losing streak of late. It was now time for a divorce.

Zach explained to her the basic no-fault divorce rules and told her to call Ginger in the morning to make an appointment. She would need to pay a retainer fee of five thousand dollars. "Small price for freedom," she said, "I'd like to get this going immediately."

She then discussed the fate of her five-year-old daughter. She didn't mind her husband taking her with him. She had a new honey and she preferred not to be bogged down with a kid during their blossoming courtship. She let Zach know that she wouldn't object one bit if her daughter remained under the care and custody of her drunken, abusive father.

Zach could use the cash flow, but as he listened to her scheme to abandon her child under the circumstances, he was sickened. As her attorney, he would have a duty to take whatever appropriate action was necessary to accomplish her selfish objectives. He would not be her attorney.

"Mrs. Sanders, I'm sorry, I didn't realize you have a custody issue. I only handle simple divorces. Therefore, as much as I'd like to help you, I'm afraid I can't."

"You've got to be kidding me. I wish you would've said so before I told you my life story. You best not send me a bill for this little conference," she blurted as she hung up.

Zach became somewhat accustomed to angry people and did his best to move on without dwelling on them.

He finished his calls then grabbed his recorder from his drawer to dictate a short letter for Ginger to type in the morning. The letter was to Nathan and confirmed their conversation earlier in the day that the estate proceeds, after deducting the payment to Ollie's landlord and administrative expenses, were to be made payable to Zachary E. Morgan & Associates, Client Trust Account. Once the funds were deposited into his trust account, Zach would pay himself twenty-five percent, per the recent pay raise given to him by Andrew, and pay to Andrew all of the remaining funds. If Andrew happened to be charged with Miss Far Out's murder, he'd retain another twenty-five percent.

According to Nathan, the judge would sign the final order allowing the release of the funds within the next week or so.

Zach placed the recorder back into the drawer. He panicked when he didn't see his gun and franticly rummaged through the drawer, believing it must be there. It was not. He nearly vomited.

THIRTY

"THE state calls Mr. Brady Abbott." Skaggs announced as he began the prosecution's rebuttal case.

Brady was tall and thin, a nice looking thirty-year-old, rare for someone living on the streets. He was prepared for the occasion: clean-shaven, white shirt with a thin lavender tie, dark slacks and shined shoes. As he took the stand, he stared at Scooter, as though happy to see him.

"Mr. Abbott, are you acquainted with Mr. Ray Mason, who is sitting over there at the defense table?" Skaggs said, pointing to Mason.

"I sure am."

"How do you know Mr. Mason, sir?"

"Ya want me to start from the beginning?"

"Sure, go ahead."

Brooks loudly objected on the grounds that the question called for an endless narrative. He didn't want this witness to have an open invitation to badmouth his client regarding matters which were entirely irrelevant.

Judge Waters overruled the objection without much thought and motioned for Brady to continue. Brooks threw his arms up as he looked at the jury, exasperated by the persecution of his client in the kangaroo court.

"I met Scooter about five months ago while working the streets trying to make a living. He came across as a pretty nice guy, and we got to know each other. After about two weeks, we seemed to hit it off and we uh… became lovers."

Je… sus… fuck… ing… christ, Brooks thought, as he dropped his pen and leaned back in his swivel chair. What the hell's next? Neither he nor Skaggs knew Scooter and Brady were gay or that they were lovers. By the sound of those in the audience, this fact surprised all. Skaggs hoped and prayed that the revelation would enhance Brady's credibility–Brooks hoped it would destroy it.

"I'm not ashamed to admit Scooter and I enjoyed a close relationship. Yes, we were homeless, but we kept each other company, and we felt as long as we were together, it didn't matter if we slept in a drainage ditch, a cardboard box or under an overpass. This may be hard to believe, but transients can be gay too." Brady smiled as he looked at the jury. Several of the jurors smiled back. The connection spelled disaster for Scooter.

"Unfortunately, our relationship ended after a few months when he viciously attacked me."

"What do you mean he viciously attacked you?"

Brooks jumped to his feet, "Objection, Your Honor, irrelevant and highly prejudicial."

"Counsel, sit down." Judge Waters ordered. "You opened the door to this line of questioning. Overruled, Mr. Abbott, you may answer the question."

"Well, Scooter became increasingly violent during our time together. If he didn't make enough money, he couldn't buy his beer and he'd take it out on me. I'd only been on the streets for a few months before I met Scooter and I felt I needed his help to survive. But he got crazy and one day he told me he killed someone. He said it as though he was proud of it. He showed me a newspaper article about Mr. Pearce's murder. I got scared and took off running with the article." Brady was animated as he spoke. The jurors sat motionless, riveted.

Scooter looked down during the testimony, avoiding eye contact with the witness, Skaggs, the jurors, the judge, the reporter, the bailiff, and his attorney, while wishing he could vaporize.

"Scooter can run like a cheetah, and he caught me and strangled me to the point where I nearly passed out. He's much stronger than I am. As I was laying in the dirt, barely able to breathe and feeling like I was about to die, Scooter told me he would kill me if I ever went to the police or said anything to anyone about the whole incident." The witness was soft spoken and articulate... very believable.

Without warning, Scooter abruptly stood causing his chair to topple to the ground. He shouted to Brady, "You're a god damn liar and you know it. I ain't ever said that to you you piece of shit liar."

"Mr. Mason, sit down and be quiet. Do not interrupt these proceedings again," Judge Waters said sternly as she stared at him in the silenced courtroom. "Ladies and gentlemen of the jury, you are instructed to disregard that outburst from the defendant. Mr. Skaggs, please continue."

"Thank you, Your Honor. Mr. Abbott, did you

go to the police after what happened with Mr. Mason?"

"No, I didn't. I didn't want to look over my shoulder for the rest of my life, scared shitless that he would come after me and do to me what he did to Mr. Pearce."

"I see," Skaggs said calmly, then continued. "Mr. Mason testified that when he fought with you he knocked out your teeth and made you bleed all over him, is this correct?"

"No sir, he just crushed my windpipe, but he didn't cut me. I didn't bleed at all. He certainly didn't knock out my teeth as y'all can plainly see." He exposed his teeth while he looked at the jurors, smiling. Several smiled back, glad that the defendant didn't kill the nice young man. Brooks slowly shook his head in disgust over the royal ass kicking he was receiving from Skaggs.

"Thank you, Mr. Abbott, I have no further questions."

Brooks began with a vengeance. "Mr. Abbott, do you recall anything Mr. Mason said about the article?" Brooks was taking a huge risk here. He had no idea how Brady would answer this question, and he hoped and prayed that Scooter didn't say anything specific about the article."

"Not that I recall," Abbott stated, as Brooks let out his breath in relief.

"So it's true, is it not, that Mr. Mason never said he killed Mr. Pearce?" Brooks yelled at the witness.

"Well, he said he killed a man and then handed me the article as though he was confirming it. So to me, he was saying he killed Mr. Pearce."

"Mr. Abbott, please just answer my question," Brooks demanded. "Did my client ever say he killed Mr. Pearce—yes or no?"

"Well, not in those words."

"You just assumed it, right?"

"Well yeah, but it was pretty obvious what he meant."

"Move to strike as not responsive and speculative," Brooks said, looking at Judge Waters, pleading for her help.

"Motion granted. The jury is admonished to disregard the witness's last comment."

"C'mon Mr. Abbott, you didn't believe a single word that Mr. Mason said, did you? You even knew that Mr. Mason couldn't even read, and therefore couldn't have read that article about Mr. Pearce, didn't you?"

"At first, I didn't believe him. But I believed him after he attacked me and nearly killed me over the article. No one would do that unless they had something to hide. Plus, the rage in his eyes said it all. He did it, he killed that poor man, no question in my mind, sir. And yes, he could read. I don't know where you heard that he couldn't. He would read books all of the time. He knew exactly what that article about Mr. Pearce said."

Brooks should have shut his mouth and sat down before he asked that question. It was pointless to object and move to strike the testimony, which the jury already heard, and no doubt accepted as the gospel truth. This witness was brutal.

"Isn't it true, Mr. Abbott, that you're telling a pack of lies here today because Mr. Mason was no longer interested in having a relationship with you and this is your opportunity to get even with him?"

"No, that is not true. I have another man in my life who happens to be very successful and I plan to move in with him in the near future. I certainly don't need that animal anymore." He glanced over to Scooter.

Brooks ignored the response. "Isn't it also true

that you were attacked by Mr. Mason because he caught you stealing things that didn't belong to you… isn't that true?"

"That is a lie. Scooter is the criminal here, not me."

"Well, we'll see whose lying. I have no further questions of this witness, Your Honor." Brooks retreated to his seat trying to appear confident. Brady had his way with him and both he and the jury knew it. He was highly troubled by his strategic decision to allow Scooter to testify, thus opening the door to Brady's testimony. But for that death-knell decision, Brady would never have stepped foot in the courtroom, and his client would not likely face execution.

Skaggs had no follow-up questions for the perfect witness. Brady stepped down from the witness stand, glared at Scooter as he passed the defense table and smiled, pleased by the way he exacted revenge upon his former abusive lover.

THIRTY-ONE

ZACH couldn't sleep a wink after searching for his gun in his office. He never removed it, and it was futile to continue looking for it after he turned the office upside down. Maybe Ginger put it in a more secure place, but this was doubtful.

The seriousness of the theft was obviously exacerbated by the shooting of Miss Far Out. He had to get to the bottom of it and he hoped beyond hope that there was no connection.

During his long night, Zach ran several scenarios through his mind. He couldn't remember when he saw the gun last and no one, other than Ginger, had access to his office or his desk. There only three feasible explanations: one, Ginger took the gun; two, someone broke into the office and stole it, which was unlikely, as there was no evidence of a break-in; or three, that Miss Far Out used her master key to gain entry and she stole the gun. This alternative was plausible. Zach recalled Ginger warning Miss Far Out about the cannon he had in his office. She knew it was there and she was just the type of person to steal it.

He waited for Ginger to arrive to tactfully inquire into the disappearance of the weapon. After beating around the bush regarding client matters, he casually asked her if she had happened to see it. She thought nothing of the question, and moved on to better things after telling him she didn't see it and wouldn't touch it if she did.

He immediately called Andrew.

"Good morning, Andrew, we need to meet to discuss an issue which has arisen. Can you stop by my office this morning?"

"I can, but why aren't you at the trial? You said it may be over shortly and you were going to keep me posted."

"Well, I couldn't make the trial this morning due to several emergencies. I do need to speak with you pronto. Can you be here in fifteen minutes?"

"No, but I'll make it in an hour. Hopefully it's good news about my money."

"I'll see you when you get here. We'll talk then."

Two hours later, Andrew arrived and was greeted by Ginger. He remembered how she offended Julie and he decided not to acknowledge her presence.

"Mornin' Mr. Morgan, what's this all about?"

"Well, I'm informed the estate may be wrapped up in about a week, at which time you should have your money. The judge has it now, and it's just a matter of days before it's over."

"Fantastic, Mr. Morgan. I knew you had some good news for me."

Zach continued, "Also, I'm missing a gun from my desk. The only person I believe would've had access to my office was Julie, since she had a key to all offices in the building. I'm curious as to whether she discussed this issue with you?"

"No, other than the fact that you told her you'd shoot her the other day when you screamed at her."

"She never mentioned being in my office looking for the gun?"

"No, she didn't, sorry," Andrew said, flippantly.

"Did you happen to see a gun laying around her house?"

"Nope. C'mon, she had nothing to do with your gun. What is your problem with her? She would never steal anything from you, man, and it's not right that you're badmouthing her when she's no longer freakin' alive to defend herself."

"Okay, okay. Well, you realize I'll have to report the theft to the police. I guess it doesn't matter if she stole it, but I'll need a police report for my insurance."

"Okay, whatever man. Do what ya need to do."

"There is one other thing I've been meaning to discuss with you, Andrew. I put this off due to the tragedy with Julie. It relates to your brother."

"What about my brother?"

"Well, the PA's office gave me a copy of the data found on his computer at the time of the murder. Most of the information he had pertained to financial matters and the stock market."

"I looked through the material and came across a file that was protected by a secret password. After discovering the password, I opened the file and found some kind of diary written by Ollie. Initially, I didn't want to give it to you, but after thinking it through, I felt you should have it."

"I printed a copy for you, but I must caution you that you'll find it to be very disturbing. You don't need to read it right now. In fact, I suggest you take it back to where you're staying. If you want to discuss it afterwards, I'll be here for you."

"C'mon, Mr. Morgan, yer freakin' me out. Just give me the dang thing and I'll read it and be just fine. I'm a big boy," Andrew said with a concerned smile.

Zach hesitated then relented as he handed him the document. "Okay, go into the lobby and make yourself comfortable. When you're done, let me know. I'll remind you... it will be very disturbing." Andrew began reading as he walked to the lobby.

Zach then called the police to report his missing gun. Due to his proximity to Miss Far Out's murder scene, several law enforcement personnel were dispatched to his office immediately.

As he finished the call to the police, Ginger walked into his office, whimpering. "Zachary, I don't know what you done gave Andrew, but he was mighty upset. He was cryin' like I ain't ever seen no man cry. He wrinkled up them papers, shoved them in his pocket and he done ran out the office. I don't much care for the man, but it was so sad seein' a grown man cry like that."

"I'm sorry, Ginger. I didn't intend for you to get upset. Andrew received some distressing news about his family that he was not previously aware of. I'm sure he'll need some time to absorb it. If he comes in or calls, please interrupt me and I'll speak to him."

At noon, Zach received a call from Nathan, who advised him of the events in court during the morning session. Brooks called Momma to the stand to rebut the testimony of Brady, but her tears and her inadmissible opinion of Scooter's innocence were not much help to the defense. She acknowledged that Scooter gave her the newspaper containing the article about the murder but insisted that he did so because she collected such articles, not because he killed the man identified in the article. She didn't remember a fight between Scooter and Brady.

Both sides rested and closing arguments were set to begin in the morning.

Zach thanked Nathan for the update and promised he wouldn't miss the arguments.

Minutes later, three deputies and two detectives entered Zach's office, crowding his small lobby.

"Hello, Mr. Morgan, I'm Detective Allen and this

is my partner, Detective Jackson. We've been assigned to investigate the murder of Miss Pharout, which you're aware of. We understand you'd like to report a weapon stolen from your office?"

"Yes, thank you for getting on this so quickly. Last night I noticed my gun missing from my desk drawer. The permit and related documents are here if you'd like to see them."

Detective Jackson abruptly interjected, "What's the caliber of the gun?"

"It's a Glock .40, why?"

"That's good news for you. I don't typically divulge this information early in an investigation, but I'll do you a favor and tell you that the gun used to kill Miss Pharout was not a forty-caliber." Zach sighed, expressing relief to the detectives. He searched news reports, but was unable to find any information as to the caliber of weapon used by the perpetrator.

"These two officers here will make a theft report for you. If anything comes up that you think may be pertinent to the theft or the murder investigation, give me a call, will ya? I'm not convinced this is a simple coincidence." Detective Jackson handed him his card and he, Detective Allen, and one of the deputies, left. The other two deputies remained to complete the report.

Zach had lunch with Sasha and Amanda at Seoul Sushi, Amanda's favorite. He was exhausted after spending the past day worrying about the missing gun, a fact he never disclosed to Sasha. He needed to be in the company of his family.

While waiting for their food, an interview of Momma played on the big-screen behind the sushi bar. The trial was coming to a close and the press was having a field day. Momma was very upset at the way Scooter was being treated. Without him, she had no one to care for her. She pleaded to the jury and the Lord to set him free. Zach and Sasha listened intently and felt her pain.

Jung Joon, the waiter, interrupted Zach's focus on the interview and asked him a question regarding a foreclosure. He owed six hundred thousand on his home, which was worth less than three hundred. "Wha' I do, attuney?" He asked while pouring tea. "I no wan' house… too big and no worth six hunda touzin dalla."

Zach suggested Jung call Ginger and set up an appointment to review his loan documents. In his view, the mortgage industry caused the massive breakdown in the housing market and the banks should suffer the consequences. "Don't pay another nickel until you see me. You'll be able to live there for many many moons without paying anyone," he said joking as he slurped his tea. Jung did a slight bow as he graciously responded, "Tank you beddy beddy much attuney."

He had only one appointment for the afternoon, after which he would play hooky and take his pregnant wife and daughter to the zoo... one of the perks of being the senior partner at his law firm.

Franco Scaletti, a big man, middle-aged, buff and sporting a long black ponytail, a black blazer and a black polo shirt, sat across from Zach in his office. He didn't seem concerned that Zach was a kid compared to him. His dark, droopy eyes, and the couple pounds of gold hanging from his neck and wrists and a few more wrapped tightly around his fat fingers let Zach know he was the kind of guy you'd never want to cross playing poker, or Go Fish for that matter.

He was arrested for possession of large amounts of crack and pot. The LAPD wasn't too interested in taking him down. Rather, they wanted his sources, and he had lots of them.

He somehow managed to get out on bail but, according to Franco, his attorney inexplicably dropped him like a hot potato once he was released. No other attorney seemed to be interested in assisting him. Beverly Chin, Zach's client who needed an emergency Last Will and Testament prepared before she would step foot on an airplane, referred him to Zach after describing Zach as the best attorney in L.A. ... an exaggeration of epic proportions. The connection between Franco and Beverly was unknown, and Zach didn't want to inquire.

With a thick, deep Brooklyn accent, Franco informed Zach that the DA was offering him a plea deal. If he ratted out his sources, he'd get a slap on the wrist. If he didn't, he'd spend the next twenty years doing hard time. Zach took copious notes, outlining Franco's prior escapades with the law, which included arrests for possession with the intent to sell narcotics, a few counts of assault and battery and an armed robbery conviction. He was also suspected of homicide after a hit on a small-time dealer three years ago. No charges were filed as the only evidence was the statement of an eyewitness who abruptly changed his story and forgot what he saw. Although Zach never asked, Franco insisted he took no part in the hit.

He gave Zach the names of his sources and other inside information making it clear to Zach that it remain strictly confidential. His sources would kill him instantly if their identities were disclosed to the LAPD or the DA. Franco had no desire to go back to prison and he instructed Zach to quietly work a deal with the DA to get him into witness protection in exchange for the information. He didn't necessarily want to be part of the cowardly witness protection program, but his hands were tied and it was the only way he'd survive snitching out his sources.

Zach new nothing about plea deals, witness protection or hit men, but fearing that Franco would lose confidence in him, and probably worse, after he just divulged his deadly trade secrets, he kept his inexperience to himself. He assured Franco he'd uphold the attorney-client privilege at all costs and that the information would be shrouded in secrecy. He'd contact the DA as soon as possible to see what he could do. But he hoped beyond hope he could do nothing so that Franco would fire him and hire a real lawyer. He wanted no part of this case, but was too afraid to say so.

When he finished meeting with the drug kingpin, he went to the zoo, looking forward to hurling peanuts at the elephants.

THIRTY-TWO

IT'S closing argument day in the case of People v. Mason. The courtroom was at maximum capacity. Zach managed to get a seat next to Nathan in the rear.

Skaggs was dressed in his Sunday best: white shirt, red power tie, and dark pinstriped suit. Brooks toned it down a tad with a white shirt, maroon power tie, and dark pinstriped suit. Scooter wore the only suit he had—the only suit he'd ever need.

Several legal commentators covering the trial packed into the courtroom, eager to broadcast their rendition of the arguments and provide blow-by-blow sideline coverage on national TV. One young man, no older than twenty-two, identified himself as an expert criminal trial attorney and an expert on capital cases, though he surely wasn't old enough to have ever participated in one. He opined that the case had some interesting twists and turns and that the jurors had their work cut out for them. He concluded, as though predicting the Super Bowl, "I gotta tell ya John, based upon my experience, the state wins this one. The defense didn't do enough to create reasonable doubt and allowing the defendant to testify was a disaster."

The courtroom fell silent as Judge Waters took the bench. "Good morning, ladies and gentlemen." She glanced around the courtroom as conversations came to an abrupt halt. "Counsel, are we ready?"

Brooks nodded that he was; Skaggs verbalized it.

"Very well, bring in the jury please."

The jurors were smiling and noticeably upbeat, no doubt because the trial was near its conclusion. As they took their seats, some of them looked at Scooter. Others wanted to, but didn't.

Judge Waters began. "Ladies and gentlemen, this is the part of the trial we refer to as the closing arguments or summations. As with the opening statements, what Mr. Skaggs and Mr. Brooks say to you is not evidence. You've seen and heard the evidence, in the form of witness testimony, photographs, clothing and other items. The lawyers will summarize the evidence for you, but their summaries and their arguments are not evidence and are not to be considered as such. Mr. Skaggs will begin for the state, then Mr. Brooks, and Mr. Skaggs will then conclude. The reason Mr. Skaggs gets to speak to you twice is because the state has the burden to establish to you, beyond any reasonable doubt, the guilt of Mr. Mason. You must not consider the fact that Mr. Skaggs is permitted an opportunity to speak twice as any indication of guilt or innocence of the defendant."

Judge Waters looked away from the jury to the prosecutor, "Mr. Skaggs, you may proceed."

"Thank you, Your Honor," Skaggs said politely as he smiled to the jurors and approached the podium situated in front of the jury box.

"Good morning, ladies and gentlemen. I realize this has been a rather long trial and you're all ready to get back to your lives. However, these arguments are very important for each side. I will explain to you why I believe the evidence shows beyond any reasonable doubt that Mr. Mason is guilty of murder in the first degree. Mr. Brooks, on the other hand, will tell you why he believes I'm wrong. In the end, you, and only you, will decide whether Mr. Mason is guilty or not guilty of the crimes charged. This will be an immense undertaking for you, so it is very important that you pay careful attention to what is presented by both myself and by Mr. Brooks. I promise you, I'll be as brief as I can."

Skaggs spent the next half hour discussing the legal issues the jury would later be instructed on by the judge. He then shifted gears to the evidence.

"It was not disputed in this trial that Mr. Mason was wearing a jacket and pants covered with the blood of the victim, Oliver Pearce. Neither was it disputed that he was in possession of shoes which also had the victim's blood on them. You'll recall that the prints from those shoes were identical–not just close but identical–to the bloody shoeprints found at the victim's home. These shoes were size twelve, the same size worn by Mr. Mason." Skaggs held up each item of evidence as he made reference to it.

"Mr. Mason also had in his possession what Dr. Benjamin Reynolds described as the murder weapon: the bloody wrench used to repeatedly strike Mr. Pearce in the head until he was unrecognizable." Skaggs grabbed the wrench from the evidence table and simulated repeated blows. He accompanied his theatrics with a look of anger and hatred, so authentic that the jurors must have believed it mirrored the passion of the killer. "This is how Oliver met his fate, while he was bound and gagged," he shouted. "This is how that man sitting right there," he pointed to Scooter, "decided to cowardly end the life of a helpless human being who couldn't even scream for mercy as he was being killed," Skaggs paused.

"Now, you heard Deputy Cramer describe to you how Mr. Mason admitted committing the crime and even said he'd do it again. The defense has tried in vain to show that this confession was not intended to refer to the murder of Mr. Pearce. Rather, Mr. Mason told you his confession actually referred to some fierce bloody attack he claims to have perpetrated upon Brady Abbott. Mr. Mason wants you to believe that the blood he was referring to when he confessed to Deputy Cramer was actually Mr. Abbott's blood that splattered on him when they fought in the park."

"However, after considering all of the evidence, the only reasonable conclusion you must draw is that the confession related to the murder of Mr. Pearce. Mr. Abbott did not shed a drop of blood on the defendant's clothes and you didn't hear a single blood expert testify that he did. There was no credible evidence presented that Mr. Abbott had cuts, open wounds, missing teeth or even a bloody lip. Fortunately, the defendant was kind enough to only strangle Mr. Abbott, not slice him up like he did Mr. Pearce."

"Admittedly, there was blood on the jacket from another person. But the defense's own witness, Dr. Bristol, testified on cross-examination that the blood was likely older than the victim's blood; in such case, it couldn't possibly have splattered on the jacket after the murder."

"Therefore, the defendant's so-called explanation for the confession was a flat-out fabrication... a bald-faced lie. The judge will instruct you that when a witness lies to you on that witness stand," Skaggs pointed to the stand, "after taking the oath to tell the truth, the whole truth and nothing but the truth, you can disregard every single word that comes out of his mouth."

Skaggs was on a roll. He paused for affect, took a sip of water, and continued with vigor.

"And how can we forget the fact that the defendant had a copy of the article about Mr. Pearce's murder and proudly presented the article to Mr. Abbott as he bragged about killing someone? Please ask yourselves—why would anyone say or do such a thing unless he perpetrated the crime?"

"I submit to you that Mr. Abbott was a credible witness... far more credible than Mr. Mason, and you should believe what he told you, every word of it."

Some of the jurors nodded in agreement. Brooks saw the nods. Fuck, he whispered under his breath. Scooter saw the nods and was tempted to hop over the defense table and shut Skaggs up once and for all.

"In short, the evidence has proven beyond any doubt whatsoever, that Mr. Ray Mason, acting alone and with premeditation, brutally tortured and murdered Oliver Pearce, cutting off his feet with this butcher knife when he was through with him." Skaggs held up the knife, looked to each of the jurors individually, and calmly put it down.

"Mr. Mason has shown you that he is a liar and his efforts to convince you that this is all some big mistake or coincidence is absurd and must be rejected. There is simply no other explanation for the evidence, ladies and gentlemen... none."

Skaggs concluded, "On behalf of the people of

the state of California, I ask you to do the right thing, the only thing the evidence warrants and that is to find Mr. Raymond Mason guilty of first degree murder. Thank you."

"Thank you, Mr. Skaggs," Judge Waters said. "The court will be in recess for fifteen minutes."

The jury left the courtroom, as did the judge. Brooks took the opportunity to fine tune his closing remarks while Scooter sat silent, noticeably distraught by the prosecutor's convincing story.

During the break, Zach checked his messages: one from counsel for DesignElec calling regarding the demand sent on behalf of Daphne Stevens; one from Randy inquiring about a new collection account; and seven from Andrew, each stating the same thing, but with increasing volume and hostility, "Mr. Morgan, call me ASAP."

Zach left the courtroom and called Andrew. "Good morning, Andrew, what's up?"

"I need to see you right now, Mr. Morgan."

"I'm in court, at Mason's trial. What's going on?"

"I couldn't care less where you are. I'll be at your office at two o'clock, be there." Andrew hung up.

Do I really need to put up with this shit from a client? Zach said to himself in the hallway, shaking his head.

Trial resumed. Brooks approached the podium with his yellow note pad to address the jury.

He began by countering Skaggs interpretation of the jury instructions and reminded the jury that much of the evidence was not disputed. He then moved to the heart of his summation.

"When I was a little boy, I had a fifth-grade teacher, Sister Timko, a nun in my Catholic school. None of us liked Sister Timko because she was always grumpy. Back in those days, nuns were allowed to smack us with a pointer if we acted up, and the grumpy nuns always smacked us." A few of the jurors smiled.

"One day, my friend Billy got whacked on the knuckles with a yardstick for passing a love note. All of us in the classroom began to laugh. Sister Timko had a strict rule against laughing when someone else was being disciplined. She became angry, striking as many of us she could reach with the yardstick as if it were a flyswatter. We laughed harder and harder and she got madder and madder. She must have swatted us ten times each."

Brooks was relaxed as he leaned on the podium and told the story. He wanted the jurors to relax too and to trust the attorney for the alleged killer. Skaggs' performance had to be erased from their minds.

"Later that day, I was in the hallway and I watched Sister Timko push a little girl named Paula down the stairs. No one saw what happened but me, and I said nothing about what I saw, out of fear of retaliation from Sister Timko. Paula was unconscious. An ambulance came and took her away. She was in a coma for about a month before she recovered."

"I was terribly upset, and I finally told my parents what happened. They called the police and informed them that I witnessed Sister Timko violently push Paula down the stairs. The police officer asked me several times if I was certain of what I saw because it was a very serious accusation. I told him I was positive, and also told him about her yardstick rampage earlier in the day."

"The officer was angry and assured my parents he would do what was necessary to punish my teacher for hurting Paula."

"Sister Timko claimed that she didn't push Paula, but instead that she was trying to catch her from falling down the stairs. The police asked me if that could have been possible, and I adamantly said no, as I saw the whole thing. No one believed Sister Timko because they didn't like her, and she was suspended from teaching."

"When Paula awoke from her coma a month later, she confirmed Sister Timko's story. She lost her footing and Sister Timko actually attempted to catch her before she fell."

"I was so very wrong and felt awful for what I had done and the mistake I had made. From my vantage point, I believed I saw her push Paula. But I wasn't really positive, like I told the officer. My dislike for Sister Timko caused me to distort what I actually saw and to assume the worst."

"Needless to say, that experience taught me a valuable lesson."

"Some of you may dislike Mr. Mason for how he acted in this courtroom during this trial, but you must put any dislike you may feel for him aside and not jump to conclusions. You must consider his version of what happened. You may not like him, but that doesn't mean he's a killer."

"Personally, I don't blame Mr. Skaggs for

assuming that Mr. Mason committed the murder. After all, Mr. Mason is a transient, he was wearing clothes stained with the victim's blood, he had the murder weapon, and he said that the SOB deserved it. He obviously must have done it, right? Mr. Skaggs was therefore perfectly justified in his assumption, as was I when I thought I saw Sister Timko push Paula. But his assumption was wrong, just like mine was wrong."

"Unfortunately, the LAPD and Mr. Skaggs felt they had their man and they never believed it was anyone else. I urge you not to make the same mistake."

"As jurors, you are required to put aside what may seem to be obvious and look solely to the evidence. If you do, as you promised you would on the first day of trial, you will have clarity and you will discover the truth." Brooks spoke gently, fatherly, as though passing down wisdom to his children.

"Now, let's first talk about the confession. Whether you believe everything Mr. Mason said or not, it is undisputed that he and Brady Abbott were embroiled in a fierce argument. Mr. Abbott said there was no bloodshed; my client said there was. Dr. Bristol testified that my client's clothing did in fact contain bloodstains from someone other than the victim." Brooks ignored Dr. Bristol's other opinion that the third person's blood may have been placed on the clothing before the murder. Why illuminate the problem by reminding the jury of it? Maybe they'd forget.

"In the end, what the blood evidence shows is that Mr. Mason's version of the events is just as likely to have occurred as Mr. Abbott's version."

"It is also reasonable to conclude that Mr. Mason found the bloody clothing in the trash, not recognizing that it was stained with the victim's blood. He then got into a fight with Mr. Abbott, and Mr. Abbott was bloodied up during that fight. When the deputy at the jail asked Mr. Mason why he had blood on his clothes, Mr. Mason admitted he had blood on him, but he was referring to Abbott's blood… not the victim's blood. Similarly, when Mr. Mason stated that he would do it again, he was referring to his beating of Brady Abbott… not the victim."

"This testimony is entirely consistent with the evidence, and I submit to you, it reflects precisely what happened."

"You've heard and observed all of the evidence

and I'm not going to go through it piece by piece. Rather, the heart of this case rests upon the lack of evidence, which I believe casts grave doubt upon the entire case."

"Specifically, Mr. Mason never said he killed Mr. Pearce and not a single witness testified he did, not even his enemy, Brady Abbott. Mr. Mason's fingerprints, his hair, and his DNA were nowhere to be found at the crime scene. Are we to believe that Mr. Mason was capable of cleaning up such evidence, after the murder? You've met Mr. Mason, and you know as well as I that it is simply not reasonable to conclude that he had the capacity to rid the crime scene of delicate trace evidence."

"The state wants you to believe that Mr. Mason wore gloves to conceal his fingerprints. This is borderline comical. If he wanted to avoid arrest by wearing gloves during the murder, do you think for one minute that he would act so careless by parading around the city with the murder weapon and the victim's blood all over his clothes? Again, that would not be a reasonable conclusion for you to draw."

"It's undisputed that no one saw Mr. Mason at the victim's home. Although Constance Federoff testified that she believed she saw his scooter in the vicinity of the crime scene, no eyewitness actually saw him at the crime scene."

"It is also undisputed that cash and other valuables were found in plain view at the scene. These were of no interest to the perpetrator as they were left behind. My client was penniless and homeless; he would have taken whatever he could have if he killed Mr. Pearce. He told you that himself. Therefore, you must ask yourselves why the victim's cash was not taken if Mr. Mason was indeed the killer. Mr. Skaggs apparently didn't think this was important and gave you no answer to this question. But I think we all see the importance."

Brooks moved on, methodically, but with only a few glances at his notes situated on the podium.

"Mr. Mason testified that he found the clothes, shoes and wrench in a dumpster. This testimony was not rebutted by the state. Mr. Mason was a scavenger. He built a make-shift vehicle to help him collect, store and lug his spoils around. He dredged things out of dumpsters nearly every day of his life while living on the streets. Picking out items which a murderer happened to toss into a trash can after committing a murder, is really not that far-fetched. Unfortunately, Mr. Mason was in the wrong place, at the wrong time, and that, I submit, is the only thing he is guilty of," Brooks paused, taking a sip of water.

"And finally, we must ask: What in the world was the motive for the murder? Again, Mr. Skaggs gave you no evidence of a motive, not even a wild guess. As we know, it certainly wasn't robbery, as Mr. Mason would have taken the cash and valuables."

"What reason did Mr. Mason have to kill Mr. Pearce the way he was killed? Are we to believe that he randomly rode his little scooter to Mr. Pearce's house, gained entry without disturbing Mr. Pearce, or the neighbors, and then brutally bound and tortured the man without a reason? No, I can't accept that explanation, and neither should you. There is a reason these types of crimes are committed. They are not random acts, as Mr. Skaggs would like you to believe. They are acts of rage targeted at the victim by the killer for something the victim did. But there was no evidence that Mr. Mason even knew the victim, or that he had any reason to do him harm... none." Brooks was throwing everything into the reasonable-doubt pot.

"Mr. Mason did not kill anyone. The person who

did is a free man who had a tremendous amount of anger towards the victim. That is who the LAPD should be looking for."

"What we have, ladies and gentlemen, is a rush to judgment which, as I learned as a boy, is taboo, particularly when a person's life is on the line."

"The state was eager to make an arrest for the horrific crime and Mr. Mason was an easy and, quite frankly, a logical target. However, once it was determined there was a plausible explanation for the evidence, the state should've continued on with its investigation until it found the actual killer."

"This is where the system failed. Mr. Skaggs is hell-bent to convict Mr. Mason. He laid out his case, using well-rehearsed and highly-trained witnesses, each taught to give you a distorted version of the events. Mr. Skaggs even personally advised one of the state's witnesses, poor Mr. Parham, that he was actually on trial and that you'd convict him if he said the wrong thing. This is a sign of desperation, a desperate prosecutor seeking a conviction at all costs."

"There are far too many holes in the prosecution's theory and these holes represent doubt.

When doubt is pervasive in a criminal case, there can be no finding of guilt."

"I know the deliberations will be difficult, but I have faith that you will not pretend to see what the state has failed to present, that you will follow the law given to you by the judge, and that you will allow my client to walk out of this courtroom a free man, which is what he deserves."

Brooks looked into the eyes of each of the jurors, then slowly sat down next to his grateful client, who broke a genuine smile for the first time since he was arrested."

Unfortunately, Andrew's demand for an emergency meeting forced Zach to leave trial before the rebuttal presentation by Skaggs. Scooter's fate would be in the hands of the jury by the end of the day. Good news for Zach. He gained valuable experience watching the trial and learning from the judge and lawyers, but he needed to spend more time building his practice.

THIRTY-THREE

ZACH arrived at his office at around one-thirty. Andrew was not there yet, so he had a few moments to catch up on his increasing workload.

He called T. Montgomery Blackstone, counsel for DesignElec. During his days at FF&W, Zach's fellow associates tried to convince him to use his first name initial followed by his middle name as a sign of distinction. Zach thought it was a sign of arrogance. In any event, he didn't feel the name Z. Elwood Morgan would give him or his career any material advantage.

Zach conducted some research into the electrical line infrastructure installed near Daphne's home. While several other deep pockets may be responsible for the deaths of Mr. Stevens and his son, Zach decided to begin the fray with DesignElec.

Once a formal demand is sent, the target of the demand usually blames someone else and sends its own threatening letter advising the other company to indemnify it against any claims made against it by the victim. The other company then does the same with yet another company, and so on, and so on. Zach figured he'd fire the first shot and let the others scramble for cover and launch their own attacks.

"Mr. Blackstone, this is Zach Morgan returning your call regarding the Stevens' matter."

"Well, good afternoon, Mr. Morgan, so glad to hear from you," he said slowly with a deep, powerful voice, no doubt designed to intimidate his opponents.

"I've been asked to give you a call to discuss your recent letter. First of all, I'd like to express our most sincere condolences to your client and her children. What a horrible tragedy. I hope she has gained the strength to cope with her loss."

"But getting to the business end of this, I understand someone from risk management discussed the claim with Mrs. Stevens, but she has yet to make a decision regarding a settlement offer."

Zach interrupted, "Well, her decision is no. With all due respect, the offer to pay burial expenses in exchange for a full release of liability was offensive. We made an offer in my letter and it is my hope your client seriously considers it or makes a reasonable counteroffer."

Blackstone's kindness abruptly went out the window and his aggression took hold. "DesignElec has no intention of paying the demand or anything close to it, Mr. Morgan. It is excessive, and while we sympathize with your client and her family, she must understand that neither she, nor you, won the lottery, Counselor."

You bastard, Zach thought then responded. "Lottery? I can assure you, Mr. Blackstone, that my client doesn't give a damn about winning the lottery. She'd prefer that you and your careless client bring her husband and son back to her so she can wake up from the nightmare she's been living in since your people killed them. But that obviously ain't gonna happen, Counsel. Therefore, she has no choice but to seek compensation for her financial and emotional losses. Those losses are far beyond anything you or those in your firm could ever comprehend."

"Calm down, son, I was just speaking lawyer to lawyer. No need to get offended or take this personally… it's the nature of the business."

"Well, I do take it personally and I'm not your son. I know how you guys operate. You'll offer small potatoes and threaten protracted and lengthy litigation if she refuses to accept. So allow me to make this crystal clear, T. Montgomery... I'm up for the challenge and whatever unethical bullshit you and your minions chose to throw at me will be met with equal and opposite aggression. Therefore, save the small talk and get to the point. Where are your people with settlement?"

"Don't play Mr. Tough Guy with me Counselor, because I'll bury you. We'll be generous to your client, not because we're afraid of you, far from it, but because my client does have a heart and recognizes that she is in need of assistance. If you really want to serve your client, you won't push my buttons. Doing so will get you and your poor client nowhere, fast." Blackstone paused, then continued. "Just so you know, my client has actually considered payment of a compensation package to your clients. In this regard, we'll pay Mrs. Stevens one hundred fifty thousand cash and another fifty grand to each of her children to be placed in blocked accounts until they reach eighteen. Believe me, Counsel, this is not the beginning of a series of offers; it's a take-it-or-leave-it proposition, so I hope you and your client consider it carefully. It'll remain open for seven days, at which time it will automatically expire."

"That offer is not going to work," Zach said. "I'll convey it to my client because I'm obligated to. However, I can tell you it'll be rejected outright. It's not even close. If your client truly wants to settle this case before it gets nasty, I suggest you and the other culpable players pass around the offering basket and get donations with lots of zeros."

Unfazed, T. Montgomery concluded softly, "Mr. Morgan, accept it while you can. Despite what you may think, this will not be an easy case for a youngster like you to win. Have a pleasant day. Oh, and by the way, Mr. J. Robert Wharton of Fleming, Fleming & White asked me to give you his regards. Seems you have quite a reputation over there."

"Well you tell him that I hope he, and everyone like him, including you, get what you all deserve, which is disbarred."

As Zach hung up the phone, Andrew approached his office, clapping slowly. "Brilliant, Counselor. You handled that well. I guess I never should have doubted your talents. You ripped that guy's nuts out. I sure hope it pays off for your client."

Andrew's presence startled Zach. He looked at the clock. It was 2:05.

"Thanks. That guy's as crooked as they come, and his client is gonna pay out the ass someday. Sorry I'm a little late."

"No problem," Andrew said, taking a seat.

"So what's the dire emergency, Andrew?" Zach inquired with a tone of frustration.

Andrew held up a few sheets of paper rolled up tightly. He glanced at them and got right to the point. "Well… this little story about my brother opened up a lot of wounds, and I wish you never gave it to me. What possible benefit did you think it would have, Mr. Morgan?" Andrew seemed suddenly mature, all business, no drama.

"Is that what this is about?" Zach looked at him, fully understanding the basis for his client's anguish.

"I gave it to you because I thought you'd want to be informed of its contents. I'm truly sorry if it upset you, but I warned you it would be painful."

"Well, I think you would have done your client a

service by keeping something like this to yourself. I don't see any good that could have come from this story. You should have known it would make me feel like shit."

"I'm sorry, Andrew. You're right, I should have thought it through more carefully. But my decision to give it to you was very difficult."

"Yeah, well it's too late now for apologies. I've already lost a lot of sleep over this and I'm still in shock by it all. To make matters worse, the cops are pestering me and want to talk about Julie. Have you spoken to them?"

"Not a word."

"Good, 'cause I don't want you speaking to anyone about me, unless it has to do with me getting my money. If I decide to meet with them, you can be with me, but until then, not a word to anyone."

"Understood. Anything else?" Zach asked curtly.

"No. I just wanted to make these things clear to you."

As Andrew abruptly left the office, a walk-in entered the lobby. A salesman type, briefcase in hand.

"Hi, my name is Darrell," he said to Zach while

extending his hand. "I'm looking for an attorney interested in taking a class action case. I have all the evidence here in my briefcase to support the case. Do you have a minute?" His eyes stretched wide open as he spoke, but retracted when he finished. He seemed to be a happy man, proud of his investigative work.

"Sure, but only a minute. I have a few things on the burner to take care of."

"Okay, I'll make it quick. I purchased a home in a tract development several years ago. A few months back, I noticed stucco and concrete cracks. I went to my neighbors, and sure enough, they have the same problem." Darrell pulled out color photos from his briefcase and handed them to Zach.

"I've heard of lawyers suing builders for constructing shoddy homes and this seems like a darn good case. There are seventy-five homes in all. I did most of the prep work, so your job will be easy. Would you be interested in taking this on? The other property owners agreed that the lawyer can have twenty percent of the settlement, and I'll get twenty percent for my work. The remaining sixty will be split seventy-five ways."

Zach spent a few moments flipping through the

pictures before he replied, "Sorry, Darrell, but to be honest, if you believe these pictures show defective workmanship, I'm not seeing it. These cracks are hairline. Homes are built with natural materials and natural materials shrink and expand. Stucco and concrete always crack." Zach almost told him that everyone and his mother knows that small cracks are normal, but stopped himself short, remembering how upset the client who hit the peanut truck got when Zach suggested he was an idiot for not having insurance.

"What you're showing me here looks like garden-variety cracking. You and your neighbors can spend lots of money pursuing these claims, but in my opinion, you won't be successful."

"You mean I did all this work for nothing?" Darrell said, deflated.

"Well, you may want to get a second opinion. Another lawyer may think you have a shot at this. But, to be honest, I really don't, sorry."

"You are my second opinion. Darn it, I thought I was gonna retire on this case."

Darrell collected his photos, thanked Zach for his time, and left.

Zach returned a few calls and then walked to June Gregory's office to get a copy of the file relating to Andrew's contempt proceeding which she handled. At some point, he and Andrew would be meeting with detectives regarding Andrew's involvement—or lack thereof—in Miss Far Out's murder. He figured it would be a good idea to have a record of his priors, including the contempt matter.

As he arrived at her office, he observed Darrell just leaving.

"Well, did ya take the case?" Zach asked her, grinning.

"Not a chance. First of all I don't handle construction defect cases, and second of all, it was a bullshit case anyway. I assume he tried to woo you into taking it?"

"He did, but the only cracks I deal with are crackpots, a la Andrew Pearce." They both laughed.

"Actually, that's why I'm here. I'm not sure if you're aware, but the LAPD has their eye on Andrew in connection with Julie's murder. Nothing there, but he and I will probably be meeting with them shortly to discuss the matter and to hopefully get them to go away.

I'd like to have a copy of his file relating to the contempt charge with Judge Waters which you handled for him. I assume it will be a topic of discussion with the LAPD."

"Oh sure, sure, no problem at all. Let me go pull that file and make a copy for you right now. There's really not much to it."

She returned a minute later with the thin file. Zach thanked her and headed back to his office.

He reviewed the contempt order and sentencing arrangement. He couldn't help smiling as he recalled his client busting Scooter in the nose the way he did. The guy had guts to do that in front of the notorious Judge Waters.

The file contained a print-out of Andrew's priors: drunk-in-public, assault, possession of marijuana, petty theft, and a few others from his hell-raising days in Texas and South Carolina. The most recent activity was a simple loitering citation which Andrew ignored, but which was later dismissed–no harm, no foul. Andrew was a small-time criminal. A punk who never did anything that would rise to the level of murder. The LAPD was barking up the wrong tree.

THIRTY-FOUR

JURY deliberations began punctually at nine o'clock. Although they listened intently to the judge's detailed instructions regarding deliberations, most of the jurors were clueless and apprehensive as they took their seats in the decision room.

The room was long and narrow, decorated with white government-issue paint, metal furniture, industrial-grade carpet and a water dispenser. It had no windows and only one door, which was monitored by an armed bailiff to prevent jurors from escaping the deliberations. Overall, rather unassuming for a place where life or death was determined.

Juror Number Eight, a dentist named Pete, took the laboring oar and suggested they discuss the election of a foreperson. Everyone unanimously agreed that since Pete brought it up, he should have the honor.

Pete let the others know he never-before

participated in a jury trial, but he would do the best he could, and if anyone disagreed with his approach, to tell him. He summarized what he believed they were supposed to do and suggested that a preliminary poll be taken. "G" would stand for guilty, "NG" not guilty, and "U" undecided. The jurors agreed. The twelve of them anonymously indicated their letter of choice on a small piece of paper and passed them back to Pete.

Pete announced the results: "Six G's, four NG's, and two U's."

"Okay, since we're so far apart, perhaps we should take a look at the evidence. Afterwards, I think everyone should share his or her thoughts with the rest of us. Remember, we can only consider the testimony and the physical evidence." Pete motioned to the table situated in the rear of the room stacked with trial exhibits.

Taking Pete's cue, the jurors gathered around the table to inspect the evidence, much like judges at a science fair critiquing an entrant's project. It was a morbid exercise for some of them, but they worked through it and resumed their seats.

"I'll start the process," Pete began. "We should allow each other to speak and not interrupt or engage in argument at this point. We'll do that later. Does everyone agree?" The jurors nodded affirmatively.

"Good. I'll begin by saying I'm in the guilty camp. I believe the state proved beyond any reasonable doubt that Mr. Mason committed the crime. He was covered with the victim's blood, he had the weapon, he was seen in the area of the crime, and he certainly seemed creepy enough to kill. To me he was a liar and said what he had to say to convince us he's innocent. I thought his boyfriend, Brady, was believable and his story about the newspaper article and confession sealed the deal for me. This guy is a killer, and I vote to convict him of premeditated murder and get him off our streets."

"Let's go around the table, starting to my right."

Juror Number Three, a disabled woman in a wheelchair, simply said, "I agree with everything Pete said. I vote to convict."

Number Nine, "I think there's doubt. Brady could be lying. He came across as pompous to me and there were no fingerprints or DNA. I just don't see how he could have done those horrible things without leaving fingerprints or DNA and I don't buy the argument that he was wearing gloves. I'm gonna say not guilty."

Number Five, "I think he's guilty, but I'm troubled by giving him the death penalty. He seems like he's had a hard life."

Pete interrupted, "The penalty phase is later. If we convict him, we'll deliberate again to determine whether he should be given the death penalty."

Juror Number Eleven, the construction worker; "I don't know; there's nothing linking the defendant to the victim, no fingerprints, no hair, no DNA. I tend to agree with his lawyer, Mr. Brooks. There might be lots of circumstantial evidence, but show me he was there. He never flat-out confessed to killing anyone and he didn't take the money. Why didn't he take the money? There would have been no motive for killing the victim, other than to steal his money, and he didn't steal his money. He was a transient and he surely would have done that. Don't get me wrong, I believe he may have done it, but to me there is reasonable doubt. I vote not guilty."

Number Seven, "C'mon, motive schmotive, he had blood all over him. He's a psychotic killer, no different from Manson. People like him kill just to kill. They have no reason for any of it. They just do it to satisfy their addiction to kill. He should fry for what he did. There's no question in my mind… guilty, guilty, guilty. I just wish the victim's brother would have given him a few more of those right hooks." Several of the jurors laughed and nodded in agreement.

Number One, "I think he did it, but I'm not too sure yet, so I'm undecided for now."

Number Twelve, "Ain't no reasonable doubt. He done it. Ain't no question about it in my mind. None at all."

Number Two, Venus, the budding actress/dancer/singer and part-time waitress, etc., got her turn and announced her rationale in a small, squeaky voice. "Okay, to me–and this is just me speaking–I think the Brady guy was honest, and cute too. But maybe when he got strangled by Mr. Mason during their fight he got cut, but didn't know it, and his blood got on Mr. Mason's clothes. And so when Mr. Mason said he would do it again to the jail guard, he was talking about what he did to Brady, not the victim, just like his lawyer said. So really, I'm not sure and since I'm not sure, don't I have to say not guilty?"

Number Seven and Number Twelve rolled their

eyes, realizing what should be a quick guilty verdict may turn into a marathon.

Number Ten, Edna, the grandmotherly homemaker, looked at Number Two and said, "Listen, sweetheart, the expert said the unknown person's blood got on the clothes before the murder. Therefore, it couldn't have been Brady's blood since the fight with Brady took place afterwards. He is guilty in my mind."

Venus jumped back in, "Oh yeah, yeah, yeah, I forgot about that, oh my god silly me... can I change my vote to guilty?"

"You can always change your vote," Pete declared.

Number Four tried to expedite the process by simply saying not guilty and Number Six joined the undecided camp.

With several holdouts for guilt, Pete began to take his job more seriously. He spent the next few hours going over the jury instructions and evidence piece by piece. He tried to get the others to focus on Scooter's courtroom demeanor, hoping to convince them it was obvious he was the killer–precisely what Brooks asked them not to do. He reminded the jurors that at any time they could change their vote, hopefully in his direction, after they revisited the evidence.

Shortly after noon, the bailiff brought in sandwiches, snacks and drinks... all on the house. Once lunch arrived, discussions about Scooter's guilt or innocence temporarily ceased. The jurors were already tired of talking about murder and decided to shift their attention during lunch to sports, movies, politics and health problems.

Deliberations began again at 1:30. Pete thought it was in order to take another poll: five G's and seven NG's. After painstakingly evaluating the evidence and reviewing the instructions, seven of the jurors couldn't come to a guilty verdict. However, the additional review of the materials solidified the guilty decision made by five of them. Stalemate.

They went around and around, each providing input about Scooter, the evidence, the lawyers, the judge, and even the court reporter and Momma. By day's end, they'd had enough of each other. The last poll... five G's, five NG's and two U's.

They arrived the next morning, cheerful and rested for the second day of deliberation. Rather than take another poll, Pete simply asked whether anyone had changed his or her position from the day before. Everyone collectively said no, except Number Eleven.

"I got to thinking about this long and hard. It kept me up all night." Number Eleven, a big, burly man, was nearly reduced to tears. "I want to do the right thing. The judge said we could consider circumstantial evidence. I was reluctant to, but I realized the law allows this type of evidence to prove guilt. I wanted to see evidence directly linking the defendant to the scene, like hair or fingerprints or DNA. At first I couldn't get a handle on it. But the evidence is right there on the evidence table."

"As Detective Cranston said, the evidence proving that Mr. Mason was in fact at Ollie's home is the bloody clothes, the size twelve shoes, the murder weapon he had in his possession and the fact that he was riding his scooter right down the street from the victim's house. Although there were no fingerprints or DNA, that doesn't mean he didn't do it. And, Mr. Brady Abbott was a very credible witness in my mind and I believe Mr. Mason confessed to the killing. Mr. Mason also acted like a psycho-nut on the stand. So after spending the night worrying about this whole thing and going over and over the evidence in my head, I now feel comfortable in concluding that this guy is a monster and is definitely guilty."

Pete responded to Number Eleven's change of heart. "Thank you—not for agreeing with one side or the other—but for taking the time to deliberate. Our job, as I understand it, is to do exactly what you've done." Pete was happy to chalk another one up for the G's.

"Well I disagree," Number Nine interjected. "Homeless people are scavengers. They hop in an' out of dumpsters all day long… saw a coupla them doin' it yesterday on my way home as a matter of fact. Mason coulda found that stuff just like he said. He shouldn't be convicted of murder for helpin' himself to the garbage left by others."

The debate intensified and raged on during the next several hours, often becoming heated and aggressive. A few times Pete threw his arms up declaring a tie game and threatening he'd let the judge know they were hopelessly deadlocked. He was yelled at for being too assertive with his opinions, but chastised for being a quitter when he couldn't get others to adopt them. The bailiff listened from the outside and occasionally tapped on the door asking if everything was okay. They would quiet down, as though being scolded by their teacher, but then quickly relapse into heated argument as they continued to piss each other off with their diverse interpretations of the evidence.

At 2:35 that afternoon, the jurors surprisingly managed to reach a consensus.

"Are we ready to let the bailiff know we have a verdict?" Pete asked.

"Yes," they said in unison. They were content with their decision, but recognized that their lives would change by having made it.

Pete completed the verdict form, passed it around to make sure everyone agreed with it, then let the bailiff know they were ready.

At 2:50 the clerk advised Brooks and Skaggs that a verdict had been reached and that it would be published at precisely 3:30. Reporters informed the rest of the country, including Zach and Nathan, who dropped everything to race to court. Zach invited Ginger. He wanted her to experience the excitement of being in the legal business.

As Zach drove, Ginger revealed the same scared-shitless look she had the last time she was a passenger. She was sweating profusely, and not a single sound came out of her mouth, except, "Uhhh huuu," which she whispered in response to Zach's effort to spark up conversation. Her eyes never left the road, her hands never released the tight grip she had on her seat.

The hallway was chaotic but through the frenzy, the bailiff recognized Zach and escorted he and Ginger into the courtroom, giving them seats in the back row. Zach owed him a free consultation.

At 3:25, Judge Waters took the bench. She reminded the spectators that if they made a sound during or after the reading of the verdict, they would be taken into custody and prosecuted for contempt.

"Counsel, are you ready?"

Brooks glanced over at Skaggs and spoke on his behalf, "Yes we are, Your Honor."

"Okay, bring in the jury."

Zach had nothing to gain or lose from the verdict, but his stomach was in knots. So was Ginger's. To outsiders, it's all about the competition... The People versus Mason, Skaggs versus Brooks, Scooter versus

Ollie, Scooter versus Brady, expert versus expert. They anticipate the reading of the verdict as though it were game seven of the World Series... ninth inning, one run down, bases loaded, two outs, three balls, two strikes, clean-up batter at the plate.

To the participants, however, the reality that a verdict is about to be read, that the defendant will lose his or her liberty, or gain his or her freedom, causes more than butterflies. For that brief moment prior to the reading of the verdict, they are physically incapacitated, nearly comatose, and hardly aware of their surroundings.

Scooter sat motionless, staring down at the table, his hands crossed, no doubt praying for a miracle. Brooks was stoic... he did his best. It was now beyond his control.

"Good morning, ladies and gentlemen, I understand you have reached a verdict, is that correct?"

Pete responded nervously, "Yes it is, Your Honor."

"Could you please give the verdict form to the bailiff?" Pete handed the bailiff the burnt orange envelope containing Scooter's fate. His handoff to the bailiff, and the bailiff's handoff to the judge, and the judge's handoff to the clerk for publication, appeared to take place in slow motion as the envelope floated around the courtroom.

The clerk opened it carefully and began to read the short and simple verdict form.

"We the jury in the above entitled cause, find the defendant, Raymond Mason, guilty of the crime of murder in the first degree."

The clerk then read the jury's findings of special circumstances and enhancements. Scooter will now face death.

The courtroom remained calm but for the reporters who managed to race out without causing a ruckus.

Scooter lowered his head to the table and began sobbing uncontrollably. Brooks tried to console him with a pat on the back, but his hand was abruptly pushed away by his client. Several bailiffs grabbed him, pulling him to his feet to place him in handcuffs. He wasn't going down without a fight; he kicked and shoved and shouted every obscenity imaginable.

The bailiffs finally overpowered him and escorted the condemned man to his cell. Those in the courtroom could hear his voice fade as he cried, "I ain't done nothin' wrong, get your hands off of me, please, oh please, I ain't done nothing wrong." He would sit in his small cell for several days, alone, petrified, as the jury considered putting him to death.

It was Friday, and Judge Waters ordered the jury and the attorneys back on Monday to begin the penalty phase which was expected to take a day, possibly less.

THIRTY-FIVE

ZACH and Ginger left the courtroom after wading through the press and other onlookers. Ginger was in tears, sad that a man might be executed. She didn't believe in the death penalty and felt sorry for "that poe man cryin' like that. The Lord Jesus Christ forgive people, Zachary, and ain't no one but the good Lord have the right to tell anyone it's time to die, no way."

Zach didn't agree with her. To him, an eye for an eye is perfectly acceptable. The deterrent effect of the death penalty may not work, but Zach believed there are therapeutic benefits for the victim's family when they're allowed to get even. Most of those families would feel even greater emotional satisfaction if the constitutional safeguards against cruel and unusual punishment were abolished.

As they approached his car, Ginger timidly asked, "Zachary, would you mind terribly much if I kin drive back to the office? I just get so scared 'n' such when I ain't drivin'. I don't know why, I jus' do. I'mma good driva, you'll see." She looked at him smiling, revealing her perfect white teeth.

He felt he had no choice. "Sure Ginger, I trust you, no problem."

They got in the car, pulled out of the parking lot, and all hell broke loose. Ginger may be terrified when others drive, but she drove like a Vegas cab driver. She weaved in out of traffic, which moved slowly through the narrow streets, all the while desperately searching for creative ways to squeeze past the cars in front of her. She was on a mission to beat everyone on the road. Speed limits were irrelevant and so were red and yellow lights. Ginger tried to calm her passenger by quietly humming "Stayin' Alive" by the Bee Gees. It didn't work.

She decided to take the freeway since it would cut a sixteenth of a mile off of the trip. Zach had no idea his old clunker could do zero-to-ninety in four seconds. She merged onto the carpool lane, assuring Zach, "Don't worry, Zachary, since you in the car, we allowed in this lane."

A few feet from the off-ramp she swerved across three lanes and onto the exit lane, oblivious to the effects her actions had on the traffic behind her. As she made her reckless maneuver, she gave a courtesy wave to the other drivers who narrowly avoided death. They waived back with one finger as their shrieking horns cursed at her. She owned the road and nobody was going to get in her way.

Zach was speechless and unable to move, holding on for dear life just like Ginger would do. Is she getting back at him or is this how this maniac drives?

They made it back to the office in half the time it typically took Zach. Ginger exited the Indy-car, expressionless and still humming. To her it was just another daily commute.

Zach remained in the car, staring straight ahead, in shock, trying to calm his palpitating heart. "Okay Ginger, you got me, I'm stumped," he shouted from the passenger seat, shaking his head. "What in God's name was that all about? Seriously? Is that how you always drive, 'cause if it is I need to look for a backup secretary? One of these days, you or someone else is gonna get hurt, or worse."

"Aww, don't worry Zachary, I drive like that all the time and I ain't never got hurt. To tell ya the truth, you drive too dang slow, and it makes me get anxiety 'n' such. I hafta hold myself from screamin' bloody murder 'cause I want you to step on it, but you don't and it keeps runnin' through my mind over and over and over. I hafta think of somethin' else, like ice cream or chocolate, to stop me from splodin' and tellin' you to git a move on it. My husband tell me that I needta git me some medication to help me through it."

Zach never heard such a story and burst out laughing. "Are you freakin' kidding me? The whole time I think I'm going too fast for you, but you're actually ready to detonate because I'm driving too damn slow for you?"

"That's about it, Zachary."

"Well, I'll tell you what, next time we go somewhere, we'll take separate cars and you can go in a different direction 'cause I ain't driving anywhere near you again." They both laughed as they walked to the office.

It was quitting time and Ginger retrieved the

messages, gave them to Zach, and said goodbye for the day.

Andrew left a message, anxious to hear how the verdict went. Zach attempted to reach him, but was directed to voicemail.

His next return call was to Nathan, who advised that the judge requested a few revisions to the final probate order, that those revisions were being made, and that the order would be resubmitted by the end of the day. The court clerk indicated that the revised order would likely be signed and processed within the next day or two.

Zach could hardly wait until payday. He still had a couple of months remaining on the six-month contract with Sasha and she would be euphoric if he didn't breach it.

He made a few more calls and dictated letters and short pleadings, all billable events. Zach was making money, but the cash injection from the Ollie's estate would put him over the top. The large fee would tide him over until he settled Daphne's wrongful death claim, which would likely be a year or two down the road.

Jake Dinkus arrived for a late appointment and

Zach greeted him with a handshake. Jake coached The Incredibles in their daughters' soccer league.

After exchanging pleasantries, Jake advised he was in need of an attorney to help him with an eviction. He had a small home in East L.A. which he rented to a family of four. The tenants refused to pay, refused to move, refused to maintain the property, and last week they refused to come out when the swat team surrounded the home.

One of the tenants was suspected of robbery and had no intention of being apprehended. The swat team pelted the place with tear gas, smashing the front and rear windows. They kicked in the front door and found the subject hiding under a bed. To vent their frustration, they proceeded to give him an ass kicking he wouldn't forget while they cuffed him. In the meantime, Jake's rental property was badly damaged.

Jake's problem worsened when the Law Office of Phillip Bunt sent him a nasty letter advising him that his clients, the wife, and adult children of the robber, intended to file suit against him for renting a home that was not habitable. He explained that his clients were experiencing significant discomfort and emotional distress since the windows were all broken, the front door was not secure, the lingering smell of tear-gas was causing them to vomit, there are holes in the walls, and blood all over the carpet. *"Demand is hereby made that you fix these problems forthwith and that you pay my clients the sum of $75,000 for the physical and emotional damages they have suffered thus far."*

"You've got to be kidding me," Zach said, after hearing the story and reading the letter. "What a piece of work this guy is."

"Okay, as to the eviction, I'll take care of that for you. Hopefully we can get them out of there within forty-five days. As to this ridiculous demand, there's an easy solution. Send this letter, and the police report, to your insurance company; they'll take care of it. You do have insurance, don't you?"

"Yes, but I called them and was told since the damage was caused by a tenant, it wouldn't be covered."

"Well, don't hold your breath waiting for coverage since insurance companies deny everything at first. Just make the claim and if they give you any trouble tell them you're gonna sue them for wrongfully denying coverage. If it gets that far, let me know and I'll jump in to help you."

The two of them concluded business matters and discussed the next soccer season; Jake promised that his team would make mincemeat out of Amanda's team the next time they played.

Zach's final call was to C.J. at C.J.'s Pawn Shop. C.J. left no message other than for Zach to call him.

"Hi C.J., this is Zach Morgan returning your call. How can I help you?" Zach asked, believing C.J. was a prospective client.

"Is this the lawyer?" C.J. responded.

"Yes it is, I'm Zach Morgan."

"Oh, great. I was looking for someone with your name and I tracked you to a law office. I didn't know you're a lawyer. Hey, I'm still holding the gun. Do you want to make arrangements to pick it up, or are you gonna let it go? With the trade-in and the loan proceeds, you'll owe me approximately two hundred forty-five bucks. So tell me what you wanna do."

Zach looked at the receiver, "What? I'm not sure what you're talking about."

"Whaddya mean, what am I talking about? You exchanged the Glock for the three-fifty-seven and I gave you a hundred bucks cash. Hey, if this is a bad time to chat, let me know and I'll call back."

"No, no, no, this is a perfect time. I never exchanged anything with you. I don't even know you. But do you have my Glock which was stolen a few days ago?"

There was a moment of silence before C.J. responded. "Are you shittin' me? Stolen? Well, that son of a bitch..."

Zach was frustrated. "Okay, let's start this over. Are you calling me about my gun that was stolen from my office?"

"Actually, I'm calling about a gun that may or may not be yours. I didn't know it was stolen. Some guy asked if he could exchange it for a three-fifty-seven and a few dollars. His Glock was in pristine condition so I gave him the dough and the three-fifty-seven. He said his name was Zach Morgan, which is the name of the registered owner, but the number he gave me was disconnected. I then found your number and I called."

"What did this guy look like?"

"He was tall, kinda thin, reddish-brown hair, grungy looking; smelled like a wet dog. I freakin' knew he was trouble. I never should have done the deal with him. Dammit."

Zach's heart skipped more than a few beats. He reached for Detective Jackson's card and instructed C.J. to call him immediately to report the stolen gun.

He then called Andrew, again, letting him know there were major developments they had to discuss and that it was urgent he return his call immediately.

THIRTY-SIX

JUDGE Waters began the penalty phase with the same rigidity she demonstrated during the guilt phase. She expected this phase to be short, as neither the victim, nor the defendant, had more than a witness or two to speak on their behalf. She instructed the jury that they must weigh both aggravating and mitigating circumstances when they make their recommendation as to whether Mr. Mason should be sent to prison for life, or be sentenced to death.

Momma testified for Scooter, sobbing the whole time. "Scooter's like my son. He does everything I need him to do. If it wasn't for him, I wouldn't be alive right now. He brings me food, water and some clean bandages. He also helps me move around the park. He's everything I have. He ain't done nothin' wrong. He wouldn't hurt a flea. That sumbitch, Brady, he's a liar, and he's gonna burn in hell someday for them lies he told.

Please... ya'll just need to spare him, please. This ain't right." She cried uncontrollably, emptying the box of tissues on the witness stand. Scooter looked at her and began to tear. He was proud to have Momma stand up for him.

Andrew failed to show up and gave no statement to assist the prosecution.

When it was all said and done, the jury had very little to consider: a heinous, vicious crime committed by a man who lived on the streets for over a decade, who showed no remorse, and who only had one friend who thought his life was worth saving to speak on his behalf.

The judge gave the final instructions to the jury and the deliberations began at 2:30 that afternoon.

Zach was not present during the penalty phase. He was busy with other matters, including meeting with Detective Jackson, who now had a great deal of interest in Zach's gun, which was exchanged for a gun possibly having the same caliber as the one used to kill Miss Far Out.

Fortunately, C.J. cleared Zach as the person who exchanged the gun at the pawnshop. Zach expressed no opinion to the detective as to who he believed stole his gun. He called Andrew several more times, without success, each time expressing urgency and frustration.

* * * * *

The jurors engaged in their customary polling: "D" meant death, "L" meant life, and "U" meant undecided. The first go-round resulted in eight D's, three L's and one U. Pete was on the side of death and was bound and determined to get the other eleven to agree with him.

The jury retired for the evening at 5:00. Before they left, the count improved to nine D's and three L's.

* * * * *

It was 3:52 a.m. when Zach's eyes popped wide open while lying in bed next to the sound asleep Sasha. He managed to slip out of bed slowly and quietly, despite his pounding heart and pumping adrenaline. He put on his clothes from the day before, left a short note to Sasha informing her he went to the office, and raced to the Culver City Professional Centre.

He darted through his lobby and directly into his office and grabbed Andrew's file given to him by June Gregory. He reviewed the record of the loitering citation several times. He confirmed what he thought he read previously, but discarded as immaterial. The loitering citation was issued by the Burbank Police Department on October 5, 2010, but later dismissed for unspecified reasons.

Zach's stomach sank and the taste of puke came to the surface. He called Andrew again, this time letting him know about the gun and the citation, and demanding he call him immediately to discuss these very important issues.

It was only 5 a.m. and Zach wasn't in the mood to work. He'd rather drink himself into oblivion, but he walked to the nearest coffee shop and ordered a tall, bold coffee-of-the-day. He sat at a small table, staring, shaking, wondering what he'd gotten himself into and how he was going to get himself out of it.

He wasn't a praying man, but the events over the last few days made him think twice about the almighty. He looked to the sky and quietly whispered to whomever was up there listening. "Will someone please tell me what the fuck is going on around here? I have a soon-to-be-rich client who is a psychopath with a very questionable past; a property manager who was murdered a few doors down with a gun very likely linked to my soon-to-be-rich client; and a career, a financial future, and a family, all of which are very much in jeopardy right about now. Who, dear lord, is fuckin' with me?"

After an hour or so of agonizing over his situation, he made the short walk back to his office, went through the dark lobby, and crashed into his executive chair behind his desk.

As he stared down at a blank yellow note pad, a voice startled him. "Good morning, Counselor, you're sure getting an early start to your day." The voice came from the lobby. It was Andrew. In his surreal state, Zach failed to see him sitting on the small sofa.

Zach rushed from his office to the lobby, "What the hell are you doing here and how did you get in?"

"Now, now, Mr. Morgan, don't be silly, I have a key to your office courtesy of my former fiancé. With the amount of money you'll be making off of me, don't you think I'm entitled to a key?"

"Besides that, you've been calling me non-stop.

I decided to be a good client and meet you here first thing in the morning to tend to your needs. So tell me, Mr. Morgan, what *is* the problem?" The lights were still off, but the whites of Andrew's eyes were visible, as were his disgusting, rotten teeth.

"You know full well what the problem is, Andrew. Why don't you tell me what the hell you've been doing over the past several months, beginning in October of last year?"

"Not sure what you mean. I came all the way out here from Texas to offer support for the prosecution of my brother's killer. I also came here to meet you personally and to assist you in getting what I deserve." Andrew spoke calmly, confidently, methodically.

"Cut the crap. I have grave concerns about your actions and I have reason to believe that every word that has come out of your mouth has been a fucking lie. You have lots of explaining to do and you'd better do it now because, as I see it, you're breaking and entering and I will call 9-1-1, which I can assure you is the last thing you'll want me to do." Zach stood behind the lobby counter as he spoke, wishing Ginger was with him for added protection.

"Bravo," Andrew said, as he clapped slowly, "you continue to amaze me with your legal prowess. I knew there was a reason I hired you. But I have a little story to tell you, Mr. Lawyer, and I'm pretty smart too. For example, I know that what I tell you is confidential and privileged. You can't and won't say a word to anyone, including the coppers. Isn't that what they taught you in ethics at Jefferson School of Law, Mr. Morgan?" He laughed demonically. Zach stared at his client, startled.

"Now, don't fuckin' move a muscle because I'll put a bullet between your eyes if you do." Andrew instantly turned violent as he stood and pulled out the gun hidden in his jacket pocket. He directed Zach to his office, motioning him to his chair behind his desk.

Zach thought of nothing but Sasha, Amanda and his unborn child. He was horrified.

"Also, pick up your phone right now and call that linebacker secretary of yours and tell her you're giving her the day off to go shopping. You'll be attending the Mason trial and her services are not necessary. Let her know she will be paid double for her day off. Don't say anything other than what I just told you or your beautiful wife Sasha will be a widow. When you're done, turn off your phone."

Zach nervously complied. He called Ginger, relaying verbatim what Andrew forced him to say. She was awake. The perks of her new job thrilled her and she thanked Zach repeatedly, unaware that as he expressed his generosity he was very close to having his head blown off by a client.

After hanging up, Zach mustered up courage to ask, "What are you doing, Andrew, and why?"

"Self-preservation, Mr. Morgan. You're a lawyer and lawyers lie, cheat and steal. That's why I need you on my team."

"So, where oh where shall I begin?" Andrew casually took a seat in one of the two chairs in front of Zach's desk reserved for clients. He was no longer hostile, but that could turn on a dime. He was just another client preparing to explain his case to his lawyer, hoping to receive sage advice.

THIRTY-SEVEN

THE morning deliberations were tense. Pete was far more dominating than he was during the guilt phase. The multiple stab wounds, the amputation and the premeditation were the only factors necessary to consider. "If Mason was simply acting out of a temporary or uncontrollable rage, why would he cut off the victim's feet? He's an animal and he has no right to be among the living."

Number Two, Venus, agreed that what Scooter did was atrocious, but she didn't think she had the power to decide whether someone should die. Pete reminded her that during jury selection, she expressly told the judge and Mr. Skaggs that she could and would impose the death sentence if there was a conviction and if the evidence warranted it. If she's now saying she couldn't, she lied to the judge and surely she didn't want Pete to tell on her. "I know, I know," she pleaded, "but when it gets down to doin' it, it's just like... so stressful."

Number Five, another hold out, felt sorry for Scooter. "He lived on the streets most of his life. If he's given food, shelter, and clothing on a regular basis, maybe he can be productive. None of us know what we would be capable of doing unless we lived under the circumstances he did."

Number Twelve responded, "The SOB tortured and killed that man. He don't deserve to be productive. He deserves to get what's comin' to him. Don't be feelin' sorry for him."

Number Five, "Well, he had a very sad and depressing life."

Number Twelve, "Good, then let's just end it for him. Put him outta his misery."

Number Eleven, "I think I'm gonna reverse myself again. As Pete said, we all agreed we would impose death if we convicted him and if there were sufficient aggravating circumstances. We can't now go back on our word. We found Mr. Mason guilty and we found special circumstances. We must all do what we agreed to do. Therefore, I'm changing my vote to death."

Pete, the scorekeeper, quickly announced, "Ten

D's to two L's."

* * * * *

"Have you ever been abused, Mr. Morgan?" Andrew asked, as Zach sat motionless, scared to death. "I mean abused by someone who should never abuse you?"

"Other than by you, no."

"Funny, asshole, but don't fuckin' try to be funny right now 'cause I'm in no mood for it," Andrew yelled.

"Well, I've been abused. And I'm not just talking about what my brother Ollie wrote in his little story. It was worse than that. My daddy used to make me do things no one on this earth should have to endure, let alone a little kid. What he did made me hate myself when I was a boy and I'm still sickened by it. I think about it every single day."

"I knew Ollie was aware of what my daddy did to me, because I could see him watchin'. He didn't stop it either. He could have because he was bigger than Daddy and he could have taken him out with one swing. I would have done it for him, but he did nothing to protect me."

"When Daddy was killed in the fire, I didn't shed a single tear for him. He deserved exactly what he got, and more."

"But when Ollie left me by myself, that's when I cried, Mr. Morgan. That's what hurt me the most. I only cried twice in my life, and when Ollie left me, that was one of them. My big brother just split and didn't give a rat's ass what happened to me. He left me to be passed around from one family to another, twenty-three in all. Most of them got rid of me 'cause they didn't like the way I looked or acted. Some of them used me and other kids as punchin' bags. The fosters got paid by the state for us to be with them and that's all that mattered to them. Giving us a safe home and a good life was not something on their to-fucking-do list."

"A couple of them fosters were sick bastards like my daddy and loved to play dirty with us boys. There wasn't anything we could do about it. I got real messed up in the head."

"When I was taken in by the Johnsons, things changed a little. They cared for me. But I had no ability to care for them. I stole from them blind and lied to them at every opportunity. Even then, they'd still send me money. I felt bad for them 'cause they always told me they loved me, but I couldn't return the favor. I'm not capable of love because of all the shit I've been through. I don't love nobody."

Zach interjected, "I'm sorry, Andrew. You're right, no one should be mistreated the way you were. But this isn't the way to handle it."

"Shut the fuck up! Did I ask for your opinion yet, Counselor? Until I do, you just sit there like a lawyer and listen." He went from Jekyll to Hyde in an instant. Zach's horror intensified.

"Now, that brings me to Ollie. He vanished after Daddy died. At that time, I thought he was perfectly okay with what Daddy was doing to me in the barn, and I learned over the years to hate Ollie for it. He left me to fend for myself and to endure the abusive treatment I received from the fosters. In a lot of ways, I blamed Ollie for what I went through. He could've stopped Daddy, and he could've taken me with him when he left... but no, he thought of himself, and only himself, and moved on to bigger and better things, leaving me behind to be picked apart by fuckin' vultures."

"Why'd you ask about the loitering ticket in Burbank?" Andrew suddenly looked to his lawyer for an answer.

Zach managed to mumble the answer, afraid that it would send Andrew into another rage. "Because you told me before that you were never in California… I just wanted clarification."

"Well, I guess I lied to you. Clients lie to their lawyers, ain't that right, Mr. Morgan? And, when they do, you're not supposed to say a damn thing about it. But since you brought it up, Mr. Morgan, I'll give you your clarification. I've actually been to California several times. I wanted to know where Ollie was and what the hell he was doing. I also wanted to kill the mother-fucker for letting that shit happen to me."

"I found him in Burbank at that little place he called home sweet home. I was jealous of his nice, quiet life. I went and paid him a little visit."

"He barely recognized me and was surprised as hell I was there. He told me to make myself comfortable and we talked about our lives. We musta spent a half-day fillin' in the blanks. He kept telling me how well he was doing and that he was at peace with himself… but I was there to kill him, and I grew tired of reminiscing."

* * * * *

After another round of discussions, Pete asked Venus whether she intended to take her duties seriously. She finally agreed that Scooter should be put to death, but she was still reluctant to take part in the decision. Pete impressed upon her the importance of honoring her duty to the court. "If you think he deserves the death penalty, you must give him the death penalty. You agreed you would, and you can't change your mind now. You need to act like a responsible citizen."

Venus began to cry. "Fine, it's just hard acting like God, okay? It might be easy for you and other people in here, but it's hard for me. I never should have tooken this job in the first place. Fine, whatever, kill him for all I care." Venus laid her head on the table, crying, defeated.

"Eleven D's, one L, we're getting closer."

Number Five, "I guess you're gonna work me over too, huh Pete? Well, I feel bad for this guy and I'm not gonna be a pushover like Venus. I need some convincing that a person should be put to death for doing things any one of us may have done if we were driven to it."

"What the hell are you talking about?" Number Three barked. "The victim did nothing to deserve what he got. Mason wasn't driven by anger to kill this man. He killed because he's callous and has zero regard for life. I could see it if he robbed the poor guy so he could buy food or feed an uncontrollable addiction, but he didn't... he killed for the sake of killing. You need to think long and hard about that. He's not the victim here, so don't make him out to be one."

"I'll cheer to that," Number Twelve toasted Number Three's speech with an imaginary Champaign glass.

* * * * *

"When Ollie turned his back to me as he sat at his computer, I wrapped a nylon rope tight around his neck and held it with all of my might. The whole time I thought of him watching me get raped by my father. My hatred exploded. He finally lost consciousness... not much of a struggle for a big guy."

"I tied him up good and waited for him to wake up. I wanted him to feel the pain he caused me and to watch me as I retaliated. When his eyes opened, I slugged him several times with the pipe wrench. Each time he moaned, I cracked him again."

"I hope you're hearing all this, Counselor, 'cause I'm enjoying getting it off my chest."

"Every bit of it," Zach said. He wasn't sure why he was being told this story, but he was quite certain that once it was over, he'd be Andrew's next victim.

"Do you think I was done with Ollie after that? Hell no, I wasn't done. I gave him a slicin' for the twenty-three fosters he made me go to. I guess you could say it was symbolic."

"But I had more work to do. I needed to pay back my coward brother for running away from me when I needed him most. That expert in Mason's trial had it right. I chopped them feet off like I was choppin' a log and I enjoyed every minute of it."

"Poor ol' Mason is takin' the rap. All he did was find my clothes and things I tossed in the dumpster. I kicked myself for forgetting the butcher knife at the house, but I had gloves on so I left no fingerprints. The dumbass experts could probably find my DNA and hair all over the joint if they just looked. Funny thing is, they focused on Mason and never bothered lookin' for anyone else. It was hysterical that I–the real killer–was able to sit in the courtroom behind the accused, while the idiots presented one piece of evidence after another to convict the wrong man. What a joke," he said, grinning, looking at Zach. "You lawyers are sure a funny bunch, I was bustin' up inside when that shit was goin' on in the courtroom."

"I really had them going when I cold-cocked poor Mason in open court. I thought that would add to the drama, and it did. So many things fell perfectly into place. I listened to every news story and rooted for Mr. Skaggs to save the day. A conviction meant I would never be suspected of anything. And that Brady fella, he was a hoot. He just lied like a carpet to get even for Mason having kicked the shit out of him. And Skaggs believed every word of it cause he wanted that conviction at all costs. Damn funny what you lawyers do to fuck up people's lives.

"So that's it, Zachary. That's how my brother,

Ollie met his fate. I didn't do it for money... I did it purely for revenge. The fact that he was loaded with cash was news to me, not that I mind the fringe benefit. I had no idea he had that kind of money until I was contacted by that Presley lady."

Andrew paused, then moved closer, "Now let me tell you about the second time I cried, Mr. Morgan, and this is where you come in."

"You were the one that gave me Ollie's little story. I read it over and over and over again. I learned that my brother killed Daddy for me. He fuckin' did it for me," Andrew was shouting, veins bulging, "because of what that son-of-a-bitch did to us. Ollie didn't condone the torture I went through like I thought; he helped fuckin' end the torture by killing that pervert. I had it all wrong and I murdered my brother for nothing. He didn't deserve to die the way I killed him. I cried and cried until I could cry no more after I read that story you gave me."

"I blame you for the way I feel right now, Mr. Morgan. Before I realized my mistake, I was good with what I'd done, ready to move on with my life and spend my money. Not now. I'm feeling pain and guilt and it's all because of you, Mr. Zachary Morgan, attorney at law. I don't like guilt and I'm not used to feeling it. You know what they'd do in the old days? … they'd kill the messenger who brought bad news, and I hate to say it, Counselor, but you *are* the messenger!" Andrew's blood-shot eyes, were fixed on Zach's.

You sick, twisted monster, Zach thought.

"I'm not sure what I intend to do with you just yet, but if I don't kill you, I'm gonna make you think long and hard about the gory details I told you about. I'm gonna make you think about poor Mason sitting in prison because you can't say a word about what I told you. I'm gonna make you think about him as he's injected with the death serum, 'cause that's what the jury's gonna give him."

"Lots to think about, Mr. Morgan. Ethics 101 was a very important class, so I hope you paid attention. And, by the way, if you forgot what you were taught and you think about spilling the beans on me, just remember that in this lovely state of California, the killer of the decedent is not entitled to an inheritance. I can do research too. What that means is that if you finger me for killing my brother, the money I'm paying you goes down the fuckin' drain. I'll get nada, so you'll get nada."

Zach felt the urge to lunge at the madman, but remained calm. "So what about Julie, why did you kill her?"

"Now, there you go, jumpin' to conclusions, Counselor; how do you lawyers say it? ... 'Assuming facts not in evidence?' I never told you I killed her, so what makes you think I did?"

Zach knew he was going to die and had nothing to lose by giving his final legal argument. "Because the pawnshop owner identified you as the one who traded in my gun for another gun; because that other gun was most likely the same gun used to kill her; because you and she stuck together like flies on shit; and because you just admitted to killing Ollie—that's why I believe you killed her."

"Brilliant. I'm so lucky you represent me. The only thing you forgot is the motive for me killing her. Don't you lawyers always want to know the motive?"

"Not really."

"Because I trusted the two-bit whore with my little secret and she threatened to go to the police unless I split the money with her, which I wasn't about to do for no woman. It's that simple."

"As to that clown P.J., he no longer exists either. The gun he gave me has a real good balance to it. It's been tried and tested on him too. As a matter of fact, I could probably hit that drop of sweat dripping down your nose right now," he said, pointing the gun at Zach.

* * * * *

By 1:45 p.m., Pete and the others exerted enough pressure to turn Number Five into a believer and move him into the D-camp. The jurors were now unanimous.

News of the quick decision spread as fast as the guilty verdict. The clerk announced that it would be read at precisely 2:15, so that the tired jurors could be excused and return to their normal lives. The lawyers scrambled to the courtroom.

Scooter didn't stand up to face the jury. He knew his fate, had no control over it, and was not about to watch it unfold. Instead, he sat at the table with his head down, wondering when he was going to wake up from the nightmare.

"We, the jury, recommend that the defendant,

Raymond Mason, be punished by death." Those words would never leave Scooter's ears. He passed out.

FINAL

IT was approaching 4:00 p.m., and Andrew appeared to be concluding his reign of terror.

"Mr. Morgan, you have a nice family, and I know you have a little one on the way. Sasha's a beauty and so is Amanda. I hear she's a great soccer player. Maybe I'll check out a game or two someday."

"Don't even think about it, Andrew, or you'll be sorry, you bastard," Zach shouted, nearly jumping out of his chair, tears running down his face. If Zach intended to scare Andrew with a credible threat of retaliation, it didn't work.

Andrew laughed, "Now, now, Counselor, calm the hell down. You play along with me, and I'll leave you and your perfect little family alone. But don't try to be a hero, because you'll die trying. I promise you that."

Andrew slowly reached in his jacket pocket and pulled out several pages torn from a yellow legal pad. He looked at them briefly as he smiled, then waived them in front of Zach. "There is one last thing you ought to know, Counselor. Your client–I believe his name is Franco Scaletti–won't be too pleased that you allowed me to have access to your file containing the identities of his drug sources." Andrew paused as he slowly thumbed through Zach's notes. "Hmm, very interesting stuff here. I'm sure you realize that if this information happens to find its way to the DA's office, courtesy of you, then you and your client, Franco–and most likely your entire little happy family–will be crucified by those very dangerous people."

Zach had enough. He jumped out of his chair and grabbed for the notes, but Andrew pushed him back viciously. He leaned over the desk and pointed the gun directly between Zach's eyes, the barrel touching him almost point-blank.

"Listen to me, asshole. If you and your family want to stay alive, with lots of money in the bank, you better keep your fuckin' mouth shut. As my attorney, you have a duty to me and if you violate it, you will see your legal career and your lovely family disappear. I hope I'm making myself clear. You better get my money now and not say a word about this conference to anyone." Andrew pushed the barrel of the gun firmly onto Zach's forehead, and paused, staring at him quietly while the anger in his eyes intensified. The momentary silence was deafening as Zach waited for the trigger to be pulled, oddly wondering at that moment whether he'd be chosen to go to heaven or hell.

Andrew abruptly broke into nightmarish laughter as he stood up, put the gun and the yellow notes in his pocket. "I've waited long enough for you to produce results, Counselor. I expect my money tomorrow morning, first thing. Don't let me down." He turned and walked slowly out the door.

After his paralysis subsided, Zach checked to see if he soiled himself. He then clicked his recorder to its STOP position.

He called Sasha, attempting to remain calm. "Hi Honey, don't worry, but I need you to pack a few things and take Amanda to a hotel and do it quick. I'll explain later."

"What?" Sasha replied. "Are you serious? What's wrong?"

He hit the panic button. "Please, I'll tell you

about it after you get the hell out of there, right now, Sasha."

"Zachary, tell me what is going on, are you okay?"

"Sasha, I'm fine, trust me on this. Please, just leave now and call me when you find a place to stay. No more talking, just go, now."

Zach darted from the office, got into to his car and drove like Ginger, but he had no destination. He hadn't had time to reflect upon Andrew's actions, but driving as far away as he could may help him sort it all out.

He heard on the radio that the jury recommended death for Scooter. He cried, laughed, screamed, punched, cursed and lost control of every emotion he had.

Sasha called him, interrupting his breakdown, and told him where she was going. He told her he'd be there shortly, hung up and headed in her direction. He was mindful of the very real possibility that Andrew was following him, or worse, following her.

After racing through the back streets, he finally managed to collect his thoughts, but not his emotions.

He met Sasha and Amanda at a large hotel on Wilshire. The three of them tightly embraced in their room. Zach was quivering, unable to release himself from the embrace.

"What's going on, Zach?" Sasha pleaded, in tears. The unknown was killing her.

He directed Amanda to watch TV while he and Sasha spoke softly in the small bathroom.

"Well, I spent the day at gunpoint with my favorite client, Andrew. He needed the entire day to explain to me in great detail how he—not Ray Mason—massacred his brother. He also killed Miss Far Out and a pawnshop owner and he nearly killed me. He made it clear that he expected me to honor the attorney-client privilege with his little bombshell confession. I don't know what the hell I'm supposed to do. I can't let Ray Mason go to prison, but I'll lose my license and probably my life and yours if I disclose what I was told." Zach was racing through the story. Sasha listened, but couldn't quite comprehend the barrage of horrific details she was hearing.

"Also, since he killed his brother, he's not entitled to the inheritance, which means my fee is history.

He knows the law, and he's banking that I won't jeopardize my family, the money, or my license by turning him in. Mason has already been convicted of the crime, so no one will ever suspect him. All he wants me to do is keep my mouth shut and live happily ever after."

Sasha was sickened, crying. "Oh my god, Zach, is this real? We need to go to the police right now. That is the only option. Everything else can go to hell as far as I'm concerned. I couldn't care less about any attorney-client privilege, or your license, or the money. We need to protect our family... and, you can't let that poor man die for a crime he didn't commit."

Why can't they arrest Andrew right now for killing Miss Far Out?"

"They could have, but he killed the pawnshop owner he purchased the murder weapon from. They have no weapon and no eyewitness. The only evidence against him is his confession to me, which I recorded." Zach pulled out his dictation recorder, flashing it to Sasha.

"What?" Sasha shouted. "How the hell did you manage that?"

"I turned it on when he wasn't watching."

"Oh great, Zach, if he caught you he would have blown your head off. This can't be happening. What a nightmare."

Sasha and Zach spent the next hour discussing the ramifications of their options. No alternative was safe, but one was a clear choice in both of their minds. Regardless of whether Scooter was or wasn't a productive and responsible member of society, or whether he chose to live in a cardboard box on the streets of L.A., he should not be condemned to die for a crime he didn't commit. Zach's law degree, his license, and the hefty fee were immaterial.

It was approaching 9:00 p.m. when he went back to his office, against the stern advice of Sasha. He had to contact Franco with the news that his confidential information was released to another client. He decided against telling Sasha about Franco or the notes Andrew stole from him.

Franco was fit to be tied and demanded to know who the thieving client was, where he lived, and what the soon-to-be dead man looked like alive. Zach didn't reveal the requested information, but mentioned he would be having a meeting with said client first thing in the morning.

He then contacted Randy, explained his disastrous efforts to run a law practice, and asked him for a favor. Randy complied.

His last call was to Andrew. His voice trembled as he advised him that he was able to get Nathan to obtain approval of the final probate order and that the funds would be wired to his trust account in the morning. Andrew wanted cash and insisted that Zach have it ready to be picked up by noon. Zach assured him it'd be ready. He also let Andrew know that, after considering their long conversation, he decided he would not jeopardize his fee, his family or his career and that he would heed Andrew's warning. The only condition to his full cooperation was that Andrew return the notes stolen from Franco's file. Andrew agreed, but reminded Zach that if the money was not all there by noon, he'd be minus his head.

At noon the following morning, Andrew arrived at Zach's office. Ginger greeted him, unaware of the events of the prior day. Andrew sat across from Zach's desk as Zach slid him a duffle bag containing over three million dollars in small, fake bills, courtesy of Randy.

Composed, Andrew reciprocated by giving Franco's secrets to Zach and extended his hand for a congratulatory shake. "Job well done, Counselor." Zach refused.

Andrew quickly walked out of the office with his head down, wanting to go unnoticed. He didn't see Franco and his several gorillas lying in wait to accost him. Franco grabbed him as he exited the office, put him in a choke hold and his assistant taped his mouth. The others swiftly surrounded and immobilized him and shoved him into their van. The entire event lasted a matter of seconds, and drew no attention whatsoever. They drove to the Mojave Desert and took care of business, giving Andrew the same treatment they gave snitches.

Zach promptly contacted Brooks and informed him of the major developments in the Mason case. Brooks was stunned at the prospect that his client was actually innocent, not a common occurrence in his line of work.

An emergency meeting was arranged between Zach, Brooks, Skaggs and Judge Waters. Zach's recording containing Andrew's admissions to various crimes, was played to the group. Zach fully understood the consequences of revealing attorney-client privileged information, but couldn't care less.

Later that afternoon, news that Scooter was wrongfully convicted and that a local lawyer turned his own client's murder confession over to authorities, consumed the airways. The legal analysts were in a frenzy. "He'll most certainly be disbarred. He disgraced the profession in a manner which undermines the very core of the practice of law."

Zach offered no statement in his defense. Someday they'd learn all of the facts and twist them as they deemed necessary to satisfy their protocol. He would not help them.

After Judge Waters and the attorneys listened to the shocking confession, it was stipulated that Scooter's conviction would be vacated and all charges would be dismissed forthwith. He was released later that day.

Scooter and Brooks publicly thanked Zach for standing up for principal at the risk of losing his career. However, this gratitude was tempered by members of the bar. They did not condone his actions. Zach knew that, given the same circumstances, some in the profession would have zipped their lips and spent their client's blood money without a second thought.

For his part, Pete, the jury foreman, defended the guilty verdict, explaining that based upon the evidence presented at trial, the jurors came to the proper conclusion. The fact that the wrong man was convicted was unfortunate, but not the jury's fault. "The LAPD should do a better job and get the right man next time."

Venus countered Pete by declaring to all that she always thought the poor man was innocent, but that she was unduly pressured by others into agreeing to the verdict. She was also quick to remind the reporters that she'd be happy to provide exclusive, one-on-one televised interviews to discuss the traumatic ordeal she experienced in the jury room.

The LAPD went on an all-out manhunt for Andrew. His remains were later discovered by a hiker in the desert. The cause of death was undetermined. Franco never said a word to Zach about Andrew's fate and Zach never asked. Justice was served.

In the coming weeks, it was established that Stanley Johnson, the cousin of Ollie's father, was the sole remaining heir entitled to Ollie's fortune. He and his wife donated much of it to a local charity for abused children.

Zach immediately resigned from the state bar, preempting an ethics investigation and disbarment. The bar assumed control over his small practice. Prior to resigning, Zach obtained the consent of Daphne Stevens to transfer her wrongful death case to Litzer/Brown, Dillon's former employer. The only condition to the transfer was that Litzer/Brown hire Dillon to work on the case while he finished law school. The managing partner graciously agreed, reiterating his promise from years ago that Dillon would always have a place at the firm, regardless of his physical disability.

Zach transferred some of his other cases, including Commercial First Bank's collection cases, to June Gregory, who hired Ginger to help with the new caseload.

Through it all, Sasha admired her husband and supported the decisions he was forced to make, in light of the unimaginable circumstances to which he was subjected. What he lost professionally and financially, he made up in respect, a quality far more important than any other.

On the way home from his new job as a branch manager at Randy's bank, Zach took a detour to Scooter's corner. There he stood, dancing around, waiving his sign, which read. *"To evrywon - Plese Help me and othurs. we all struggle won way or anothr and nead just a litle help sumtimmes!!!"* He finally had some truth to his advertisement.

Zach pulled over and gave him a fifty as he had done the past few weeks. Scooter was grateful to the point of tears and promised to use the money to build himself a new "ride."

Zach then went to NorthStar Residential Care. The publicity from the trial caught the attention of the county's adult protective services, who quickly located Momma, made sure she received medical attention and placed her in a permanent care facility. Zach made a few visits, bringing Momma books he collected from friends and family. He'd sit by her bed listening to the Beatles while they chatted about nothing of significance. He was perfectly content with the simple life.